Nessie Out Of Water

Stacey Wooten

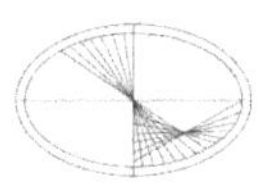

DIVERTIR
PUBLISHING
Salem, NH

Nessie Out of Water

Stacey Wooten

Cover design by Kenneth Tupper

Published by Divertir Publishing LLC
PO Box 232
North Salem, NH 03073
http://www.divertirpublishing.com/

ISBN-13: 978-1-938888-16-8
ISBN-10: 1-938888-16-2

Library of Congress Control Number: 2016948980

Printed in the United States of America

Contents

Chapter 1

A petite Martha Stewart wannabe with monogrammed oven mitts cradled a perfect quiche in my doorway. Her hair was the reason shampoo commercials were invented, as evidenced by its immunity to the infernal humidity that invaded my air-conditioned foyer. Against all odds, her wheat-golden locks managed to stay silky straight before gently curving up to meet her chin. My gaze lingered on the rooster apron she wore over her polka-dot dress, red as candied apples. The hemline stopped below the knee, shadowing conservative heels that inched towards the threshold of my apartment.

"You must have the wrong door," I offered with a pitying smile.

Her lips curved up in a Cheshire cat grin, jolting my brain into realization. Three things became apparent.

1. Somewhere on her body was a caffeine pump, supplying enough energy to be bouncy around the clock.

2. The lipstick she wore was sold to either a septuagenarian or June Cleaver.

3. She was indeed at the correct address.

Lord, help me.

My visitor inhaled deeply and squealed, "Oh, you must be Agnes. What a card!"

I considered shutting the door but figured I should at least be as kind to her as to the toaster salesman that constantly visited the complex. My mother would have said it was the Christian thing to do. Me? These days I was more concerned about catching a double-wide toaster on sale.

Her fingers reached through the portal separating my sanctuary and the outside world, gesturing to the camo tank top and cargos I wore. "Oh Agnes, you must tell me where you got that hilarious outf—"

My fists clenched at the name my mother had bestowed upon me while doped up on high levels of labor drugs. "I go by Nessie, please."

She laughed. Well, I suppose one could deem those sounds a laugh; it was more akin to a pig grunting. "You jokester! Isn't that some mythical sea creature? Why on earth would you want to be called that?"

I checked her face for secret wrinkles, chin hairs, or anything that might indicate she was much older than the twenty-five years I'd credited her with,

1

since the only people who liked my given name shopped at the local Piggly Wiggly for Polydent. Add the facet of outdatedness to memories of childhood bullies taunting me with "Angus," and it wasn't hard to figure out why I adopted a nickname. "It really is just Nessie. Now, I assume you were the one who responded to the newspaper ad?"

Mini-Martha chortled again. "Of course, honey. Who else would I be?" I opted not to answer that question and let her continue. "The name is Betty."

"Let me guess, Crocker?" I snorted, unable to help myself.

Her Botoxed face never showed any signs of creasing, though I could have sworn her fingers flinched. "Huh?" She waved her hand. "Oh, posh. You and your jokes, Agnes."

For the record, I had never met this woman in my life. Yes, I received a handwritten letter in the mail announcing her arrival to check out the apartment, but I just figured she was a little old-fashioned. I didn't realize she had stepped out of a black-and-white television rerun.

Betty nudged me out of the way and turned a sharp left towards the kitchen, as if the location was wired into her brain. Her free hand rifled through the drawers with both speed and grace, looking for something.

There is one thing I should mention: I was not a big cook. My kitchen contained a fridge, microwave, and a toaster, purchased from the toaster salesman in a moment of weakness. There were a couple of dusty pans from Goodwill, bought when I made a pact to start cooking my own food every night, but the empty takeout boxes in my trash were witnesses against me. I didn't go into shock when Ms. Homemaker's search turned up empty.

"Where are your cooling racks, dear?" she inquired.

Cooling whats? I shrugged. "Don't think I have any."

Her face twitched. "Oh. Really, now? Well, I'll just set this on the counter. It's probably cooled by now." Betty began her investigation of the kitchen drawers once more. "And your pie servers, hon, where might those be?"

"Um, none of those either," I admitted.

A bead of sweat, my first clue that she was indeed human, slid down her forehead. Her hands jittered restlessly at her side. "No pie servers…" she murmured under her breath.

My short-but-sweet Girl Scout training kicked in with peacemaking strategies flooding to my brain—negotiation, redirection, anything to keep this woman from having a complete meltdown on my dusty vinyl floor. "Why don't we let it cool while you take a tour? I'm sure you'd love to see the apartment."

Her posture straightened and she whirled around to face me with renewed vigor. "Oh, that would be delightful, Agnes!"

So much for that peacemaking side. "Um…why don't you take a look around? I'll…look for a pie server." Betty beamed at me as if I was her little hostess protégé.

There was no way my small two-bedroom apartment would be featured in *Better Homes and Gardens*. A few kitten-themed motivational posters aside, my decorating motif was an expression of winter: bare. The living room had a futon, a dinged-up coffee table, a dusty bookcase, and an ancient, chunky television. That was it. There were no lovely Thomas Kinkades gracing the walls, no cutesy bumper sticker sayings in the kitchen, and no photographs of me and my nonexistent friends doing fun things like traveling the world or going to amusement parks.

If I had a therapist, she would probably tell me my lack of décor reflected my denial and unwillingness to accept the direction my life had taken. But I didn't have a therapist, so I just told myself I was cheap and utilitarian. That was good enough for me.

However, I had thoughts that it might not be good enough for Betty, who was pacing the living room, clicking her tongue disapprovingly. She opened her mouth, but a sudden bang against the wall interrupted her. Muffled shouts sounded from the next apartment over.

"Tommy, get your soccer shoes!" resonated through the thin walls.

Betty raised her palm to meet her lips. "Goodness."

"That's Felicia from next door. She has four children." I said nothing more, taking Betty could infer the rest.

"Oh, I adore children, Agnes!" Betty's eyes glazed over.

Panic set in. What if she never left? I needed a roommate, but not this bad. "Quiche?" I offered and quickly stabbed a butter knife through the pie, hoping a speedy transfer from dish to plate would ensure an equally fast departure of Ms. Betty Crocker.

She walked into the kitchen humming but froze in horror when she registered the butter knife. There couldn't have been any more terror in her expression if I was chain-sawing a crippled kitten. Her scream startled me, and I dropped the knife, cringing as it clattered against the floor.

"What. Have. You. DONE?" she roared and lunged to snatch the dish from my marble counter, her nostrils flaring.

Betty marched toward the front door, but not before whipping around to shower me with a look of disgust. "Were you raised by wolves! Never use a butter knife to serve quiche! NEVER!" She paused her angry tirade long enough to grace me with a pitying chin quiver. "How will you ever marry?"

With a haughty sniff, she was gone. Barely registering the waves of humidity, I stared out the rectangle frame long after she stomped down the three flights of stairs. Her words failed to compute in my brain. Utensils? Getting married? What was the connection there?

With a sigh, I gently closed the door and shuffled over to the bathroom to nurse my wounds. A splash of frigid water from the sink shocked me back into reality, and I peered into the mirror.

I wasn't a gorgeous girl. My short pixie cut, dyed so dark a brown the DMV marked my hair color as "black," was always disheveled because of my anxious tendency to ruffle my hair. I lacked the necessary patience for makeup, so my lips usually rested in a pensive line rather than the award-winning smile of a Maybelline girl. Though I had the height of a model, I somehow lacked the fashion and poise to go with it, rendering me clumsy and awkward. Another check in the mirror confirmed my suspicions: the girl looked weary and weathered.

A knock sounded on the front door made my breathing quicken. I stalled in the bathroom, afraid Betty Crocker returned to chastise me. On the other hand, she had the tenacity of a pit bull and making her wait could prove to be more dangerous than avoiding her.

Creeping softly across the carpet, I gathered my courage and yanked open the door, like ripping off a Band-Aid. The toaster salesman on the other side jumped at the sudden movement. He was a familiar sight in my complex, and my heart lifted at seeing his slicked-back hair and kind eyes. Maybe he would understand my pain. My hope lessened when he held up a shiny toaster.

"I already have one," I explained halfheartedly.

He smiled with his lopsided grin. "But they're a low, low price."

I bought another toaster, just because it had been that bad of a day.

Chapter 2

I went inside and made four pieces of toast for lunch, just to prove I was not the horrible cook Mini-Martha-Stewart insinuated I was. To demonstrate my wise acquisition of a second toaster, I timed how long it took the toast to pop up. Two minutes and thirty-six seconds. It would have been over five minutes if I had only one toaster. The thought relaxed my tense forehead, and I slathered some jelly on the toast, counting it as nutrients.

I ruffled my short hair while munching. The roommate search left me a little bummed out lately. Rent on the two-bedroom apartment was too much to keep paying on my own since my last roommate decided to leave.

Two weeks ago, she knocked on the door to my room while I slurped Ramen and watched cartoons. "Nessie! I need to tell you something!"

Our solemn meeting took place on the futon. Sitting there with long noodles streaming oh-so-attractively down my face, I cringed when she told me, "Nessie, the Northern Bobwhite Quail is calling to me. Can you hear it?" She looked out the window stoically. I paused munching out of respect, though I didn't expect to hear anything. She dramatically outstretched her hands in the air, as if she had been choreographing some weird nature dance to commune with the quail. "Nessie, I must preserve their habitats."

The bird girl moved out two days after her "revelation."

Perhaps it was the name "Nessie," but strange people were drawn to me. At least the bird girl didn't call me "Agnes" or think I would need a huge dowry to find a husband. Better yet, I was able to use butter knives in her presence without fear.

I looked heavenward. *God, you have to help me. I'm struggling here.* The white ceiling offered no response.

God cared about me and my struggles, right? So many Sunday Schools ago, a young Nessie would have blurted "yes" with unwavering confidence. These days, the stacks of bills, monotonous work routine, and empty pantry met me with raised eyebrows until I started to doubt myself.

Was this my life? My only purpose to wake up, go to work, come home, and eat toast? A heaviness not explained by carbs settled in my stomach.

Sighing, I pulled out my laptop and forced down the rest of the toast, unsuccessful at keeping the crumbs out of the keyboard. I winced. Phil, the half-balding tech at ValuComputer, always shook his head at me, sending his pitiful comb-over flopping in all directions. "Do not eat over the keys, Ms. Burgh. This is why your space bar keeps sticking." At that point, I would hold my hand up high and say, "Nevermore. Scout's honor."

Ha. The joke was on him. My troupe leader kicked me out of Girl Scouts for being an ineffective cookie seller, which I blamed on my passive aggressive tendencies and sweet tooth. These combined traits were my fatal flaw in the realm of Girl Scout cookie sales. What could I say? With all those crates of unsold cookies lying around in my room, it was only natural for me to want to drown my little girl sorrows in a box of Thin Mints.

My mother explained the situation to the director, believing she would understand the weakness of my will. The director understood that my mother would pay $52.87 for the boxes of devoured cookies. You would think that with all that understanding, things would have worked out better. Sadly, it did not, and I was the first child in the county kicked out of Girl Scouts. Who knows? Maybe I was the first person in history.

Regardless, my honor as a scout was tarnished, and Phil should have known better than to chide me for the inevitable. Logging onto my e-mail, I deleted the junk, scanned an advertisement for sweaters, and then saw there was a new message.

To: Nessiemonster@email.com
From: Mysticalunicorn@email.com

I paused. Cutesy e-mail address with a childish ring to it. Promising.

Greetings. Your advertisement appeared in my newspaper. I noticed it while meditating in the sunlight this morning. I believe our souls would coexist peaceably in your abode. The winds of fate will bring me to your doorstep tomorrow if that harmonizes with your being. Respond as your heart guides you.
Peaceably,
Mystical Unicorn

Oh. That was her name and not a silly e-mail address. My cursor lingered over the delete button, but hesitated when I spotted the rent notice on the coffee table. She couldn't be worse than the quiche woman. I began to type before I changed my mind.

Hey Unicorn,
Sounds radical. Be there or be square.
Just,
Nessie

Send button. Done. Surfing the web brought a new sense of fulfillment. There I was, finding roommates without trying hard. Maybe God was on my side after all. It was then my spacebar started to stick. I could see the crumbs peeking out from underneath the key. Oh, how they taunted me.

§ § §

One stern lecture later, I was out of ValuComputer's parking lot vowing once more to never eat bread products over the spacebar. Yeah, right.

There was still time left in the afternoon to visit King Arthur's Shopalot next door and peruse the shelves out of boredom. Back in my younger days, wandering the aisles of oddities had made my eyes grow big and my jaw drop. These days, I was less impressed and more amused, but the store still had a strange charm to it.

An advertisement on the sliding doors broadcasted the special in bold letters: GOLD PLATED BLOWTORCHES, BUY ONE GET ONE FREE. I made a mental note just in case I should need to set something on fire.

Once inside, the distinct aroma of incense, rubber, and lemons mixed with a tad of unwashed body odor assaulted my nose; it was clear a few choice shoppers thought soap was for decoration only.

Scenes of dragons and thrones graced the walls, a sight that would have been beautiful had the owners not commissioned middle school students for the task. The princess on the wall in front of me was a glorified stick figure holding what I assumed was a harp. Instead of the squeaky shine of white linoleum, fake cobblestone paths paved the way down aisles of lava lamps and maces. A simple stroll through the store was like visiting a tacky museum of randomness. I nodded politely to an old woman checking out the blowtorches.

My eyes drew to the medieval section where Renaissance dresses and imposing thrones were available for purchase. I admit I am a bit of a geek. The enchantment the Middle Ages held over me with all their princesses, rogues, and swords started when my third-grade crush, Billy Carpenter, dressed up as a knight in shining armor for career day. Looking back, I can only chastise myself for being interested in the one kid whose career aspirations were based on an ancient feudal system and amounted to clanking around in metal armor.

Still, the die was cast, and the era of the Middle Ages would hold my fascination for years to come. My mother had hoped that I would grow out of it. But the older I got, the more mundane my life became, and immersing myself in a book filled with quests and kingdoms became routine. I often reminded her, whenever she sighed in disappointment at my reading selection, there were much worse coping mechanisms.

Passing whoopee cushions, ventriloquist dummies, wigs, and decoy ducks, my gaze caught something shiny. An ornate golden hilt peeked out of a leather scabbard on a shelf, practically begging me to slide the long gleaming sword from its depth. Runes were carefully engraved into the blade. My fingers skated along the symbols, curiously tingling when they touched the metal. The prickling sensation caused me to jerk my hand away at first, but when I picked it up again, the fuzziness coursed through my fingers anew.

That's strange, I mused. It had some kind of weird static electricity. Oddly enough, when I returned the sword to its sheath, the tingling stopped. I couldn't shake the feeling I needed the blade. That it was made for me.

Yes, there had been accusations I tended to impulse-buy, such as when I bought a second toaster…earlier that day. Lest you think I lacked reason altogether, I remembered a voice in the back of my head that said, *What in the world do you need a sword for?*

It was at that moment I remembered all of the crime in the world. A girl couldn't be too protected, even if a sword was her weapon of choice. Who knew? Perhaps the purchase would save my life one day. The argument seemed reasonable enough and settled the matter in my mind.

"Lords and ladies of King Arthur's Shopalot," a nasally teenage voice greeted dully over the intercom. "The store shall closeth in ten minutes. Make your way over to yon check out. Kay. Thanks."

The announcement was sufficient motivation for me to haul buggy towards the front of the store, not wanting to be stuck in a long line of creepy people. On my last late-night visit, I was sandwiched between an Elvis impersonator and a twitchy man who talked to me for fifteen minutes on the perils of owning a gerbil; I would do anything to avoid a repeat of that night. Unfortunately, speed was my downfall. Sword in hand, I collided with a man turning out of an aisle, and for a moment all I saw was red. Much to my relief, I realized the splash of color had not been blood, but rather a billowing red superhero cape my co-collider wore.

"Hey, watch out," I admonished, though the wreck was both of our faults. "I could have poked your eye out."

"Is that you?" a familiar voice asked—a familiar voice that sold me a toaster in the middle of an emotional breakdown. In front of me was the man with black, slick-backed hair, shiny dark eyes, and lips that were a little too far to the left.

"Oh, hey….toaster…guy," I bumbled, slightly embarrassed.

"The name's Eric." He grinned lopsidedly and held out his hand. I took notice of his tall, slightly lanky stature. Never before seeing Eric sans toaster, I was distracted by how nice he was on the eyes. The small dose of awkwardness he projected prevented him from being a GQ model anytime soon, but he fit the criteria of tall, dark, and handsome. His down-to-earth ease made the tilting smile seem playful and friendly. *Whoa, there. Focus, Nessie.*

"Nessie," I offered, and gave him a clumsy high five instead of a handshake. It seemed like the right thing to do while holding a sword.

We stood in silence for a moment.

"So, how's the new toaster working out?" A dimple creased his cheek.

I shuffled my feet on the faux-cobblestone floor. "Great. For lunch today, I made twice as much toast in half the time."

"Awesome."

More silence.

Behind Eric, a man wearing a half-disco, half-cowboy outfit sashayed to the front of the checkout line. Panic rose when he turned around for a second and met my eyes. This one was definitely a talker, and I refused to endure more speeches about anyone's back hair problems, pet iguana relationship drama, or fears they may have killed Santa Claus. Yes, I met these customers before in line at King Arthur's Shopalot.

"Um…well it was nice seeing you, Eric, but…uhh…I…uhh…I have to pee." I bolted away from him towards the front. The last glance I got before darting off was him saluting me like Superman of the army.

I hurried over to the nasally teenage cashier with my spoils of war. Catching my breath, I noticed the disco cowboy distracted by the blowtorches—the line was empty.

Good, I could make my purchase and get out before any weirdos got in line with me. I gave the tingly sword to the cashier, but he was in turtle time. As if moving through molasses, he reached for the sword to scan it. Tapping my foot impatiently had no effect on his speed, even when I hummed the Jeopardy theme.

His dark emo haircut obscured his left eye, but the right was framed with black eyeliner and lazily glanced from the sword in his hand to my face. "Oh my," he said, with all the enthusiasm of a comatose person. "Are you over the age of fourteen, milady?"

I snorted, stamping a foot. "Yes, I'm twenty-four."

He raised a pierced eyebrow. "I'll need to see some ID."

Oh, the sarcasm that welled up in me. "Will my Chuck E. Cheese membership card suffice?"

His facial muscles twitched, but no change. I sighed and pulled open my purse, flashing my ID before his eyes. He took on the arduous task of ringing up the sword. An eternity later, he gave me the total.

"That'll be $19.46. Oh, no, wait. The time is now 5:33. We're closed." He slowly reached up to turn off the register light.

Somehow, my restraint kicked in and prevented me from breaking the teen turtle's arm. "Wait a minute!" Wrath gathered like a dark storm waiting to pour out into a flood of verbal abuse.

"I'm joking, milady. Ha. Ha." His face never altered its flat expression.

"I thought you had to pee."

I yelped in surprise, whipping around to face Eric the toaster salesman, who was apparently just as sneaky as he was tacky. Unfortunately, grace was not my forte when struggling for a response. "I just went…in my pants."

This time, Eric was the eyebrow raiser.

And my mother wondered why I never had a date on Saturday night.

My emo friend never missed a beat. "Depends are on aisle three."

"I don't need—"

He grabbed the intercom, with the most efficiency I'd witnessed in the whole transaction. "Doris, will you grab some Depends for the young woman in line here."

The pronouncement echoed through the store, and the few remaining shoppers turned to look at the incontinent woman in question. The disco cowboy winked and nodded approvingly. *Shudder.* Suddenly, a package of Depends was in front of me, and I didn't have the courage to deny them. Paying for the order as quickly as possible, I made a beeline for the exit.

While the sliding doors parted for me to escape, a voice stopped me. "Hold on," Eric called, his superhero cape fluttering as the afternoon breeze invaded the store. "Let me walk you to your car."

Unable to take more of the already pitiful evening, I held up the sword. "I'm good. If anyone gets near me, I'll skewer them."

An elderly homeless man sat on the outskirts of the parking lot and smiled gratefully when I gave him the package of Depends. Glad he didn't take the gift as an insult, I got behind the wheel. At least someone had a good day.

§ § §

Later that night I donned my pajamas, ready to be done with the strange day. My fingers flipped the light switch and darkness flooded my bedroom. Flopping down on my pillow, I concentrated on the ceiling. The clock told me it was past time to go to bed, but something stopped me from counting sheep. Bedtime prayers had been a part of my nightly repertoire since childhood, and, as they said, old habits die hard.

The ceiling fan swished overhead. Was that all it was now? An old habit just taking its sweet time to die?

It wasn't that I didn't believe anymore, but my grip on life and faith was slipping. Life had become a droll recipe for survival, and the endless cycle of "lather, rinse, repeat" was unbearable. *God, there has to be more to life than this. Don't let me waste away here, missing the purpose You have for me.* The ceiling fan continued to spin air around the room. *Because You do have a plan, even when it doesn't make sense.*

My eyes fluttered sleepily in the dark, vaguely making out a strange glow by the closet where I remembered placing my newly-purchased sword. Glow? Must have been reflecting a streetlight from outside the window.

Then again, I couldn't get that tingling feeling the sword had emanated out of my head. Before I could think, I found myself stepping out of bed and shuffling towards the closet, eyes fixated on the dull glimmer. My knees lowered and I reached out for the illuminated weapon, bracing for the electric sensation when I grasped the hilt. Nothing. The room went dark again, making me wonder if I'd just imagined the whole thing.

A deep sigh escaped my lips and I went back to bed. Was my life so pitiful I had to invent a magic sword just to have some sense of excitement? I snuggled further into the warm covers. No time for hallucinating when I was having life dilemmas.

Rolling over, I closed my eyes. Change was in the air; it had to be.

Chapter 3

The doorbell rang three times. *Here we go again.* Clenching my eyes and whispering a prayer, I opened the door to Mystical Unicorn's beaming grin. "Three is the number of completion," she stated.

Why did the fates of roommatery dislike me so?

Her hot pink hair cascaded to her waist, where cheetah print capris assaulted the eyes. It was a wonder she wasn't stopped by the fashion police. They would have arrested her for the zebra striped shirt with puffy sleeves, not an article on the "Acceptable Patterns to Wear with Cheetah Print" list. As if this was not enough to display eccentricity, her bare toes wiggled in anticipation on my welcome mat. Hygiene much?

"Don't worry," she assured. "The skins are fake. I would never hurt a real animal. I only try to commune with nature by wearing the patterns of my fellow animal friends."

I pinched my "Puns Not Guns" t-shirt. "I wear…uhh…cotton to commune with plants."

Her smile brightened and she craned her neck to look past me. "Oh, radical! So, this is your abode, Nessie?"

I bit my lip hesitantly. Mystical Unicorn was odd but friendly, and despite her lack of footwear, she appeared to be clean. Furthermore, she didn't berate me for my lack of cookware and pleasantly complimented the living arrangements. Stepping aside, I let her into the house.

"Sorry there aren't many decorations," I apologized, but she shook her head and sat cross-legged in the middle of the floor.

"I feel simplicity is a major element in meditation. My soul is in harmony in this room because of the pure white walls unmarred by commercialized art."

Okay, time to figure out if she was as creepy as the man down the hall with a bald cat. "I know this kind of sounds weird, but with all this talk of spirits and stuff, you wouldn't be holding séances in the living room or anything, would you?"

She waved her arms. "Oh, no way. I don't mess with any of that. It's just my language, Nessie." Mystical Unicorn smiled, and I returned it. "Actually, I'm more into parallel universes," she added.

Well, then… "Does that require tearing up the furniture or disturbing the neighbors?"

Her brow furrowed in concentration. "It surprisingly has little effect on the worlds in between."

"Uh-huh," I offered. "Will you pay half the rent and utilities?"

"Providing financial support is not turbulent to my soul. We can split everything down the middle." She paused. "Just like a commune!"

"Uh…sure. As long as we keep everything PG," I stipulated.

Thus went the tale of how a girl named Mystical Unicorn came to live under my roof.

§ § §

6:47 a.m. The muffled blasting of the SpongeBob SquarePants theme song and wrathful shouts of, "Mikey, if you don't turn that television down right now, I will come over there and…" jolted me from the most wondrous dream concerning cupcakes. When the tireless yelling match next door failed to cease after fifteen minutes, I forced myself out of bed and shuffled towards Felicia's apartment. Nothing like a kindly worded "Come to Jesus" meeting to start the morning right.

While scooting past the vanity mirror, the reflection of a disheveled, sweaty woman clad in Disney princess pajamas startled me. Snow White's figure on the material looked back judgmentally.

Oh, those pink footies. My journey to obtain them had been as perilous and complicated as a Tolkien trilogy. Sadly, they didn't come in adult sizes, which meant I had to ask the snippy store lady for a special order in a youth quadruple extra-large. The image of her raised tattooed eyebrows haunted me, shaming me like an obese child. Well, in a way, I was. Though I was a few donuts away from being trim, Youth XXXXL fit me like a glove.

Still, that searing glance had been the price to pay in order to obtain my fat-kid pajamas with Cinderella, Belle, Ariel, and the rest of the gang. And for what? I was the only one who saw their beautiful faces smiling up at me before climbing into bed. No, now was the time to show the world my darling PJs and let them become green with envy. Sliding into my bunny slippers, I marched to the apartment next door and rang the doorbell.

The door, scuffed from multiple run-ins with small children, opened to a harried blonde in her mid-thirties. Her hair was clipped up in a moment of desperation and spouted every direction at once like a dysfunctional fountain.

I was not alone in my pajama fashion statement; she was wearing ones with a cat pattern. I had seen Felicia at my church a couple of times, always sur-rounded by a flurry of active children, but never in cat pajamas. There was a first time for everything.

"Oh, hey, Nessie," she greeted me distractedly and then jerked her head away. "Peter, stop pulling your sister's hair!" Turning back, Felicia fiddled with her black-rimmed glasses and offered a wan smile. "Did you need something?"

All my indignation at being woken by shouting vanished. Felicia was just a single mom trying to raise her four kids without any physical or psychological casualties. Her deadbeat husband left her after two sets of twins in two years, and though that could be enough to make anyone go crazy, he had no excuse. The two older boys, Mikey and Tommy, were six, while Peter and his fraternal twin, Susan, brought up the rear at four years. Their matching white-blond hair and blue eyes always creeped me out, reminding me of a mob of clone children speckled with dirt and syrup.

A girlish scream and crash sounded from inside the apartment. What was that dilemma I was having about lack of purpose? "Uhh…I was just coming to see if you needed a babysitter."

The tension in her forehead melted and her mouth parted with a hesi-tant smile. Looking up and down at my princess pajamas, she rubbed the back of her neck. "Right now?"

I reached up to ruffle my sweaty hair. "Whenever."

Raising her arm high, Felicia inhaled the armpit aroma. "Well, I don't remember the last time I had a shower. If you wouldn't mind sitting with them for just…I don't know, ten or fifteen minutes…"

"Not a problem," I assured and walked into her apartment where World War III had apparently taken place between a herd of Barbies, monster trucks, and action figures.

With a stern command aimed at the children to be good, Felicia vanished into another room. Four pairs of beady eyes assessed my weaknesses as I dis-located some stuffed animals and sat down on the couch. Susan leaned close to Peter and attempted to whisper, "She's wearing my pajamas."

Punk. That kid could never understand the trauma I faced for those pink footies.

"Why is there a girl with pink hair in your apartment?" a child's voice blurted from inside a pillow fort constructed in the corner.

Nosy kid. I raised an eyebrow and looked for the boy who owned the voice. "She's my roommate."

Mikey's bleach-blond head popped up in between two sheets, compromising the structural integrity of his fort and bringing a mass of blankets and pillows tumbling around him. "Why does she have pink hair?" he inquired, unsatisfied by the many mysteries of Mystical Unicorn.

"She dyed it, I suppose."

Mikey's replica, Tommy—or maybe I had them mixed up—cast aside a monster truck he was using to run over Barbie. "You suppose?" he asked snottily.

That did it. Every scary movie I'd seen as a child returned to memory and infused in my voice. "Yes, that is, unless…" I paused for dramatic effect and all the kids sat down at my feet.

"Unless what?" Peter ventured, taking a seat beside his sister on the couch.

"Unless…" Why was I so bad at making up names? Only seeing a crayon and a G. I. Joe on the floor, I went with my gut. "Unless Joe-Crayon got her."

Eight eyebrows went into the air. "Joe-Crayon?" Susan asked incredulously. She twisted a lock of her almost white hair.

"Yes, Joe-Crayon. Now be quiet and listen. Joe-Crayon has eight arms, three eyes, and ten toes."

After some quick counting, Peter protested. "But I have ten toes, too!"

I frowned. "Well, he has ten toes on one foot and none on the other."

Peter's jaw dropped. "Wow. That is crazy!"

"Anyway," my voice lowered to ghost-story pitch, "Joe-Crayon comes into the homes of little boys and girls through the refrigerator, and he colors their hair different colors while they're sleeping."

"So what?" Mikey had fully emerged from the fort wreckage and was listening with hands on his hips.

I scrunched my face into a ball and shouted my next words with vigor. "And then the werewolves come and eat you!"

They screamed simultaneously, and the shower cut off. "Kids, is everything okay?" Felicia called.

Oops. "We're good," I assured and waited until the water resumed.

"What do werewolves have to do with anything?" Peter said with arms crossed. The show of bravado wasn't quite as effective with his face drained of color.

"Werewolves can only see bright hair, so when they see children with neon green and tangerine-orange curly locks, they know it's time for dinner."

"What about the girl next door?" Susan whispered. "She's hasn't been eaten by a werewolf yet."

I shrugged. "She's really nice. Werewolves don't really like to eat nice people, even if they have bright pink hair."

Susan slugged her brother in the arm. "That's why you gotta not pull my hair! The werewolves are gonna eat you!"

Peter looked sheepishly at the ground. "Sorry, Susan."

The shower stopped for good. Time to wrap up the tale. "Well, you should be nice even without the werewolves," I offered. "You know why?" Four children stared at me intently, and I couldn't help but feel like Mr. Rogers. "Because your mom loves you and gets sad when you all don't get along. So, try to love each other instead of punching someone in the spine. Okay?" They all nodded and gave me their word.

Felicia came into the room wearing fresh clothing and combing wet hair. She glanced at the children sitting peacefully at my feet and turned to me. "Nessie, you're a miracle worker!"

Peter ran up to hug his mother first with the other three children following suit. Gratitude seeped out of her, much like the tears beginning to gather. "What do I owe you?" she asked, quickly wiping at her eyes.

"Oh, nothing," I said, heading for the door. "These kids gave me something I've been lacking for a while."

She cocked her head. "What's that?"

"Perspective."

It was odd. For years, I'd cycled around in a mundane existence, going back and forth to work, never getting to know the people around me further than the mandatory pleasantries required of acquaintances. Yet there I was actually being useful, showing love to my neighbor.

If I didn't know better I would say something shifted in me ever since the tingling touch of that sword in King Arthur's Shopalot the day before. Purpose welled up inside of me, and I opened the door, relishing the winds of change blowing in the breeze.

Standing outside, I watched the morning sun rise up over the world and marveled that maybe God wasn't through with me. After all, if He could use me, groggy and dressed in Youth XXXXL Disney Princess footie pajamas, maybe that meant He wasn't ready to give up yet.

$$\mathscr{Chapter}\ 4$$

Back in the sanctuary of my apartment, I discarded the princess pajamas for a T-shirt, jeans, and boots. With a satisfied sigh, I plopped on the futon, propping my legs out onto the coffee table. A thick, dusty Bible sat on the shelf, neglected for so long I'd forgotten it was there. Since the whole roommate fiasco, I had gotten out of my habit of reading in the morning. It was a day of new starts; why not add that to the list?

Mystical Unicorn emerged groggily from her bedroom and nodded politely before heading to the kitchen. I reached for the Bible, flipping it to where I left a bookmark ages ago.

"Be strong and courageous. Do not be terrified; do not be discouraged, for the Lord your God will be with you wherever you go. Joshua 1:9"

I sighed. My life wasn't really in danger, but fear was still a major motivator in my life—fear of being alone for the rest of my life, fear of living without making a difference in the world, fear of what people thought of me. Discouragement—now that was something I could relate to.

My career was virtually nonexistent. I worked for a portable toilet rental company called *The Emperor's Throne.* I spent my days as a secretary, coordinating deliveries, answering phone calls, doing my nails, and staring off into space. The only real difference I made in the world on a daily basis was providing a place for construction workers to urinate—which I supposed was better than the alternative.

My degree was in Art, which would be wonderful if I lived in the seventies or ancient Greece. However, there were surprisingly few jobs around for an art major, and people in my community would rather buy Thomas Kinkade's snug wintery homes than my paintings of ducklings. The first ninety attempts to sell my masterpieces discouraged me from that career path.

Once I tried to spruce things up at work, just to feel some sense of accomplishment, but the Fates were against me. When I approached my manager, Steven, and cleared my throat, he was munching on a burrito and talking to one of the delivery men—at the same time. It wasn't a pretty sight.

Steven, who looked like Rhett Butler with a bald patch and a unibrow, glanced at me and sighed. "What is it this time, Aggie?"

I shuddered but let it slide. "Okay, you know how some porta-potties are called Port-a-Johns? That's really sexist. I mean, no woman would want to do her business in something with a man's name. So, what about a new type of porta-potty? The Port-a-Jane—for women. We could do a completely new line in pink, with indoor plumbing, a baby changing station, and a powder room. It would be a hit!"

Steven's thick, all-encompassing eyebrow lifted. "So, basically, a women's restroom on wheels?"

I nodded excitedly.

"Agatha, believe it or not, women are not really that interested in porta-potties—not a target market if you know what I mean."

A frown spread across my face. "Perhaps that's because no one's ever targeted them before."

"Besides," Steven continued without acknowledging me, "if we hook up indoor plumbing, it ceases to be portable."

"What about cordless plumbing?"

His condescending smile made my skin crawl. "It doesn't work like that. Just keep answering the phones, sweetheart."

I'm gonna "sweetheart" your face, I thought, but calmed down, hearing my mother's "What would Jesus do?" in the back of my mind. Jesus wouldn't have threatened His manager. He would have been kind to a butthead like Steven. Furthermore, He hadn't abandoned me to an empty, discouraging existence, even if—

The smoke alarm pierced my peaceful meditation. I bolted from the futon, heart racing, into the kitchen where my pink haired roommate stood by a smoking toaster. After we silenced the smoke detector, she shrugged her shoulders.

"It caught on fire."

"Oh," I replied. It seemed like a better response than, "Duh, I can see that."

"Solar flares," she explained.

"Mmhmm." I tried not to sound completely incredulous.

"It burned out by itself."

Mystical Unicorn unplugged the toaster and scraped charred bread into her blender. She saw me watching and pointed to the concoction. "It gives carbs."

Nodding, I began my retreat, but stopped. "Umm, how about we don't use the toaster until the…uhh…solar power—"

"Solar flares," she corrected gently.

"Yeah, those. Let's wait until they're done."

She waved her hand. "Of course. I wouldn't have used it if I had remembered to look at the celestial bodies weather report this morning."

"Good to know," I answered and retreated to the safety of my room, shaking my head all the way.

§ § §

Three soft knocks sounded on my door.

"Come in." I put down the Bible on my Disney princess bedspread (hey, it had to match the PJs) and sat up straighter. Mystical Unicorn entered with two glasses of a green colored liquid.

"There's enough for two," she grinned.

The concoction was less than tempting, but politeness kept my nose from wrinkling. "Thanks, that's really sweet of you. If you want, you can set it on the table over there."

"Wow, this is quite different from the rest of the apartment," Mystical Unicorn noted, browsing the walls crowded with my artwork. She placed the glasses on an end table and settled onto a cow-spotted beanbag, playfully poking the strings of a guitar I never learned how to play.

"One room needs to be cozy, I guess." My arm reached up to tousle my hair, but I caught myself.

She noticed the Bible on my bed. "Pretty sweet reading."

"Oh, are you a Christian?" My eyebrows resisted the urge to rise.

Mystical Unicorn nodded. "Yeah, I know it's a little surprising. Most churches don't really welcome me as a sister. I'm not quite like the other people there."

Guilt poured over me for judging her so quickly. How long would it take before I realized what was on the outside didn't reflect the inside? "Well, if those same churches actually practiced what they preached, they might find that He uses the most unsuspecting people."

She smiled half-heartedly but fixated her attention on the floor as she spoke. "I'm pretty new to the area and I've been living with a bunch of hippies, which is why I talk differently. As for my interest in parallel universes, it's not necessarily unbiblical. God is so infinite—who's to say that He didn't make worlds other than this one?"

While I didn't necessarily agree, there was no value in debating the issue.

With a sigh, Mystical Unicorn stood up from the beanbag and walked towards the door. "Well, guess I should be going before—"

She tripped by the closet and mumbled apologies, stooping down to pick up the offending object. Unicorn emitted a high-pitched gasp and the color drained from her face. She held up my most recent Shopalot purchase. "Is this—is this…" she stammered. Her fingers gently closed around the hilt. "Do you mind?"

"No, go ahead," I shrugged, confused at her outburst.

With great care, she unsheathed the blade and caressed the runes, mouth agape. "Where did you get this from?" she whispered, her eyes riveted to the sword.

This is getting really weird. I reached for the green smoothie and took a sip. Not bad, actually. "King Arthur's Shopalot. Why? Is it special or something?"

She waved the sword excitedly and took a step towards the bed. "You're telling me you don't know what this is?"

I scooted back for safety when the hyperactive woman inched dangerously close with the weapon. "It looks like a sword, but I'm going to guess and say that it's a tape recorder."

The attempt at humor had little effect on her. "This is one of the Blades of Remiel." She paused, waiting for a response, but the excitement was lost on me. "It's one of the portals to a parallel universe!"

"Oh," I nodded, unconvinced.

She continued inspecting the blade, unperturbed. "Legend has it the ancient king Remiel sealed up the gate between worlds with this sword. Only when the bearer said the correct words on the blade would the gate be open."

"Well, that doesn't help," I smirked. "I don't have my Rune-to-English dictionary handy."

"No! I know what these mean." Mystical Unicorn carefully slid the sword back in its leather sheath and sat beside me on the bed. "It says 'Eethi andre canasi,' which means 'Enter with Him.'"

"That's odd." I frowned. She shook her head, pink hair bouncing.

"Remiel taught the people to fear and love the same God that rules over every world. So, the words mean to pass between worlds with God's blessing and remember that He is with you."

"Uh-huh." It made me wonder if there was a housing agency that sent the crazy roommates directly to me. My fingers massaged my throbbing temple while I searched for the right words to say. "And how did some magical sword from a parallel universe get here in present day America?" I used my best of-course-I-don't-think-you're-crazy voice.

Mystical Unicorn fell silent, her smile fading. She gingerly set the sword on the bed and walked back to her green smoothie, her voice soft and slow. "I've read a lot about these swords; according to legend, the Blades of Remiel have a way of…showing up."

An uncomfortable quiet filled the room and I picked up the sheath, staring at it sternly. Again the allure, the static electricity, the sudden purpose I'd felt since acquiring the sword… The words emerged haltingly, almost unwillingly, from my mouth. "When you—when you touched the blade," I began, "did you feel…I don't know…a tingling?"

Frowning, Mystical Unicorn cradled her glass. "No, I don't think so. Why do you ask?" The oven timer went off, and Mystical Unicorn perked up. "That's my tofu celery." She downed her smoothie and sighed, casting a longing glance at the sword. The insistent beeping continued. "Guess I should get that. Do you want any?"

I declined, glad for the interruption. "No, thanks. I'll eat my Fruit Loops."

"Oh, really?" She cocked her head. "I didn't see any milk in the fridge."

"Well, we're out. I'm just going to have dry cereal for lunch."

She shrugged and opened the door, leaving me and the mysterious sword in an unyielding staring match. "What's your deal?" I whispered, unsheathing it just enough to touch the blade. The tingling coursed up my arm in what was becoming a familiar sensation.

Parallel universes? Magical swords? I pushed the sword back into the leather case and tossed it onto my pillow. I clearly let my imagination get the best of me; it was time to bury the fairy tales I wished were true and snap back to reality.

But with the soft *click* of Mystical Unicorn closing the door, reality took a turn for the weird.

Chapter 5

Vertigo hit me first when my room spun around in wobbling circles. I gripped the headboard to steady myself. Dizziness…nausea…could it be? *My appendix!*

Ever since the third grade when Theodore Strider did a presentation about exploding appendices, complete with graphic photos of operations—the teacher hadn't checked the projects beforehand—I pointed a finger at that tricky tissue every time I felt pain. Eat too much ice cream and feel nauseous? Exploding appendix! Develop a headache after listening to children's music for three days straight? It was the darn appendix, I was sure of it.

Too bad I couldn't remember which side my appendix was on. Releasing the headboard, I stabilized my shaking hands against the wall. There was only one place to consult when facing medical mysteries. I wobbled over to the laptop on my desk, and clicked over to WebMD, but the tingling was different from the sharp pains I would be experiencing if my appendix were going to explode.

A rustling sounded came from my bed as the pages of my open Bible fluttered. The lights flickered around me before cutting off completely. Well, that definitely wasn't related to my appendix.

"Mystica—" I started to call for my pink haired roommate, but a pulsing light in the darkness distracted me. Turning away from diagrams of the large intestine, I peered through the shadows to my bed where a dull glow, muffled by the leather sheath, reverberated from the Blade of Remiel.

Suddenly, breathing didn't seem so necessary. The room continued to spin. A force pulled on my limbs like strong magnets sweeping back and forth over my body. I stumbled out of the computer chair. The magnetization directed me to the sword. Somehow, my legs carried me steadily towards the bed, surprisingly stable despite the endless spinning of the room.

I flailed my arms—which, unlike my traitorous legs, were still under my control—for something to latch onto, ultimately clinging to the closet doorknob. My fingers turned bone white with the effort of holding on while my legs tried to pull me away. With a crack, the doorknob broke off in my hand, ricocheting me to the bed. The assumed instigator of all of this mess, the Blade of Remiel, continued to glow on my pillow.

Pick it up, a sweet voice whispered. Was the sword some sort of mythological siren drawing me with uncontrollable allure to my doom?

I squeezed my eyes shut. *This is my room, my refuge from the world!* Breathing came in rapid bursts, and my fingers went numb. I knew I was hyperventilating but didn't care. Maybe if I passed out, my brain would reboot and wake up to my normal, non-tingly, wind-free bedroom.

The sound of shattering glass jolted me to attention. Gusts of air flung papers and picture frames off my desk, sending them flying into the middle of the room. Tears, whether from the intensifying breeze or my bewilderment, stung my eyes. I was unable to wipe them away because my arms chose that moment to have a will of their own.

This is REALLY, REALLY weird, my brain screamed, watching the scene like a supernatural horror movie. A wave of nausea rolled over me, but I was powerless to stop my fingers, reaching, begging to touch the sword.

When I grabbed the hilt, the electrical shock burned my hand. Dropping the sword, I cradled my palm protectively, noticing that

1) I was no longer hyperventilating

2) My fingers were glowing.

Under normal circumstances, this would have been disconcerting, but the jolt wiped away all of my nausea and fear. As much as a part of me demanded to stay far from the unearthly weapon, my glowing hand reached down and curled around the hilt again.

Although I heard them just a few moments prior, the words came out effortlessly. "Eethi andre canasi." *Enter with Him.* The mantra curled around my tongue, giving me the strength to endure the pressure of needles against my skin. The words were lost in the rushing wind. My fingers itched to trace the runes, and I saw no reason to deny them. Instantly, the writing turned crimson, and my voice sounded of its own free will.

"Eethi andre canasi," I repeated. The wind reached hurricane speed and, like an angry child, ripped papers and books from shelves tossing them about. My words echoed against the walls, gaining volume at each utterance until they reached an overwhelming crescendo. Fireworks exploded in my brain, melting the colors of my room until only a bright white consumed my vision.

§ § §

A drop of moisture hit my forehead. I reached up to brush it away.

"Sire, she's moving," a voice shouted.

My eyes opened to a man dressed in a purple tunic and lime green stockings leaning over me. A silver insignia of a fork and sword was embroidered on the fabric. Sweat dripped off his shoulder-length dark hair, flecked with gray.

I touched the wet spot on my forehead. Gross! Studying the beads of moisture gathered on his brow, a more pressing issue caused my stomach to turn. There was a man in my room! A quick reach for the pepper spray I had stashed inside my nightstand caused me to realize that:

1) My furniture was gone.

2) There was not one man, but many. Just how many people could fit in my room?

Behind their scrutinizing faces was a crisp blue sky, clearer than I had ever seen. Better question. How did the sky fit in my room?

When I shifted positions, a sharp point scraped against my shoulder blade. I reached behind to examine the cause. A rock? That was not what my carpet looked like. Memories flooded in, one after the other. Mystical Unicorn, a glowing sword, foreign words.

"No," I proclaimed, sitting up on my elbows. "Parallel universes do not exist." However, the five men, all dressed in the same garb as Señor Sweaty and shooting me paralyzing glares, were living proof against me. They grabbed for the swords at their belts when I pushed myself off the ground, holding my hands up in surrender. Weapons? Matching uniforms? They had to be some kind of guards, but how they got here was the bigger question. "Easy now. You could poke someone's eye out."

Intriguing as sitting on the wrong end of pointy blades was, I needed to find my sword and figure out how to get out of this crazy place. Past the soldiers, a lush grassy hill sloped down into what appeared to be a marketplace. Oddly-angled buildings that resembled skinny books jutted out from the ground, and people far off in the distance scurried in and out of them, all wearing the same bright purples and greens of the soldiers. Beyond the scene of a busy village was the outline of…a castle? That couldn't be right.

Everything was brighter than I was used to; my senses seemed amplified, hyperactive even. I could smell the perspiration dripping off the man beside me, blended with the earthy scent of grass. Every touch, every sight, every sound was clearer than I had ever experienced before.

With my ever-so-keen hearing, my ears registered an impatient cough from the tallest soldier with cropped black hair, a silver pendant around his neck, and a scar running down his cheek. He kept his hand on the sword drawn at his side.

"State your name, homeland, position," he barked in a deep command-ing voice.

As a 5′ 7′ female, I had never regarded myself as short, but the fierce man loomed over me. I shifted back and forth on my feet. "Uhh…Name: Nessie. Homeland: United States. Position…" How to describe a porta-potty to some-one from…shudder…another universe? "I…work…with chamber pots?"

One of his lime-legged companions whispered in his ear—thank you, enhanced senses—"What are these…United States that she speaks of?" He continued to stare at me. "And what manner of clothes are those?"

Another soldier shook his head. "Maybe she found them in a trash heap? All I know is that I do *not* want to find out what a 'chamber pot' is."

My nose wrinkled. "Look, I know I'm not the most stylish person, but jeans are always acceptable to wear."

"If you choose to be uncooperative," the tall one barked, "you can spend the night in the dungeon."

That was not how I envisioned spending my first trip to a parallel uni-verse—because, you know, I had imagined it oh-so-many times. "My apologies, sirs," I said, adding a smooth curtsy for flourish. "The low altitude was making me woozy." My eyes winced against a refraction of light—the sun reflected from the Blade of Remiel lying not far outside of the circle of guards. The solider with the pendant shifted, providing a gap big enough to squeeze through and giving me an idea.

"I'm just so dizzy," I continued, holding a hand to my head. With a fake stumble towards the opening in the circle, I caught myself and sprinted for the sword, snatching it up by the hilt.

An angry roar erupted from the guards, and a rush of wind blew past my arm as one took a swipe with his sword. I ran down the grassy hill, my body propelled by adrenaline, sword swinging wildly. Children playing on the hillside jumped out of my way, pointing at the crazy foreigner who almost skewered them. "Sorry!" I shouted. The grassy terrain suddenly turned into cobblestone streets. A quick glance over my shoulder told me my pursuers were falling behind, but an angry shout snapped my attention to a man driving a horse carriage headed straight for me. The sound of my high-pitched squeal and his cursing filled the street before he narrowly swerved.

Okay, no more checking on the guards. Sweat dripped from my brow but I focused on weaving in and out of traffic, this time paying attention to the maze of horses and…mopeds? The stress was either making me crazy or this was a much stranger parallel universe than I originally thought.

Crowded streets opened up into the town square, an area hemmed by brilliant flowers and statues of elegantly dressed men and women. Townspeople strolled around, buying and bartering at market stands while children played games of tag. In the middle of the throng was a stage-like platform with a wooden frame—were those gallows? A shiver ran up my sweaty back, but the villagers, cheerfully chatting and milling about, seemed oblivious to its ominous presence.

My shirt clung to the wet patches of perspiration on my skin, and I forced myself to slow to a walk. Running would be out of place in the leisurely environment, and my best bet would be to blend in. Which meant I should probably peel my white-knuckled fingers off the hilt of my sword and hide it somewhere. "But then I'll be completely defenseless," I muttered, hesitant to let go of the only link to my world. Deep in my dilemma, I had stopped in front of the glass window of a cobbler's shop and nearly peed myself when a hand clamped on my shoulder. My scream filled the street, earning me the stares of nearby villagers, but I was already whipping my weapon around to the attacker.

"Woah, there," the man cautioned, holding his hands up. "You could have stabbed me with that." He indicated the Blade of Remiel in my hand. In a fluid motion, the stranger swiped the sword from me, examining it with interest. A whistle escaped his lips. "Now, where did you get this?"

"I'm sorry, sir, but I have to go," I panicked, scrambling to grab the hilt, but he held a firm grip on my wrist. "Give it back!" I gritted my teeth, slapping his hand away without success. Even worse, the guards had noticed me in the scuffle and were headed straight for us.

That was it. I would meet my doom in some parallel universe at the fate of men in bright green tights because a champion wrist wrestler captured me. Maybe I should have died of embarrassment and saved them all the trouble. My fluffy-haired kidnapper watched the soldiers approaching and secured the sword onto his belt before the men arrived.

"The lady comes with us!" the tall one panted, drawing his weapon.

"I go wherever you take my wife," Scruffy directed authoritatively, a possessive hand on my shoulder now.

Wait. What? Was this a weird parallel universe trick? Had I some other-world doppelganger married to this man? A graceful, stylish lady who knew how to cook? Just wait until he found out the truth.

The men lowered their swords hesitantly, the one with the scar last of all. "Your wife, you say?" By now, the cobbler and some of his customers had exited the store to see what all the commotion was.

My "husband" sighed slowly. "She's…" he paused, winding his finger around his ear. "A few *flurrins* short of a *bolsar*, if you know what I mean. Didn't know until after marriage cord was tied, but she's actually quite sweet when she's taking her herbs."

The sweaty one nodded. "I thought she was a little off."

Mr. Scarface looked unconvinced. Time to persuade him. "Honey," I drooled, twirling my arms fanatically, "are these men here to take me back to Ponyland where I can ride carousels forever and ever?" Disturbing how easy it was for me to pretend to be crazy.

"What is this nonsense about a…carousel?" said one of the men.

Finally, the one with the pendant withdrew his sword. "Alright, she's fine for now. But if I have another run-in with her," his voice lowered, "and I have a feeling I shall…" He stepped closer. "She comes with me."

My "husband" nodded solemnly. "Of course, sires."

The soldiers marched off. Scruffy and I walked away from the center square and nosy bystanders. "Here," he whispered when we reached the opening of an alley. Lines of laundry stretched between the buildings above us.

Amidst the trash bins littering the alley, I faced him for the first time. "Thank you so much, sir, for—" I stopped when I saw his face. "Do I know you?"

He grinned. "I would hope so if we're married." He winked, and I released a sigh. Good, no doppelganger.

Something about his face was so familiar. Inky eyes…deep voice… "Your hair!"

The smile faded. "Yes, how do you—"

I reached for his curly locks and swiftly yanked. The wig fell into my hands, revealing dark, slicked back hair.

He snatched back the hairpiece and affixed it to his head again, but it was too late. I knew exactly who the man before me was. My rescuer was none other than superhero-cape-wearing Eric, my two-time toaster salesman.

Chapter 6

"Eric, what are you doing here?" I hissed before his sweaty palm clamped over my mouth.

"Shhh! Do you want those soldiers to come back for us?" He let go of my mouth to comb his hand through the rumpled wig before affixing it back to his head. "Besides, my name is Bran." He shifted on his feet, clearing his throat. "I don't know anyone named Eric."

I crossed my arms. How could this man look like Eric and yet try to disguise his identity? But a more important question arose. "Your name is Bran? As in…Bran Muffin?" A laugh escaped me.

"And I don't suppose you would tell me what your name is?"

My chuckles stopped. "Nessie," I whispered bashfully.

His mouth opened for a retort but shouting in the streets distracted us both. Grabbing my hand, he pulled me to the town square where villagers had gathered around the commotion. I craned my neck to see over the crowd.

Guards dressed in the same fork-embroidered garb escorted a young woman through the streets. Her radiant red hair shone like fire against the lime green dress she wore. When the snarling soldiers gave her a shove towards the platform in the center of the square, she whipped her head with an angry scowl. She marched forward regally, occasionally turning to survey the crowd. Jaw stern, head high—she was not some guilt-ridden criminal. No sooner had the thought registered than her fierce gaze locked with mine.

I shuddered. Me? What did I have to do with anything? At the notice of Bran's subtle nod, it clicked; rebel lady was giving him the interested look, not me.

Just what crazy mess had I stumbled into?

"C'mon." Bran didn't wait for my response before jerking forward to grab the shoulder of a bystander on the outskirts of the crowd. "What's happening?" he demanded, keeping his other hand firmly around my own.

The man stroked his beard, not tearing his attention from the scene. "Treason. She was caught helping the half-breeds. The soldiers are preparing to execute her."

Bran scratched his head. My arms squirmed to break the connection he

31

had on me, but my companion—*captor? It was hard to tell at this point*—was too busy muttering under his breath to care about the bruises I would be wearing as a bracelet later. Seriously? Did this guy take hand steroids?

"That's it!" He snapped to attention, pulling me behind him through the crowd. I stumbled, jogging to keep up with his long-legged power walk. Maybe the sweat forming around my wrist would help me escape…

"Where are we going?" I managed to get out, breathless from our break-neck pace weaving in and out of the crowd. "And why must you always hold my arm like you're a trash compactor?"

He turned back and flashed a grin. "Well, I am going to save her, and if you're the kind of girl that I hope you are, you're coming too."

The square filled with hushed chatter of bystanders; villagers barely registered the rudeness of our jostling when we pushed past them. *Going to save h*—surely I had misheard. "What was that again?"

"We have to keep up the pace if we're going to follow the plan I've cooked up. Let's walk and talk."

My breath caught, but from exercise or panic, I couldn't say. "I work at a place that sells toilets! I don't know anything about saving people!"

Bran stopped for a few blessed seconds and finally released me, giving me time to rest my hands on my knees and suck in glorious gulps of oxygen. "Look, this is the last pause I'll allow. I sense that you want to make a difference, don't ask me how. Some part of you wants to take a chance and come with me." He leaned in close. "You're not obligated to come, but if that's your choice, get going now."

The sunlight caught on one of the soldier's swords and glinted in my eyes. I looked up at the sky and remembered pleading with God, begging for my life and faith to be rejuvenated somehow. Was this that moment? *"Be strong and courageous. Do not be terrified; do not be discouraged, for the Lord your God will be with you wherever you go."*

Did that include a rescue attempt in a parallel world, God?

In the middle of the throng, soldiers pushed the redhead up the steps of the platform, where others fitted the wooden frame with a rope. A heaviness settled in my chest, and I struggled to breathe. Surely, heroes didn't have panic attacks; it was better to leave the adventures to the professionals. But a muscular guard on the platform was already tying a noose, and there weren't any professionals around. The time for indecision was past.

Focusing on calm, even breathing, I held out my open palm. "If I'm going to help you, I'll need my sword."

Bran's lips stretched into a wide grin. "That's what I thought." He looked at my jeans, and shook his head. "We're going to need to get you some different clothes."

§ § §

"Here goes nothing," I muttered, tugging a gray riding cloak around my shoulders to keep out the wind blowing through the town square.

Knowing I was not the sharpest crayon in the box, Bran repeated my instructions fifteen times before leaving me with his last piece of advice. "Take account of your surroundings, Nessie. Things can get out of hand in a moment and you need to know your exits."

Not the best advice to give someone in the middle of a crowd. I perched on my tiptoes to look over the mass of curly black hair—apparently 80's hairstyles were alive and thriving in parallel universes—belonging to the woman in front of me. A horde of townspeople pressed together around the wooden platform where the accused stood rigidly, hands balled in fists at her side. Conversations around me were hushed and terse; even the children stopped their games of tag to look on with solemn faces.

Most important was the man cloaked in a monk's habit at the front of the crowd, hands clasped together. Everything was in position.

My stomach clenched, and I reached for the hilt of the sheathed sword at my waist. There was something comforting about its heaviness, especially now I had traded my familiar jeans for the standard uniform of a lime green tunic and purple trousers. While villagers no longer stared at me as if I showed up to a Christmas party in a Halloween costume, I missed my pair of good old Earth denim. Still, it was nice to blend in and be able to listen to the conversations around me.

"Second hanging this month," a man whispered to the curly-haired woman.

The woman clicked her tongue disapprovingly. "Why can't they just leave those half-breeds alone? Helping them isn't worth your life, I can tell you that."

"Leander certainly likes watching them die," the man nodded. "Makes you wonder what they ever di—"

The woman shushed him. "Keep your voice down, Harold. You don't want to end up on the other end of that noose, do you?"

What had I dragged myself into, and how did I think I was qualified to be a part of it? Recon Missions 101 was not a class I had taken in college. Managing to balance my checkbook on a weekly basis was hard enough. What if I forgot something important like the escape route? I peeked at a figure casually brushing two horses on the outskirts of the crowd. Whew. Our getaway mounts—never thought I'd say that—were right where Bran told me they'd be. Eyes closed, I inhaled deeply. No use thinking of everything that could go wrong.

Trumpet fanfare directed the crowd's attention to the herald approaching the platform. "The criminal, Atalanta of Tinner," his shrill voice carried over the hushed whispers, "is hereby guilty of treason against His Royal Highness, King Kermit of Spoons, by fraternization and lending aid to the dangerous half-breeds. Her sentence is death by hanging."

The executioner pushed her towards the noose, but Atalanta jerked her shoulder away, walking freely towards the rope. The tall soldier from earlier with the scar running down his cheek stood next to her, beaming with glee. What could she have possibly done to make him hate her so much?

The executioner placed a possessive hand back on Atalanta's shoulder and reached for the noose when a voice cried out. "Hold! Hold!"

Bran approached the platform, lowering the hood of his monk habit. "I find it ironic that you of all people don't know the laws of this kingdom, Commander Leander," he spat, pointing an accusing finger at the tall man I had recognized.

Is that really his name? I chuckled to myself. *Is Doctor Seuss secretly behind all of this?*

Leander scowled. "What is it this time?"

"The same thing that it is every time," Bran retorted. "You're killing innocent citizens."

"Treason," Leander reminded him. "This woman has been convicted of treason. Or do you want criminals against the King to roam around freely? Do you like chaos?"

Bran stepped onto the platform. "Even criminals are granted confessions."

"Oh, yes, yes," Leander waved his arms. "Get on with it, will you?"

That was my cue. I turned to the man on my left who was enthralled with the proceedings. "Sorry," I muttered, and punched him in the side as hard as I could. Before he could react, I kicked the curly-haired woman in front of me in the ankles and elbowed the man behind me. Then I ducked and ran towards the horses, hoping none of them caught a glimpse of me as the actual instigator. It all went down like a John Wayne movie; after the first punch was thrown, everyone got in on the action.

It reminded me of my time as a delinquent second grader. Unfortunately hooked on Mutant Ninja Turtles, I injured seven classmates that year, much to my poor mother's chagrin. If only she could see me putting my fists—feet and elbows, too—to good use.

While chaos moved through the crowd, I pointed to some far off, unseen villain and began shouting hysterically. "My baby! My baby! That man just took my baby!"

Heads swiveled left and right, villagers looking for the kidnapper in question. "Who would do such a thing?" a woman shouted. Some of the soldiers ran after the invisible perpetrator. Confusion moved through the crowd like the wave in a football stadium.

"You hit me!"

"The woman who's going to be hanged stole a baby!"

"You hit a baby? That's despicable!" More punching, biting, and clawing.

I surveyed my handiwork. *Wow, I did all of that.* Let's just say it wasn't something I wanted to take a picture of and hang on my refrigerator. I ducked as someone threw a punch over my head and continued pushing until, with a final shove, I stumbled out into fresh oxygen.

The man brushing the horses nodded to me, and I dug around in my cloak for a coin. He pocketed the change and tipped his hat before heading down the street. That was the nice thing about bribing people: they didn't ask questions.

Leander's voice rang out over the crowd, adding to the din. "Everyone calm down!" His fingers snapped angrily at his soldiers. "Go break up the fights and find missing babies and whatever else needs doing." The crowd bumbled about while Leander barked orders and roared at the people. "Everyone, be quiet!"

Bran grabbed Atalanta's arm and yank her away from the executioner's grip. He ran behind Leander and pushed, sending him headfirst into the mosh pit below. Soldiers watched with puzzled faces, going back and forth from the escaping prisoner to their fallen leader before finally rushing off in Leander's direction.

On the outskirts of the riotous crowd, I saddled two horses we procured for our exit. Now all to do was—

Bran vaulted onto a horse, his curly wig askew, and hoisted Atalanta up after him. "Let's ride," he gasped breathlessly and kicked his mount into motion.

"Right behind you," I called and tried to copy his motions. *Place foot in the stirrup…swing leg over the saddle…and urge the stallion onward.*

Easy, right? Except I got the faulty horse that apparently didn't respond to commands. "Go, pony," I shouted, digging my heels into its side. No reaction.

"Do something!" I slapped his flank forcefully, this time getting results.

With a start, my mare sprang into action and I…well, I fell onto the hard cobblestone street.

A sharp clang resounded in my head. Everything went blurry and faded to black. The last thing I thought before losing consciousness was, *Wow, that's got to be the stupidest way to end a rescue attempt.*

Chapter 7

oke. Poke. Poke.

PMy brain, though foggy, registered the repeated jabs in my ribs. Cold fingers pulled my eyelids back, but I slapped them away. "I'm awake," I muttered.

Where was I? Sharp pain reverberated in my head, making it hard to remember. Something about falling off a horse… Oh, yes. My glorious rescue attempt. I slowly pushed myself off the hard surface, which upon further investigation was a kitchen table. Definitely not what I expected.

Glass jars, piles of old clothing, and empty boxes cluttered the walkway in what appeared to be a cramped cottage. A tattered chair upholstered in an ugly orange print sat next to a hammock that hung near the fireplace. The walls had no windows, but moonlight flooded through a ceiling made of a transparent glass-like material.

Pale luminescence reflected off two people beside me in the room—an elderly woman stroking her chin with long, bony fingers and a teenage boy—eighteen, nineteen? I was never good at guessing—with blond, floppy hair. The woman stared at me until I looked away uncomfortably.

"Yes, Elbert. She will make a fine wife for you," the woman decided, smiling like a crocodile. She held out a knobby hand. "I am your future mother-in-law, Ferny."

An incredulous snort escaped me. Elbert looked like he belonged in a preteen-worshipped boy band, and I had been over that sort of thing for about…oh, let's see…ten years? Yes, I spent a few months in sixth grade leading a cult of Backstreet Boy fanatics, but we all made mistakes, right?

For instance, my backside was regretting the mistake of falling off a horse. With an oh-so-graceful grunt, I tried moving away from the table but was stopped by a shooting pain behind my forehead. "Uhh…I'm not for…sale… or marriage or whatever," I muttered, delicately massaging my temples.

"What eloquence and beauty, mother!" Elbert beamed up at me with complete sincerity. Poor guy.

The crone shot me a dirty look. "Nonsense, girl. You have no marriage cord on your wrist. My son will make a suitable husband."

The teen got on his knees. "I promise I will be the Best. Husband. EVER."

I winced at his shameless display before me, a woman he hadn't met until…well, until my horse threw me onto the street, assuming my crowd-brawling abilities hadn't attracted him first. Biting my lip, I shuffled towards the door, but a bony finger drove into my chest.

"Stay put," the woman growled. She lowered her voice to a grating whisper. "If you break my son's heart, I will break every bone in your body."

Okay, was I the only normal person in this entire galaxy? Who did that? Who picked up some unconscious girl from the road and said, "She'll do?"

My eyes narrowed at the old woman. I was hungry, in pain, and tired; the only thing I wanted was to eat whatever the parallel-universe version of a hamburger was and crawl into a warm, fluffy bed. Even the ugly chair looked appealing compared to the table with its unforgiving hardness.

But Ferny, hands clasped together under her chin, looked more interested in dissecting me than making me comfortable or, more importantly, letting me go.

Forcing a yawn, I rubbed my eyes sleepily. "Your son looks like a fine match, but I simply can't talk about wedding details while I'm this tired." Ferny glared at me suspiciously, saying nothing. A good future mother-in-law would have offered me a more comfortable bed, but the crone just nodded once, handing me an old shirt for a blanket. I retreated to my table/bed and laid down, wincing when my sore muscles made contact with the wood.

Eyes closed, I listened to Ferny and Elbert's conversations about wedding decorations and guest lists before they settled in for the night.

For what seemed like forever, I lay motionless on the table, occasionally peeking under my eyelids. Dim light faded to black and the sound of soft snores reached my ears. Slowly, I propped myself onto my elbows, still aching for some ibuprofen, and surveyed the scene.

Elbert, curly locks cast askew in sleep, snoozed on the hammock. Ferny was sprawled out on the chair drooling over the orange fabric. I tiptoed towards the door, emitting a loud *creak* from the floorboards. My head whipped behind to check on the pair, still peacefully dozing. Good. I leaned over to clear a pile of glass jars and continued my trek. Getting to the door wasn't an issue; arriving there, however, I faced a dilemma.

Where the heck is the doorknob? I strained my eyes and caressed the doorframe, taking care to listen for Ferny's breathing. My fingers found a barely noticeable indentation in the wood and traced the pattern softly. Why would someone carve that into the door?

Beneath my touch, the pattern glowed a dim blue and the door slid back into the wall, closing after I stepped through. If I ever met back up with Bran, I would need to ask him about that. My breathing quickened, producing misty clouds into the cool night air. "If…" That was the pivotal word.

Where to go from here? Cobblestone streets spread out like a grid map, running in perfect lines on either side of me. With a quick turn of the head to ensure Ferny hadn't emerged from her coma, I started briskly down the road. Strings of white lights hung along the roofs of shops, giving a warm glow to the chilly night. Painted in pastel oranges and yellows, the buildings were compacted together like skinny townhomes and advertised wares of bread and clothing in small glass windows.

The scene was devoid of life. More importantly, the streets lacked the gallows and marketplace of the city square, meaning I was lost. I swallowed, trying to ignore the heaviness growing in the pit of my stomach with each step. Nothing looked familiar—not that I'd been in this world long enough for much to be imprinted to my memory. What was I supposed to do now? I turned my eyes heavenward.

God, You put me here for some purpose, but I'm pretty disoriented right now. Show me wh—

"Going somewhere?" a grating voice filled the night. I whipped around and faced a crazy-eyed Ferny, framed by a butcher's shop and coming towards me with a skillet. That image would haunt me for years to come.

When did she get there? "Lady, you have problems!" I blurted.

I know. *Come on, Nessie. Be a woman; it's just an old lady, for Pete's sake.*

But, no. Standing under a street light, gray hair frizzing out on all sides, sharp nails digging into the handle of the skillet—she was a not your friendly neighborhood old lady.

Her teeth glinted. "Oh, more than you'll ever know." She took a step towards me, sending my pulse off the charts. Considering the skillet situation, when it came around to picking fight-or-flight, I went with flight. My legs pivoted underneath me, and I took off down the cobblestone path.

Through narrowed vision, I focused on the road, avoiding empty produce stands and traffic signs. *Ignore the burning in your muscles, Ness.* I gave myself a pep talk. *To give up means either being kidnapped or skillet-ed. I'm not sure which is worse.*

A burst of wind passed over my back, and my stomach clenched. Was she already that close to me? Calling on all the reserves of my strength and speed, I pushed forward, swerving down a side street by the fish market.

Great, because strong fish odor was exactly what was needed to motivate a nauseated runner.

The flickering streetlights made me squint. I tripped, not once, but twice over carelessly discarded empty trash bins and carts. If I survived, I would make a PSA about keeping the streets tidy in case someone needed to make a mad dash for their life.

However, road obstacles were the least of my problems. My lungs burned and the sore muscles I'd decorated with bruises earlier cried out for rest. Instead of an Olympic sprinter, I resembled a limping antelope that had been in a car wreck. A bright white light stretched out in front of me. Was my time on earth over? Would this be the end?

I lost my balance, stumbling out of the alley into a well-lit street. False alarm. The light was just a street lamp; I wasn't going to die yet. Or at least, not from running.

I pushed myself up with a groan and caught a glimpse of Ferny behind me, her gray hair flopping like a mad scientist, frying pan raised in a threatening salute. One could only wonder how such seemingly frail bones sustained that kind of cardio. It was time to ignore the agony in my muscles and get the heck out of dodge.

The wind whistled past my ears, blending with the sound of my drumming heart and…? Rhythmic clicking echoed off buildings, the sound belonging to a quickly-approaching figure in front of me. The face was too far off to see. A soldier on a warhorse? Was being captured by him better or worse than the psycho matchmaker? The closed shops and wire benches held no spaces to hide from either peril.

Lord, a little help here?

The horseman raced down the road with incredible speed, too fast to make out even when it passed under the street lights. On a more pressing note, he was headed straight for me.

Everything happened so quickly. One minute I was huffing and puffing, running away from a crazy lady; the next I was snatched from the street and slung onto a hard, bony surface that felt like…a horse? Yes, a quick whiff concluded that it was indeed a horse, and a moving one at that. Frantically, I clawed at the strong arms that pinned me to the galloping steed. My scratch marks earned me a "Hey, cut it out, will you?" Why did I recognize that voice?

The buildings rushed by in a blur, but I managed to make out a frail woman shaking a skillet at us before turning my attention to my second kidnapper that night.

The rider released the pressure of his arm and pulled me into a sitting position on the mount, a delicious toaster smell wafting from him to my nose. If I wasn't so grateful at being rescued, I might have eaten him.

His soft laughter was like music in the quiet night. "I see you've made friends."

I wilted—due to tiredness, no doubt—and basked in Bran's warmth that shielded me against the cold night full of crazy, skillet-wielding matchmakers. The back of my head rested against his broad shoulders, and I closed my eyes, letting the wind rush by. "How did you find me?"

He shrugged. "Mostly luck. It took me a bit to notice you were missing I was so caught up in the adrenaline. I just assumed you were behind us and didn't think to check. When you weren't there, and your horse was just following us without a rider, I sent Atalanta ahead. I've been going back and forth along the roads, hoping to find some clue of where you'd gone. I was starting to think the soldiers had found you."

"Thank you." I nestled against his chest. Once again, my prayers were answered. Why did God never work in my life like that at home? Or was I just never paying attention?

Bran didn't say anything for a while. Then I heard soft chuckling. "It's not a problem, Nessie. But I am going to tell everyone that I saw you get chased down by an old lady."

I jerked up. "That woman can hardly be classified as human! She has—"

He shushed me. "I was teasing. Just get some rest because we have a lot to talk about when morning comes."

Maybe it was just me, but that sounded ominous; just my kind of anti-bedtime story. I sighed, remembering the rescue. Crazy did not even begin to describe the day it had been. Before nodding off, I continued my habit of bedtime prayers but with a different attitude. *God, help me stay alive tomorrow.*

§ § §

Bright sunlight invaded my thinly-squinted eyes. A stretch tested my ability to deal with pain. From the way I grunted and winced, one would assume my body was made of stiff boards. The only plus to the muscle strain of sleeping on a horse was the comfort of Bran's warm presence behind me. Staying as still as possible, I tried to sneak a peek at him and noticed his shirt was wet…from my drool. *How attractive.* Without appearing fully awake, I tried to wipe the saliva off my face before—

"Sleep well?" he asked, his deep voice vibrating in his chest behind me.

Noticing he'd deemed it safe enough to ditch the wig, I was both comforted and puzzled in the eerily familiar sight of his gelled-back hair. He had to be some kind of toaster salesman twin.

I nodded with the smile that came after just waking up. He returned the grin, but it faded when he gestured around us. "We're here."

Silence was the only response I could muster at the sight of the dirty homes clustered so close together; they were practically overlapping. Weathered boards hung at odd angles, exposing the dark insides of houses where milky-eyed children peeped out. Sounds of a young girl's wail echoed through the dusty streets, causing the hair on my arms to bristle.

Dressed in black ragged dresses and tunics—was this an emo village—women lined the street while children peeped out from behind skirts, looking on with curiosity. I ventured a small wave, hoping to gain their confidence, but it only made their shy faces disappear into the folds of their mothers' frocks. One young girl with hollow cheeks and red hair reached out a frail hand to tug on her mother's arm.

A gust of wind whipped through the village, twisting scraps of flimsy metal that served as roofs. The wailing child quieted, leaving the raking of the metal shingles the only sound when we urged our horse into the village.

"I just see women and kids. Where are the men?" I whispered to Bran, but he shook his head. What happened to these people? This seemed to be worlds away from the comfort of the city square where clean, sturdy shops displayed fresh-baked goods and tailored clothing. Even Ferny's dump of a house had been warm and structurally intact.

Bran took the horse past a tall oak offering precious shade to a few homes and stopped in front of a shack. It had seen better days. The wooden beams were splintered, sporting stains and discoloration where rot had settled in. Nearby children watched a mouse scurry out of a hole in the baseboards and dash down the street.

Bran was intending to go *into* the house? My stomach growled like something from Jurassic Park. Right…food. Maybe they would have that inside. However, judging from the villagers' gaunt looks and loose dresses, I wasn't so sure.

He slid off the horse with ease, and I was aware of how far away the ground was. Horseback riding was never my specialty, obviously, but Bran was looking up at me expectantly. I smiled, summoned all of the grace and confidence within me, and swung my legs to one side. The sudden momentum forced me off balance. Houston, we had a problem. Gravity took its course and I fell off the mount flat on my butt. Sprawled out unattractively on the ground, I could hear stifled giggles nearby.

Ha! Signs of life, after all. "I'm all right. I'm all right," I assured everyone as I hoisted myself off the ground, gingerly rubbing my bottom. Bran had his hands over his face, failing to conceal his laughter. He grinned when I playfully punched his arm, gesturing to the open door in front of him.

"Ladies first."

Inside, someone had tried to make the dank, leaky space into a home with sparse furnishings arranged as neatly as the tight room would allow. Like Ferny's house, the walls were devoid of windows. The ceiling was made with the same transparent material, but metal shingles covered patches where holes had formed.

Two straw pallets topped with neatly-folded blankets took up half the area in the one-room dwelling. The other side was occupied by a few buckets of water, rudimentary cooking supplies, and a small blanket that covered the dirt-encrusted floor.

Hand-sewn cushions took the place of chairs and were propped against the wall where three people sat waiting for us. I recognized one as the fiery redhead we rescued the day before. She jumped up to embrace me before I joined the cushion party. See? I was making friends already. A shiver made me pull my cloak closer to keep out the constant draft.

Bran gestured to a middle-aged woman with emerald green hair and firm jaw. She wore a tattered black tunic and a black cord tied around her wrist, which reminded me of Ferny's comment about a marriage cord. Was that what she was talking about? "This is Beryl. She is the governor's wife."

I didn't quite know what to make of the unique hair color, but her wave and motherly smile put me at ease. The next one in line for introduction was Atalanta, whom Bran informed me was Beryl's daughter. My gaze shifted from the older woman's emerald locks to the younger's ruby curls. Perhaps genetics didn't work the same in parallel universes. Brushing my questions aside, I nodded at Atalanta and waited for the final and most out of place person in the room.

Well, perhaps that was a little too extreme; I was the most out of place person in the room seeing I had come from an entirely different universe. Regardless, the man before me was the first male I had seen in the village besides Bran. He was tall, six feet and then some, with long tousled golden hair. I doubted they had gyms in whatever land I had swept myself into, but the man looked as if he had worked out his whole life. His serious face gave way to a smile ever so slightly when he was introduced. "This is Fletcher, Beryl's nephew."

I raised my hand in a high five, but Fletcher left me hanging, staring at my hand like it was going to do a trick. "No, you raise your hand, too," I explained. He slowly brought his hand up in the mirrored position, and I smacked his palm.

He jerked his hand back, cradling it protectively, and turned to Bran. "She hit me."

Bran shrugged. "Nessie's a work in progress. I picked her off the street yesterday."

I crossed my arms, glad to know that I was Bran's dump puppy that had followed him home. He offered no further introduction for me. "So, when will I get to meet the governor?" I asked.

No one said anything. Fletcher looked at his feet. "I managed to escape after the edict was passed. I'm the only one who has been able to elude them."

Edict…elude…what? By Bran's strained expression, I realized I hit a nerve, and the conversation fizzled into silence. Three pairs of eyes looked at me, while I chewed on my lip and watched Bran for direction. Fletcher tossed his hair behind his shoulder and pointed to me. "What's her story?"

A white grin came to the mouth of my toaster salesman lookalike. "She's come to save you all."

The group focused on me, their faces frozen in hope, intrigue, and disbelief. I, of course, knew what eloquence such events required and punched Bran in the arm. "Well, that would have been kind of nice to know before you told everyone else, don't you think?"

Everyone let out a collective sigh. Oh, one of *those* heroes.

Chapter 8

Bran excused us by grabbing my elbow and dragging me outside of the house. The angry marching didn't stop until he'd pulled me under the shade of an oak tree. Guess that meant I was in trouble. Nothing new there. In fact, it seemed like ever since I picked up that sword, I was constantly jumping out of the frying pan and into the fire. Well, bring it on, Bran Muffin.

"What was that?" he seethed, letting go of my arm to ball up his fists. "You're supposed to be giving them hope, not acting unstable." A village woman in a garden by the oak tree raised her head before reaching for a handful of weeds.

What an impression we are leaving on these people. I took a step closer to Bran. Planting my hands on my hips defiantly, I said, "Oh, don't even try that, mister! You've given me no explanation about this, so excuse me if I'm a little concerned when you tell the leaders of a village that I'm here to save them. In fact, you've been keeping me in the dark about your grand plans since we met."

He laughed bitterly. "I'm sorry if you've been too busy falling off of horses and getting kidnapped by old women for a heart-to-heart chat!"

Oomph. That was a below the belt. I pointed an accusing finger at him. "Leave my horse-falling tendencies out of this! My muscles hurt like I've been hit by a dump truck, I haven't eaten in a day now, and I'm so tired I could curl up and sleep under this tree." I unsheathed the sword at my waist and tossed it on the ground. "I want to go home."

Bran held his hands out. "Let's not be too hasty." The words had lost their hard edge. "Blades of Remiel are hard to come by, and I still haven't heard how you stumbled upon it. Besides," he reached down and gingerly lifted the weapon, "legend says that these swords only come to the right wielder in a moment of need. I wasn't puffing you up back there; you've really come to save us."

"Well, I've done a bang up job of it since I got here," I huffed and lowered myself to the dusty ground. It was time to tag out and let the next hero take my place, someone who actually knew what they were doing. *Now, how to get the sword to take me home…*

Bran sat beside me, resting the sword on the ground between us. "Just hear me out, okay? You say I haven't told you what's going on; let me lay everything out for you."

Ugh. How could I argue with a man that smelled like toast? Maybe if I let him tell his story, he would find me something to eat. I crossed my arms. "Go ahead, but this doesn't mean I'm giving in."

Bran scooted to face me. "Well, let's start at the beginning. When you fell out of your realm, you landed in the kingdom of Spoons."

"Spoons? But all the soldiers had pictures of forks on their uniforms."

Bran looked over his shoulder and lowered his voice. "Don't say that word."

"What? Fork?" In one swift move, he clamped his hand over my mouth.

His voice was the barest of whispers. "We are called Spoons, but we're feuding with the kingdom of Forks." He let the hissed word fade.

"Let me guess," I rolled my eyes. "Their emblem is a spoon?"

"What are you talking about? The kingdom of Spoons' emblem is a spoon— a utensil with four tines you use to eat. The…other realm has the insignia of a…fork—a utensil with a little shallow bowl on the end."

Where was Wikipedia when you needed it? I guess there was no use arguing with a backwards alternate universe. "So, how did these kingdoms get such…unique names?"

Bran shrugged. "King Reed founded our nation hundreds of years ago. Having been chased by wolves for twenty-three days and nights, he stumbled upon the land our country is built on. The first thing he saw was a utensil, so he stabbed the wolves that were chasing him. After that, he held his small weapon in the air and proclaimed triumphantly," Bran's voice reached a falsetto. 'This item saved my life! I shall call it a "spoon" and the kingdom that I build in this place will be named after it.' Or so the history books tell us."

"What about Fo—the other kingdom?" I inquired, catching myself.

"King Reed's brother, Diggory, was the one who unleashed the wolves to kill Reed. He thought his brother was dead but found out he was the king of this small realm. Diggory became jealous, so he found his own land and named it after the utensil he used for the construction of his new kingdom, which he called…well, you know."

I sighed and leaned back against the oak, letting my eyelids close. Stabbing wolves, digging with spoons…who cared? And how could Bran prattle on when it was such a nice day outside…and such a cozy tree to lean against…

"Nessie, are you even listening to me?" Bran startled me from the beginnings of a nap.

"Unfortunately, yes." I crossed my arms. "Your ancestors were resourceful and violent; what does that have to do with me?"

"King Reed and King Diggory were at each other's throats. They were separated in age by only a year, but opposite in every way. King Reed liked architecture and military strategy. King Diggory preferred the arts and literature. They couldn't see eye to eye on anything, especially the Volumes."

My eyebrows rose. "The whatsits?"

Bran reached into his pocket and produced a small rectangular screen. He poked the face of the white box and instantly words burst forth from the device, hovering over the rectangle like a hologram.

My eyes scanned the letters. *"But God demonstrates his own love for us in this: While we were still sinners, Christ died for us."*

Why did those words sound familiar? After a moment of fighting early-onset Alzheimer's, memories of sitting in Ms. Helen's Sunday school class flooded my brain. The sweet silver-haired woman had read those words to me, which meant Bran had a holographic…Bible?

"The Volumes hold the words that God Himself gave to our people when our universe began, but each side twisted the words to meet their own opinions instead of reading them as they were intended."

"God is so infinite—who's to say that He didn't make worlds other than this one?" My mind was going to explode trying to process Mystical Unicorn's words from what now seemed like ages ago. How could she have known?

He returned the device to his pocket. "Even today, the ruler of Spoons, King Kermit, and the king of…the other country, Alfonso, bicker over the very same issues their great-great-great-great grandfathers disputed. It never ends." Bran looked back to the dingy homes around us. "And the innocent are caught in the crossfire."

The nearby woman bent over her garden, trying to coax life out of the crumbling dirt. Beads of sweat dripped from her brow and rolled off her face. "Do all the townspeople of Spoons live in this kind of poverty?"

He shook his head sadly. "Not all. This group of people is looked down upon by the rest of society, referred to as half-breeds. They are part-Spoon and part-Fork."

A smile tugged at my lips. "Sporks!"

Bran buried his face in his palms. "Um…that's not what we call them."

I shrugged. "Well, it seems pretty difficult to say 'Fpoons'."

Muttering to himself, Bran massaged his forehead and continued. "Through-out the history of our kingdoms, half-breeds have been treated poorly because of the relentless feud on both sides. However, that treatment was usually limited to haughty looks and upturned noses. Their families were never compacted into shacks like these on the outskirts of town. You asked about the men earlier; they've been carted off to work camps. The women have to look after the children so they can't work, meaning there is barely enough food to fill their bellies."

Bran smiled ironically. "You want to know the funny thing? The half-breeds have an understanding of the Volumes and the God they reveal better than the kings or rich subjects."

"Why the sudden change in attitude towards the half-breeds?" I asked.

"Do you remember the soldiers you saw when you first got here?" he asked. How could I forget? With my nod, Bran carried on. "The tall man with the long scar on his face and the silver pendant—his name is Commander Leander."

Seriously, he needed a different title. Maybe General Leander?

A snort escaped me, but Bran ignored it. "King Kermit has been ailing for quite some time."

"I hope he doesn't croak," I blurted before I could take it back.

Crossing his arms, Bran gave me a dark look. "Do you want me to explain or not?" His words brought me back to sobering reality. As crazy as all of this sounded, this was his life, not a game. Even I wasn't hungry enough to be that heartless.

With my humble apology, he carried on. "There's…suspicion that Leander had something to do with it. Regardless, he's taking the king's weakened power as an instant promotion and does whatever he wants, like proclaiming the edict to gather the half-breed men into work camps.

"Rumor has it Leander used to love a girl from Forks, but something happened with their relationship. Either way, he hates Forks and the half-breeds with a passion. He's out of control on his rampage against them. Recently he's upped the ante by executing leaders of the half-breeds. That's why Beryl's daughter, Atalanta, was on the chopping block yesterday. She would have been the second leader executed this month." He paused. "I've heard rumors once he takes control of the kingdom, he plans to eradicate them completely."

The statement left his face pale. He reached up to rub his temples and slumped against the trunk of the oak.

Eradicate. Completely. Meaning mass genocide. People dying. The faces of Atalanta, Beryl, and Fletcher came to mind, and the gravity of the situation hit me. I traced a path in the soil by the oak tree, swallowing the lump in my throat. "So…where do I come in?" Please…please say I was here to find the real hero. Maybe hang up fliers, make a few phone calls, and call it a day?

Silence overtook us, leaving only the rustling of the leaves. The village woman continued to work the earth, occasionally dropping a small, withered seed into the coarse dirt.

"I had a dream that started a few months ago," Bran said. All right. We were now in the dream-sharing segment of the conversation. "Leander was standing at this thick tree with an axe chopping at it. His swings made deep cuts in the wood, but it wouldn't fall down. Finally, it looked so weak, one more swing would collapse the tree. A voice whispered, 'Eethi andre canasi' and suddenly the ground liquefied around him! Out of nowhere," Bran stretched his hand out, "a sea serpent emerged from the water and swallowed Leander." He paused, huffing and puffing from the excitement. "At first I thought I had just eaten too much for dinner, but then the dream kept occurring. First once a week and then every night."

Sitting in my room, my fingers run up the blade of the sword, sparking life into the glowing runes. Coincidence, right? "That doesn't mean I have anything to do with it."

He went completely still, and I squirmed under the earnestness of his dark eyes. "The dreams stopped the night before you arrived."

"Happenstance?" I ventured. Heat rose to my face, and my breathing quickened. No. Want me to change a lightbulb? Maybe I could handle that. Need me to save a race of people from dying? He had the wrong girl. I stood up from the ground and started pacing.

Bran's voice raised an octave as he pushed himself up to join me. "Nessie! Don't you see? The oak is the half-breeds! Leander is chipping away at them, trying to kill them. You were brought here for the purpose of saving them! The sea monster is you, Nessie!" He waved his arms wildly.

I growled, pinching at my skin. "Do I have scales, Bran? I'm not a reptile, and I don't have gills. Why would I be the sea monster in your dream?"

A slight smile touched his lips. "Your name: Nessie. Like the Loch Ness monster from Scotland. Get it?"

Arms crossed and brow furrowed, I let his words sink in. Didn't I feel like God was calling me here for a purpose? Was He announcing my arrival months before I even considered the possibility of an alternate world? And why—I whipped my head around to face Bran. "Wait a minute! How do you know about the Loch Ness monster? How do you know about Scotland?"

His eyes darted around quickly. "Um…well…you know. There's…uhh…"

I inhaled a gasp. "You *are* Eric. You're my toaster salesman. And you lied to me." While I was still on a roll, I jabbed my finger in his chest. "And guess what? Your little toaster you sold me the other day—IT DIED. Kaput. Mystical Unicorn tried to blame it on solar flares, but I think you're really selling faulty equipment!" I sucked in a deep breath and turned away from him, the gears turning frantically in my brain. "It all makes sense now. You weren't even fazed I was from another world. That's because you're from another world, too."

Eric/Bran looked like a puppy that had just been kicked by its owner. "Look, Nessie. I was afraid that if I told you the truth from the start, you wouldn't come with me. I—"

I balled my fists angrily. "And you figured once you told the leader of the village I was their savior, I'd have to help? Nice move. It definitely won *my* trust."

The puppy dog face was gone, replaced by an angry Eric. "Do whatever you want, Nessie. I'm not going to sit here and beg."

"You know what I want to do?" The words came out hard and bitter.

He leaned his face in closer. "What, Nessie? What do you want to do?"

"I want to punch you in the face," I seethed.

He crossed his arms and smirked. "Go ahead. I don't think you have the guts to do it."

Technically, I had his permission. That's what I told myself when I slammed my balled knuckles into his smug look. We both gasped in unison. Eric because he didn't think I would really hit him, and me because…well, the same reason. I brought my lethal weapons to my open mouth. "I…uhh…Eric, are you okay? I'm so sorry! I don't know what—"

The gentle sound of his laughter caught me off guard, but I guessed laughter was better than crying. He cradled his eye gingerly. "It's okay. I guess we're even now." He stepped closer, the proximity causing my face to flush. "I'm sorry for lying to you."

Ugh. His intentions were well enough; I mean trying to save people's lives was as noble as it got. Besides, how could I stay mad at that lopsided smile? "Yeah, we make a great pair of examples for God—a liar and a brawler."

A breeze rustled the leaves of the oak above us, and I turned to face the dilapidated house. It was time to make a decision. *Everything happens for a reason, Agnes,"* my mother used to say after flunked tests or break-ups, but did the same apply to an otherworldly Mission Impossible situation? I had to admit that a freaky glowing sword transporting me to another universe was a bit out-of-the-ordinary to be a coincidence.

Why me, God? Why not some brave, ninja bodybuilder instead? I reached down to pick up the Blade of Remiel. Guess I had to stick around long enough to see what the reason was. "Shall we head back?" I turned around to face Eric and cringed at the red swollen flesh around his eye. "That's not good."

"What's not good?" Eric asked. I stepped towards him, gently rubbing the angry skin.

How could I have lost control like that? "I'm really sorry, Eric," I pulled back, staring at my feet.

His fingers tousled my hair and raised my chin up to face him. "No worries. Besides," he winked, "I think it makes me look more manly. Don't you agree?"

Now that he mentioned it… "You mean more like a criminal," I smirked, heading back towards Beryl's home.

The woman working in her garden stood up to acknowledge us as we passed next to her, but she gasped at the notice of my compatriot's battle wound. *Definitely* leaving an impression there.

Eric knocked on the door, and after a brief moment, it slid away, revealing Beryl with her emerald hair. "Bran, I was just wondering where you—" she brought her hands up to her mouth. "What happened to your face?" Everyone looked from Eric's swollen eye to me.

Eric rubbed his neck thoughtfully. "Well, you see—"

"We had a disagreement," I blurted.

Beryl poked her lips out. Atalanta looked at me approvingly. Fletcher held up his hand for a high five.

No one spoke until Beryl broke the silence. "Are you two married, by any chance?"

Eric's face turned pink, but I shook my head. "We were yesterday, but not today."

"That explains a lot," Fletcher commented with a real smile.

"That's not really what she means," Eric protested, but everyone was already wearing Cheshire cat grins.

"If your appearance gives any indication of what you've talked about," Beryl chimed in, "I'm not sure I want to hear."

"It was just a misunderstanding," I assured. The room quieted and waited for more. Here went nothing.

With a deep breath, I found my words. "Something that everyone can be clear on is the fact that I will do whatever is in the power God gives me to help your people."

A hush fell over the room. Beryl, Fletcher, and Atalanta exchanged guarded looks. I had no idea what passed between them, what fears or hopes they communicated through those silent glances, but after a moment their attention turned back to me. Beryl stepped forward and placed her hands on my shoulders. "'But God chose the foolish things of the world to shame the wise; God chose the weak things of the world to shame the strong,'" she quoted. "Daughter, we will be behind you every step of the way. May God bless the path you take."

Atalanta clasped her hands together. "If you are committed to this, we are with you. Have you thought of any plans yet?"

Eric ran a hand through his dark hair. "Well, we haven't really—"

The words possessed my tongue before I even contemplated their meaning. "We're going to rescue the men from the work camps."

Beryl and Atalanta gasped and hugged each other, while Fletcher closed his eyes. I glanced heavenward. *Well, God, that was unexpected.* Watching the tearful hope gathering in the room, I decided to add more: *please don't let me disappoint them.*

<h1 style="text-align:center">Chapter 9</h1>

"L et me get the door for you," Eric offered. The noon sun beat down over us, beads of sweat sliding down our foreheads. The cloudless blue sky offered little relief from the heat while we picked crops from Beryl's garden. Her weathered shack looked more appealing the longer we went without shade.

Eric wiped at his forehead and attempted to hand off the basket of *kolyas*, purple carrot-like vegetables that I'd found were quite delicious. A gentle breeze cooled the perspiration on my neck from working the soil. Though the patch of dirt behind Beryl's home was brittle and dry, the kind woman somehow brought life to it, nursing a meager selection of colorful vegetables.

"No, I have it," I insisted, but instead of grasping a doorknob, my fingers slammed into the wooden frame, earning me a splinter in my knuckle.

With a groan, I took the basket from Eric and banged my head against the worn door, my hair flopping in all directions. "I just want to get inside. Why doesn't this world believe in doorknobs?"

He patted my shoulder. "Just have patience. Watch." Eric placed his index finger in the center of the smooth door and effortlessly traced three circles and a triangle. The symbol glowed and the door slid to the side, as it had in Ferny's house. "All private homes are protected by rune keys. One has to know the correct symbol to trace on the door before it will open."

Countless memories of losing my keys and having to shimmy through my apartment window replayed in my mind. "But how do you remember it?"

Eric shrugged. "Some people carve the symbol on the inside of their door, while others write it down in a secret place. After the first couple of times, it becomes second nature."

Inside Beryl's house, we stepped around the straw pallets. Fletcher was reading suspended words from his copy of the Volumes. He touched the white box and new words replaced the existing ones. The sudden movement made me dizzy.

We made our way to the corner where a rudimentary wooden counter was nailed into the wall. Guess that was the kitchen. The countertop held what looked like a silver microwave with a square dial on the face and a bowl attached to the top. Instead of a sink, bowls of water, supposedly drawn from a well I had seen by the field outside, lined the floor. Eric splashed some of the water onto the eggplant-colored vegetables and placed them into the silver bowl on top of the "microwave."

A subtle headache kicked up, my brain struggling to keep track of all the new things I was learning. "So anyone can get into your house if they know your rune key?"

Eric shook his head and added more of the kolyas to the bowl. "No, you can set the outside of your door to respond only to the fingerprints of certain people. It's very effective technology."

My lips poked out in a pout. "So many things to learn."

"Oh, it's not that bad," Fletcher said, putting his white box in his pocket. He got up from the pallet and stepped into the kitchen area. Backed by the straw bedding and dirt floors, he reminded me of an income-challenged Fabio. "For instance," he said, twisting the square dial on the microwave, "You just put your ingredients into this *cofana*, set the timer, and it does all the work. Come back in a few minutes and you have warm, vegetable porridge."

"I prefer my toaster," I mumbled.

Fletcher sat on the counter and laced his hands behind his long blond hair. "So, do we have the beginnings of a plan yet?"

I twisted the material of my leggings around my finger just to have something to fiddle with. Eric and I had talked of strategy while picking the *kolyas* but quickly realized how little we knew. "We need some more information. What do you know about the work camps?"

Fletcher's face lost color. "More than I would like." He raised the edge of his tunic to reveal long scars stretching across his side, echoes of deep gashes that had once split flesh. "I spent an unfortunate amount of time in one of Leander's work camps before managing to escape."

My forearms prickled with goosebumps, unrelated to the constant draft in the home. Work camps, torture methods…it all sounded like terrors foreign to my comfy frappuccino-filled existence back at home. How could such cruelty exist when townspeople knew?

But maybe there was a bright side to all of Fletcher's pain. "So you already have a plan to break the others free?" I ventured.

Lowering his shirt, Fletcher shook his head. "It was only through luck I was able to leave that horrifying place." Without further explanation, he pushed himself off the counter and sketched a rudimentary map in the dirt floor. "There are three compounds where the men are located, two on the outskirts of the city, and one right in the heart of the capitol."

He leaned closer to the map drawing. "At the compound in the middle of the capitol where I was, I counted roughly thirty armed soldiers surrounding a barricaded building. The prisoners are held in locked cells when they're not working." He shot me a devilish grin. "Lucky for you, I've been doing some free-lance investigating in my spare time, concocting a plan to save the remaining men. The other compounds have half the number of guards, but they also hold fewer half-breeds." Fletcher paused and walked towards the door. "I took Atalanta with me on my last visit. Let me see if she can remember any more details that will help us."

Glad we have someone on our team who knows what they're doing, I thought, watching him leave. I cradled my aching head in my hands. "God's pulling another David and Goliath, and this time we're David."

Eric ruffled my hair "It's not an easy path by any means, but remember we're part of a bigger plan. You're not alone in this."

His comment was met with my frustrated groan. "Why is it so hard to trust, even when we know God's faithful?"

Eric shrugged, opening the *cofana* and pulling out the finished vegetable porridge. "I guess our memories are never as clear as the problems in front of us."

Up to this point, my life had been cushy and safe, never "needing" God because I handled everything myself—that was, if ending up alone, depressed, and empty was considered "handling it." But charging into some prison with armed soldiers based on the notion I was called here for that purpose? Not a safe move at all.

A question crept up I couldn't shake. I was never confronted with any-thing difficult in my life; what if I found my faith wasn't strong enough? Did I trust God with my life, my plans? Worse still, what if He let me down?

"Are you okay, Nessie?" Eric nudged me, handing me a bowl of purple mush.

I stirred the mixture absentmindedly. "Yeah, I'm fine." *Just fine,* I tried to convince myself, but my unsettling questions subsided under the surface, begging to be answered.

§ § §

The sun sank down into the horizon, washing the compound below in pale blue. The wooded hill Eric, Fletcher, and I nestled on provided us with a perfect view of the grounds. Razor wire fence wrapped around buildings with solid, cement ceilings, the first I had seen since arriving.

Fletcher crouched beside me, his silver helmet and mirrored visor catching me by surprise. Despite Eric's earlier explanation of the headgear as standard for the compound soldiers, I couldn't help but think they belonged on the head of a motorcyclist. Fletcher removed the helmet and pointed to the gray building furthest from us, where two guards stood post outside the south doors. "That's the prison where the men are kept when they aren't working," he whispered. "The one connected to that," he indicated a square building, painted deep red, "is the soldiers' quarters."

Okay, so we just needed to sneak through the razor wire, past the buildings, trick the guards…and…The air seemed thicker. I sucked in deep breaths, trying not to hyperventilate. *Strong and courageous*, the thought coursed through my mind, and I reached for the comforting hilt of my sword. Maybe I should have taken some combat lessons before we came here. *Strong and courageous.*

Eric edged closer to my position in the foliage and pulled up the visor on his silver helmet that matched Fletcher's. "Everything's coming together, Ness." His proximity and whispered words twisted my butterfly-filled stomach into knots.

Nope. No time to think about that. It was hard enough to keep the panic attacks at bay without considering how his deep voice stirred joy inside of me or how his nearness kept the chill out of the air.

Distractions were a luxury I couldn't afford. For better or worse, I was married to this rescue mission—a union that was, pardon the cliché, till death do us part. Ignoring the probability of that happening, I pushed aside branches obscuring my vision and took one last dusk-lit survey of our target.

"What's that?" I pointed to a large, swampy pool located near the closest edge of the compound.

Fletcher's face grew somber. "That…that is where the men work, wading day after day into the acid swamps to collect *millenium* for the Captiol's power-houses." He rolled up the sleeves of the guard uniform Beryl sewed for him, chemical burns stretching across his arm.

I closed my eyes, clenching my fists. We had spent days surveying this camp. Spork men were herded into the swamp like cattle. Luckily, the distance we were at was too great to witness the pain on their faces as they stepped into the burning pools, but we saw the weaker ones fall into the sludge when the noon sun scorched the earth. Soldiers seemed to take pleasure in whipping the tired workers mercilessly, their feeble cries drifting on the wind in vain. No one ever came to save them.

For Fletcher's sake…for their sake, this had to work.

South, trees served as a barrier to a neighboring community, with houses clumped together as if huddling for warmth. With the right angle, one might have seen through their transparent ceilings and watched families settling in for the night. How could they be sitting down for dinner when innocents were tortured just across the street? Did the sounds of wounded men become second nature, like the rattling of trains by a railroad?

"They're changing the guard soon. It's time." Eric clamped a hand on my shoulder, rumpling the dark cloak he loaned me. My job was to blend in with the shadows. If all should fail, resorting to the sword was my next option.

Really regretted not taking those lessons…

Mindful of our presence, we crept down the hill until we were up close and personal with the razor wire fence. Fletcher produced a heavy-duty pair of cutters from his pocket and clipped a small section. Though he provided ample room to pass, I couldn't help but wince at the dark stains on the wire where some unfortunate person stepped too close.

"If it's so easy to cut the wires, why has no one broken into the compound before?" I'd asked Fletcher during our planning sessions, and his response haunted me.

"They don't need to keep people out because no one dares to break in. Those work camps hold only death and darkness."

Death and darkness was right. There were no guards standing post anywhere besides the outside of the jail. Who would want to break into this place? The smell of roasted flesh permeated the air surrounding the bubbling pools we passed. I was careful not to step in the mysterious piles and puddles that littered the barren dirt. Feces? Blood? Human appendages? My imagination was having a field day.

Our trek towards the jailhouse was painfully slow, every door slam and shout freezing us in our tracks until all was clear. Once we reached the red building, my prayers went into overdrive. It was go time. Pressing up against the shadowed walls, I gave Eric's hand a quick squeeze for good luck.

Two short men wearing the same silver garb as Fletcher and Eric were in clear sight.

"Almost done for the night," one sighed, fiddling with the visor on his helmet.

"Yeah, if our relief ever gets here," the other grumbled. "Always late, messing around at those gambling houses."

Eric took his cue, lowering his visor and boldly striding out of the darkness with Fletcher at his side. Still scooted up against the wall, I held onto the hilt of my sword in case things went south.

The first guard took off his helmet and gave his flattened hair a fluff. "Well, isn't this surprising." He gestured to Eric and Fletcher. I wondered if the guards could hear the sound of my heartbeat, now blasting from my chest. "Someone's actually on time."

Eric nodded. "Ended our games early. Lady Luck was not on our side tonight."

The soldiers chuckled and gave Eric a slap on the back. "Keep her locked up tight."

"Will do." Eric and Fletcher took their posts by the door. The men started heading in my direction.

Pressing harder against the wall of the red building, I squeezed into the corner and held my breath. They walked past, oblivious. Time stretched on and my racing thoughts made concentrating difficult. I tried keeping track of the seconds but lost count in the hundreds. What if Eric and Fletcher were discovered?

Raucous singing filled the silent compound. A new pair of guards sauntered up to the jailhouse doors, too drunk to notice me in the shadows.

"Okay, fellas. We're here to take over," the first one slurred at Fletcher and Eric. He attempted to salute but stumbled.

His companion tottered over tipsily and jostled his helmet askew. "At ease!" The partner's words sparked a giggle fit between the two.

"We have sentry duty tonight," Fletcher informed the pair sternly. "We've already changed out for the night shift."

The first soldier looked at his friend and launched into more hysterics. "Benny, you told me we had sentry duty tonight. You crazy blockhead!"

The soldiers wandered away from the jailhouse towards town. I waited until their boisterous chatter faded before peeling off the wall. Fletcher swiftly traced the rune key on the door panel. His eyes lowered when I looked at him questioningly. "Every day, I watched the soldiers come and go. Never forgot the key symbol."

Without a word, Fletcher opened the door and we stepped into the dimly lit hallway where the odors of unwashed bodies and vomit made my stomach turn. Candlelight flickered off the walls, and I noticed a dank, slimy substance coating the corridor. A feline-sized rat skittered dangerously close to my foot. I kicked at it and watched the creature scamper towards the door. Good riddance. The narrow hallway was wide enough for two to walk, but that was only if both were comfortable brushing up against wall gunk.

My mother always chastised me for being a germaphobe. I never believed her until now. Trying to avoid the ooze on the walls, we walked single file down the curvy hallways. If I didn't think too hard, I could imagine our trek a game.

Believe me, I could get into games. When my kindergarten teacher, Mrs. Peters, made us creep like mice down the hall, I was that one kid crawling on all fours, scuttling through the legs of my classmates and trying to chew on the baseboards. My dedication to delusions knew no bounds, which was helpful when the game was "Don't Die While Sneaking Into A Torture Camp."

A piece of sludge dripped off the ceiling onto my head, and I bit my lip to keep from screaming. See? I was already winning.

Fletcher tiptoed around puddles, occasionally halting and tilting his head. "I don't think we're far now," he finally whispered, waving for us to follow. Before the words left his mouth, a rhythmic clanking echoed in front of us.

No, no, no. Sweat gathered at my brow, and I squeezed my eyes shut. *Please, God, just make it go away.* My eyes opened to man-shaped shadows stretching out across the flickering walls. Apparently, God wasn't having any of my prayers tonight. Heart racing, my hand searched frantically behind me for Eric. If this was how it was going to end, I needed a dose of that warm comfort his touch seemed to lend.

The walls seemed to close in as the clanking grew louder; there was no furniture to hide behind, no cubbyholes to sneak into. Squeezing against the discolored, oozing walls wouldn't save us. My fingers found Eric's hand in the dark and clasped around it tightly.

Fletcher yanked down his mirrored visor, and a bearded guard, helmet missing, came into view. Lucky for him, the life of a solider didn't require a charming appearance. His furrowed unibrow and snarling lips wouldn't have gotten him very far as a Walmart greeter.

"What are you doing here?" he barked, reaching for the hilt of his sword.

Eric's gentle touch turned into a squeezing wristlock. His deep voice behind me took an angry, bitter turn. "Saw her trespassing, sir. We were escorting her to a holding cell for now to see how she'd like to live among the jackals."

The smell of beer invaded my space when the guard stepped past Fletcher and leaned in close. Were those flecks of meat in his beard? Gross. "What would bring a…defenseless girl like you into such a godforsaken place?"

His warm, stale breath made my arm hairs bristle. *Um…umm…resort to ditzy girl!* Borrowing the blank facial expressions of a mindless cheerleader, I tilted my head. "Uh…what?"

Rolling his eyes, the guard sneered, mere inches away from my face. "What are you doing here?"

If Eric hadn't been practicing his wrist-wrestling moves on me, I would have included a hair twirl. "So my best friend—well, she's not my *best* friend, but we've gone shopping a few times—she said there were some guys in here. And well…I was like, 'Well, are they cute?' and she was all like 'I don't know.' And I was like 'Well, you should check.' And she was like, 'No way.' And I was li—"

The soldier glared at me, but a thin malicious smile began to spread across his face. "I understand. I'll take you to your cell."

The smirk on his face made my stomach sink. There was definitely an excess amount of testosterone in the cramped hallway. I squirmed in Eric's grip, no longer comforting or warm. *God, please…do something.*

Eric's deep voice flooded the close quarters. "I've already have a special one picked out for her."

My skin crawled despite the deception but his words had the desired effect. The other soldier backed up, his smile thin and haunting. "I'll just have to interrogate her…later." With a lick of his lips, he pushed past us and marched on. The tension in my shoulders eased when his metal clanking faded into silence.

Once we were out of earshot, Eric released my wrist and rested a hand on my back. "Maybe you should wait outside for us."

He was right; it was foolish for a Batman-wannabe like myself to try to take on the world. Would anyone blame me if I turned around and waltzed out the door now? My leg stretched forward to pivot, but the weight of the Blade of Remiel tugged at my belt. Didn't Eric say the sword only came to right wielder in a moment of need? If that was true, turning back wasn't an option, even for a receptionist at a Port-a-John rental company.

"No," I took a step forward in the darkened hallway. "This is something I'm supposed to do."

Fletcher nodded and led us down the corridor and into the jail where the undeniable stench of filth and neglect made my stomach lurch.

My appetite didn't improve when I took notice of the rat-infested cells housing wraith-like men. Behind iron bars, a group of haggard and weary prisoners watched with sunken eyes. The only sign of color against the dingy walls was their hair, once vibrant hues of orange, crimson, and emerald, now muted with sweat and dirt. The prisoners' clothes were a dismal shade of gray, ripped and burned, exposing mottled flesh and bony ribs beneath.

Silence overcame me, and for a moment, I forgot I was supposed to be afraid, that it was my life on the line if we were caught. My imagination conjured stories of these men's lives, loved ones they had left behind, and pain they endured on a daily basis. What could it be like to be torn away from family and forced to live in such conditions? How could these guards come to work every day, ignoring the horror before them? How desensitized did they have to get to turn a blind eye to such depravity?

Guilt, triggered by the most mundane memories, washed over me. Lounging on the couch, watching television, stuffing cereal into my face, painting my nails at work—did I really live such a meaningless life when there was this kind of suffering? After twenty-four years of blessing upon blessing, what had I accomplished besides being depressed and malcontent?

Eric snapped his fingers demandingly, waking me from my reverie. Ahead of us, five soldiers stood near the cells, four of which were in the middle a card game.

"Soldiers," Eric barked, "we have a new prisoner." The four scrambled to put away their cards while the youngest soldier, maybe seventeen, with cropped blond hair and soft features snapped to attention. "You," Eric pointed to the teenager. "What's your name?"

"Uh…S-seth, sir," he shifted nervously.

"Seth, I want you to open the door to a cell—an empty one." The teen's hands shook, fumbling for the keys on his belt to unlock the door. Perfect.

The cell door creaked open to an eerily-moist space with scratchy pine straw thrown carelessly in one corner. Though the lump was supposed to mimic a bed, I was not interested in fighting the three hand-sized rats that had decided to call it home. When I didn't step into the cell, Seth grabbed my arm, ready to throw me in.

"Where are the other guards?" Eric inquired.

Seth made a quick glance at the other four soldiers who were now standing at attention. "It gets boring down here…sir. Most of them go off to gamble and leave us to watch the prisoners."

Eric feigned a look of disgust. "Gamble? Where do they go off to do this?"

"The tavern in the town just south of here," he admitted. "They go after dark so they can't be spotted easily."

Eric nodded. "I will report this to my superiors. Thank you for your cooperation. And as for you four," he turned to the card-playing quartet, "if guarding prisoners is not *exciting* enough for you, I can find you a new job cleaning out cells or scrubbing walls. However, you also didn't run off gambling with your compatriots." Eric paused, rubbing his chin. "You four will step into the corridor where you will wait for me to deliver your punishment."

The four scurried, heads down, past Eric and into the hall we had come from. Go, Eric. Taking charge and kicking butts, he was a man after my own heart. Seth escorted me into the cell, but before leaving, I felt him lean in close and breathe deeply.

"Are you smelling my hair?" I shouted angrily, batting him away. Weird kid.

He turned red, stammering for an answer, but I noticed the ring of keys he left in the door. Calling upon my inner damsel-in-distress, I threw my arms around his neck. "Oh, please don't lock me in here!" My fingers furtively reached for the keys, unsuccessful in my first attempt. He stood motionless for a moment and looked to Eric.

Pushing me away, a frown crossed his face. "Get in your cell, woman," he growled unconvincingly.

Reattaching, I tightened the embrace. "But I'll die in here," I whispered dramatically. A little further…and yes, I pilfered the means to my escape. With a pretty little pout, my pleading hug came to an end, and I fell to my knees in desperation, careful to hide the keys in my fist. "I guess it's no use," I sighed. He marched out of the cell, slamming the door with a resounding *clang*.

"I'm just doing my job," he explained.

Eric turned to the young guard. "I find the behavior of your fellow soldiers unacceptable and will make sure you receive a promotion. My fellow officer," he nodded to Fletcher, "will keep watch over matters while I speak with you and the other soldiers waiting in the hallway. Follow me." Caught up in his new persona, Eric puffed his chest out, his firm chin giving him a regal air. The confidence he exuded could have made me swoon. Where was the nervous toaster salesman who knocked on my door a year ago?

Like the obedient soldier he was, Seth marched after Eric, his face beaming with excitement. Fifty pairs of hungry eyes zeroed in on the ring of jangling keys in my hand. No one spoke a word or moved until Eric and the soldier disappeared. Once he was gone, an older prisoner with a dirty, scraggly beard, stepped forward to the edge of his cell.

Time to move. "What is Eric doing?" I asked, handing Fletcher the keys

"He's going to take them out," he whispered. My eyes widened.

"Like *take out?*" Visions of Eric in Mafia get-up made me shudder. Was he driving them down to the docks now? Tying a cement block around their feet before they went sleeping with the fishes?

"Not like that. Beryl mixed up some sleeping dust. It won't be hard for him to knock them out for a little while. Once he's done, he is going to cut the fence on the eastern side so we can sneak the prisoners out that way without going all the way back across the compound. I'll go back through the corridor, make sure there's no one coming, and then lead the men to Eric. You let them out and then meet us outside."

He disappeared, and I wiggled the keys in locks, trying out multiple keys to find the right ones to open the cell doors. "Your wives and children think it's high time you come back to them," I whispered to the Sporks. Their faces brightened with hope, and one by one, (once I found the right key) filed out into the dim hallway to meet Fletcher. Finally all of the prisoners were out except for the last one: a middle aged man with green hair speckled with gray. *Beryl's husband,* I thought with a smile.

His eyes filled with tears as he kissed my cheek softly. "You are an angel of God," he whispered.

The comment made me blush. "I don't know about that; I gave someone a black eye earlier this week. We'll give credit for your rescue to God alone."

He nodded and set off down the hallway. I glanced around to make sure there weren't any stragglers. Nope, all clear. But then I noticed something in one of the cells. Bending down, I traced a crude engraving in the stone floor.

"HE IS FAITHFUL."

To think that I was so close to turning around and leaving the rescue for someone else. Did God really use me as the answer to countless prayers from these men and their families? How many nights had they pleaded for relief with no answer and yet still trusted? Oh, to have that kind of belief, to know that God wouldn't leave me hanging. My problems here were larger than bread crumbs stuck in my keyboard; I had a feeling God would teach me about His faithfulness before my time was done.

I did a quick sweep and retreated back down the corridor, ready to be rid of the dirty prison. In my hurry to exit, I collided with a wall. *Ow, guess I should look where I—*an iron grip clamped onto my shoulder. I saw, not a wall, but two men. The first was the soldier with the unibrow I'd had the pleasure of meeting earlier, and the second was none other than the amusingly-named Commander Leander. Neither looked very amused.

Chapter 10

*O*h crap oh crap oh crap. *They found us. It's over. They're going to torture us and the Sporks. The mission has failed, I'm dead. We're all dead.* The thoughts sent me hyperventilating, and a wave of nausea rolled over me.

"What are you doing here?" Leander snarled, the pressure of his hand tightening on my shoulder.

No "aha, we've found you," or "Where have all the prisoners gone?" That was a good sign. They didn't look hurried or frantic; Leander's cropped black hair was seamlessly in place, and the creep of a soldier beside him had not even a wrinkle in his uniform. So, the prisoners were safe for the moment. My fingers tingled, and I flexed them to regain feeling. Above all else, I needed to calm down and handle this. Deep breaths.

Eric and Fletcher needed time to get as far away from the building as possible. In a flash, I unsheathed my sword…which Leander seized from me and cast aside. In a karate move, he shifted his grip to my forearm and whipped me around, wrenching my right arm behind me. Pain coursed through my shoulder, and I bit my lip to keep from crying out. *Can't let him know he's getting to me*, I thought to myself.

"Would you believe I'm looking for the bathroom?" I ventured, sweat gathering at my forehead.

His acrid voice whispered into my ear. "I don't know who you are, but ever since you've shown up, there have been problems in this kingdom. Something gives me the impression I'm going to enjoy your interrogation."

My breathing sped up, tripping over itself as Leander pushed me towards the jail. I had seen every *Sixty Minutes* episode about kidnappings, and if I'd learned anything, it was that you never went anywhere with the kidnapper. The grimy guard beside the commander rubbed his beard, smiling cruelly. Nope, wasn't happening.

My sword was on the floor. I hadn't paid attention in self-defense class, and I wasn't strong enough to fight them. But I did have one thing going for me: my keen understanding of a temper tantrum. Still wrenched in Leander's crushing grasp, I went limp.

With a grunt, Leander caught my weight and squeezed my arm harder, twisting it until the pain in my shoulders seared. Was my arm still attached? My eyes watered from the pain, and I heard a gasp escape my lips.

"Nessie? Was that your name?" Leander leaned in closer and the angle afforded me a look at the jagged scar stretching from his cheekbone to chin. "Face it, Nessie. It's a dead end and you have nowhere left to go." His stern features were unyielding, commanding…spelling my defeat out for me. My shoulder burned like fire, and a desire to surrender surfaced. It was over.

But it couldn't be over. Not when we were so close. Not when these men had suffered countless atrocities. Even after all of these things, the Sporks had somehow still carried hope, holding on to the promise that God was faithful.

Well, that was a firm promise, and that day, He was going to use me to carry it out. I conjured up images of violent linebackers for inspiration and slammed my elbow into Leander's stomach. He didn't end up sprawled out on the floor as I intended, but his grip loosened enough for me to jerk free and jet past him, grabbing my sword before I bolted down the hall.

For the record, I wasn't a big runner in my usual life. However, sprinting past the oozing walls taught me that literally running for your life was sufficient encouragement for that level of exercise.

Candlelight flickered off the wet stone, illuminating a crossroads. *Fletcher told me to meet him where we came in, but…*

Further away from the prisoners meant more time for them to escape. Well, the plan was messed up already, so why not? I swerved left, dodging puddles of mire lining the floor. With every crossroads, I picked a new direction. One of them had to lead out, right?

Air rushed past my ears, blocking out the sound of everything except my pounding heart. Had I lost Leander and the sleaze ball? And more importantly, was that wooden slab up ahead really a door? My eyes darted around, searching the panel furiously for the handle before remembering this stupid world didn't believe in doorknobs. *What did Eric tell me about rune ke—*

Leander's swears echoed off the stone, growing louder.

I ran my shaking hand across the wood, looking for any kind of indentation, but apparently soldiers don't like to keep their rune keys openly displayed. In a moment of desperation, I pulled out my sword, raising it above my head like a mighty warrior. "Open, you stupid door!" I hissed and swung the sword down, hoping to decimate the wood. The blade landed with a thud, not even leaving a scratch.

Why? After all this, was I really going to be defeated by a door?

Leander appeared at the end of the hallway, and, noticing my entrapment, slowed his run, teeth bared like a bulldog. In an easy minute, he could have been at my side, dragging me back to the jail, but instead he stalked forward, toying with his prey. He wasn't here for the kill; this was a game.

"Having some difficulty there?" he smirked.

I leaned my head on the wood. Every step Leander took was a step closer to my death and there weren't many paces left between us. *God, you've got to help me! Strike him with blindness, give me inhuman strength, or maybe you can just open*—My eyes darted to a glowing blue rune in the middle of the door, matching the hue of the shimmering stones on my sword.

The door rushed open, and I stumbled forward. Never had I been so happy to see a bubbling acid swamp. Sliding the sword back into its sheath and running into the cool night air, I didn't stay to ponder the mystery, but headed for the opening in the razor wire fence we first entered through.

At high speed, I couldn't afford the same carefulness I'd entered with. The sharp edges of the cut wire tore through my cloak, nicking bits of flesh. Glancing behind, I smiled excitedly. The cuts were worth Leander's look of frustration. He slowed at the torn fence, not quite as willing to rush through the dangerous obstacle.

"Someone stop that girl!" Leander's cries rang out into the empty night. Instead of waiting to see who took up the commander's call, I bolted towards the thinly wooded area south of the compound.

A group of large, sturdy trees separated the work camp from a cluster of homes. My sprinting led me to the largest of the trees nestled up against the side of a yellow house. Hide and seek behind the trunk was not the wisest option…unless… In fourth grade, Jimmy Adamson got mad that I wouldn't let him into my fort and took his psychotic Rottweiler off the chain to chase me around the neighborhood. The only reason I didn't become dog food that day was because of my superior tree-climbing skills. Really needed those abilities to come in handy.

Seizing a thick branch, I hoisted myself up into the leaves, scrambling close to the top. I shifted away from the branch poking into my thigh and glanced over to the transparent roof beside me where a family was getting ready for bed.

Hope they don't look up and see me sitting up here like a stalker. That would give their kids nightmares.

Directly connected to the yellow house were numerous other residences where I imagined moms and dads reading stories to their kids to get them to fall asleep. A small street jutted out in front where a few stragglers were walking home. If only they knew what was going on just outside.

Sweat gathered on my palms as sounds of angry shouting drew closer. Stilling my breath, I clung to the rough bark and watched Leander and his posse march beneath me.

Their fruitless search resulted in frustrated cries of what I assumed were the Spoons' equivalent of PG-13 four-letter words. Hopefully, Leander would give up as easily as I had in the quest for my missing library book. Eight years and counting—that book was still lost to the world.

Among the chorus of curse words, a single word resounded, a thousand times worse than any curse I could think of. "There!" The bearded soldier pointed a finger in my direction, and heat rushed to my cheeks. My stomach, heavy and tight, felt like I'd eaten a stone.

Leander smiled in triumph, his guards circling like vultures. Outnumbered, the situation was hardly fair, but alas, parallel universe battles were rarely just. Crossing his arms, Leander looked up at me with his eyes glinting in the moonlight. "You have to come down sometime, Nessie."

False. At nine years old, the term "tree house" was one that I misunderstood. For two days, I perched in the oak tree in our yard before the fire fighters removed me forcibly. Still, I didn't have a stash of cheese crackers in my pockets like back then, which meant I needed to find another way out. Under the transparent roof next to me, a woman was scrubbing plates at the kitchen sink.

My eyes followed the branch supporting me to its end on top of the houses. Bingo.

Muttering insults under his breath, Leander took hold of the tree trunk and began his ascent, but—no worries—I was already on top of the first house. For a split second, I peered through the transparent roof to see the woman, a half-washed dish still in her hand, staring up at the mysterious person walking on her house. Oops.

Imagining myself as a cloaked ninja, I hopped from roof to roof atop the clustered homes while Leander snarled from the tree behind me. Jack be nimble, Jack be quick, Jack jump over the—

A moment too late I realized I stepped on a thatched roof instead of a hard, transparent one and, lucky as always, found a weak spot where the straw wasn't reinforced. With a resounding crash I landed butt-first, raining straw and me onto something surprisingly soft. The throbbing in my derriere kept me from springing up from the couch beneath me as spryly as I would have liked. I lay staring at the hole in the ceiling for a moment. "Argh," I grunted, rubbing my bottom delicately and pushing myself up. Just add that to my growing list of bruises.

Through the dust and debris now swirling in the air, I gaped at a family eating a late dinner. Correction: they *had* been eating a late dinner. Now, forks were down, jaws open, and eyes riveted on the weird cloaked girl that crashed through the roof and landed on their couch.

"Uhh…I didn't mean to do that," I said, pointing up at the hole in their ceiling. "I'll find a way to help fix it. Until then," I wrestled out of my cloak, wincing at the ache in my lower back, and threw it on the floor. "This is water-proof and will keep the rain out."

Hurtling out the door and down the narrow street, I ran in the dark paths beside houses until my legs quivered beneath me. I scanned the road behind me, content that Leander and his men were nowhere in my sight. With the cursing and shouting out of earshot now, I could safely say I had outrun them. In a tapered grassy strip between two homes, I caved in to my burning lungs and came to a stop, panting for air with my hands on my knees. Leander or no Leander, my legs were done with running, and I was lost.

Gingerly, I lowered my aching body to the ground, lacing my arms behind my head and greedily sucking in the cool night air. The stars twinkled brighter in this universe, far away from fake lights to pollute the dark. I closed my eyes for a moment, amazed at how the night had turned out. My doubts had quieted for the time being, and I found myself talking aloud, giddy and laughing. "God, that was amazing! How could I ever think my faith is misplaced in You?" My fingers reached down to massage my tender shins. "I should know by now that You'll always rescue me."

Crickets chirped in the grass beside me, and I closed my eyes, reveling in the afterglow of victory for a few precious minutes.

However, I knew I couldn't linger; I had to get back to Eric and the others. Resting for an extended period was not a luxury I possessed. I pushed myself up, my hands flattening the grass beneath me, and took a deep breath. *You can do this, Nessie. You've got to keep moving if you—*

A shadow stretched across the road in front of my hiding place. Soldiers? My heartbeat thumped noisily in my chest, and I was sure anyone around could hear it. Holding my breath, I scooted closer to the house at my back, hoping its silhouette would cover me.

Crickets stilled around me. *One Mississippi. Two Mississippi. Three Miss—* The figure, shrouded in darkness, walked past the opening, and I breathed a sigh of relief.

No soldiers, no robbers. I was safe.

The crickets started their chirping again, and I gave it a few minutes before deciding to keep moving. No sooner had I stepped onto the road than a strong arm grabbed my waist and pushed me face-first against the house. A blood-curdling scream filled the night before I realized it was my own. My attacker didn't waste any time moving his hand up from my torso to my mouth.

Don't panic. Do not panic. Was that the coldness of sharp steel against my neck? My breath came in deep shuddering gasps. Maybe it was time to panic.

I reached for the hilt of my sword, but the metal pressed deeper into my flesh. "That would be unwise," a deep voice hissed into the night.

A joyous laugh erupted from me, muffled by the hand; I knew that voice. My head twisted towards my captor, breaking free from the fingers clamped over my mouth. "Eric!" I gasped. Thank goodness it wasn't Leander. But, Eric, what a jerk! Here I was worried sick, and he was playing games? "How did—"

The blade nicked the edge of my neck. "What did you call me?" his voice growled.

I paused, reconsidering my first assumption. It sounded like Eric—was it some sort of trick or test? "I called you Eric because that's your name. Or do you want to go by Bran now? I never know when—"

The knife bearer released me and stepped into a patch of moonlight. I reflected on his features—the same Roman nose, wide eyes, and slicked-backed hair—though, when I squinted in the shadows I saw that it was blond instead of black. In the scant light, it was hard to tell the difference. Tilting my head, I acknowledged the strange inconsistencies—he was taller than my Eric, lips different (as in perpetually frowning), and more muscular than lanky.

"No," I whispered to myself. "You're not Eric. You must be…" I considered his approximate age and the similar features. "His brother."

The knife went back in its sheath, which I took as an improvement until he picked me up and threw me over his shoulder. The strength of his grasp reminded me of Eric, the Wrist Wrestler. Definitely a relation. Disregarding my cuts and bruises, I squirmed in his grip, trying to break free. "Let me go! I have come too far to be killed by some psycho Eric doppelganger." The strain of the day pushed me into panic mode, my breaths coming in short, rapid gasps. I frantically beat his back with my fists.

Remember that *Sixty Minutes* rule about kidnappers, and not leaving with them? My legs kicked his chest violently, and I even managed to sink my teeth into his shoulder, but he just grunted and kept walking. "You can't do this!" I shouted, tears stinging my eyes.

"I think I can," the man laughed. "Now, let's go for a walk." And like a sack of potatoes, I was carried off into the darkness.

§ § §

I had never seen a home, so…unhomey. The one-room house looked like a prison warden had been the interior decorator.

The monochromatic color scheme, devoid of mess and clutter, held no hint of comfort. Even the hard gray stool I sat on was just so…cold. Eric's brother slammed his palms down onto the black table I sat at. "Tell me your name and how you know my brother!"

My head collapsed against the hard surface. The cool wood soothed the throbbing in my temples. "Look, I've already told you. My name is Nessie, and your brother is the toaster salesman at my apartment complex." I lifted my face to glance at the glass ceiling, the stars I had seen hours ago beginning to fade into the pale dawn sky. The interrogation was never going to end. My wrists chafed against the scratchy rope, and I banged my head back down onto the table.

"Do you live here?" My words were stifled against the wood. "Because that would explain a lot."

His growl echoed in the small space. "That's none of your concern." He paced the room, breathing heavily as he marched. "Really, if you're going to make up stories, why not something believable? Who would name their child Nessie? And in the name of Spoons, what in the world is a toaster?"

I beat my head in succession now. Maybe I would knock myself out from the blunt force trauma. "You question my name, but not someone called Commander Leander? And a toaster is a kitchen appliance that you put bread in to make…toast."

He should have worn holes in the floor with the amount he was pacing. "That doesn't even make any sense."

Tears gathered in my eyes. Isolate feelings merged into a single existence: hunger, hurt, stress, weariness, exhaustion. Up to that point, I tried to maintain composure, to focus on the mission, but my barriers were melting down. "It doesn't matter what I say to you. You're never going to believe that I'm from a parallel universe where I met your brother or that I came here by a sword or that Eric saved me from Leander and his goons. You probably won't believe that we freed all of the men from the Spork work camp and that Eric and Fletcher are currently transporting them—"

"Stop," he barked "I heard shouting from the compound as I was doing some…investigating."

My head shot up from the table, tears sliding down in relief. Unable to wipe them because of my bonds, I let them fall. "Really? Are they okay? Did they make it out safely?"

His brow knit together, a puzzled frown deepening the crease lines in his face. "I can't very well answer that question when I don't know if you're speaking the truth." The grumpy man turned away from me and began pacing the floor once more. "Breaking into the compound, such a thing would be…" he rubbed his chin, "preposterous. Still, I can't deny that I heard shouting from a place that has been locked up tight since King Kermit started ailing. I guess there's only one way to find out. We're going to go find Eric."

Joy flooded in at the mention of his name, and I couldn't help but smile weakly when I considered being reunited with the one person in this world who offered me some sort of comfort.

Woah there, Nessie. Don't overreact there; just a friendly homecoming with your neighborhood toaster salesman. But when I thought about his lopsided smile and that goofy slick-backed hair, the grin on my face hurt my cheeks.

With efficiency, Eric's brother unsheathed his sword, sawed through my bindings and led me out of the dismal house. Out front was a bike that resembled a two-seater moped without electronics or exhaust.

"What, no horse?" I indicated the bike, but he just snorted and ordered me to get on. Tired, sore, and dirty, I took refuge in the good things that had occurred: rescuing the half-breeds from the compound, evading Leander and his entourage, and finding and earning the trust of Mr. Grumpy Man, whatever his name was.

"Oh, one more thing," his voice chilled my bones despite the roar of the moped coming to life. "If you try to run away, I *will* hunt you down and it will not be pleasant for you."

I rubbed the goosebumps on my arms. Well, maybe not that last one.

§ § §

"My kingdom for a bed," I muttered to Mr. Grumpy's back. His moped tore down the street, blowing my pixie cut into a jumbled mess. We passed a quiet sleeping village, bathed in yellow morning light and framed by the forms of mountains far in the distance. The thought of families snoozing away under cozy blankets sparked a yawn.

During the long night, my drowsiness won the battle against awkwardness, and I had slumped against my captor's stiff back, surrendering to cat naps. However, my body, not surprisingly, needed more than a couple of hours rest to function. Maybe just a few more minutes… My forehead slumped down on his shoulder.

"My name is Veli," he said, breaking the silence at last.

His words perked my head up. Conversation and gossip: my morning dose of caffeine. "Eric didn't tell me he had a brother. In fact, he hasn't told me much about himself in general. He seems to walk around in disguise." At times, quite literally.

Veli shrugged, not turning around. "It's best to carry secrets close to your belt. That's the only way to survive in this turmoil-filled kingdom."

An isolated home flew by in a blur, and I sighed. "Why did I feel like you would say something like that instead of offering more information?"

"Why would you need more information on my brother?" Veli countered, a slight edge in his voice.

Okay, stepping back out of dangerous sibling territory. "We could play twenty questions all day, but it wouldn't get us anywhere." *And where exactly are you trying to get, Nessie?* After just a short time here, my perception of Eric had morphed from some awkward door-to-door peddler to…I wasn't sure.

The wind whipped around us, pulling at the sweat-stained tunic I wore. What was it about Eric that tugged on me so curiously? He was an enigma wrapped up in a toaster salesman, my one link to the world I came from; a companion and a rescuer in this strange and foreign land. Thinking of him made me feel warmer on the chilly ride.

Since Veli banned further questions, I didn't see any reason to rouse him from his thoughts. After the chaos of everything, I nestled down onto his back once more for a nap. The hilt of my sword jabbed into my side, but I was too tired to care. Sleep came in broken fragments and was interwoven with strange dreams of Sporks and swords and Leander. Instead of finding answers, I was left confused and restless. What did it all mean? Finally giving up on the effort, I groggily scanned the landscape, no longer surrounded by fields but the thinly-wooded beginnings of a forest. The sun was in full morning mode by now, its rays annoyingly bright.

"Where are we?" I yawned to Veli, my voice coming out more like a croak.

He shrugged without taking his eyes off the road. "Almost there."

"Not a man of many words, are you?"

He didn't respond. Incorrigible man.

We turned off the dirt path and headed deeper into the thickening woods until the foliage became too dense. Dismounting, Veli walked the moped ahead of me, wheeling it around tree trunks and roots. I leaned over, stretching my arm out over my head. Man, my muscles were tired. Sunlight peeked through the leaves above; its gentle warmth seeped through my skin and dissipated the tension in my shoulders. I listened to the muted rustling of animals scampering in the brush and the mellow call of a whippoorwill.

Much to my surprise, Veli answered with a bird call of his own. Suddenly, a voice bellowed through the trees, but it was impossible to tell which direction it came from. "WHY'D THE CHICKEN CROSS THE ROAD?"

I laughed at the seriousness of the caller, and Veli elbowed me. "It's a password. What's your problem?"

Still giggling, I raised my hands to my mouth and giggled, "TO GET TO THE OTHER SIDE!"

Veli considered me with amazement before fifty or so men emerged from the behind trees and shrubs. Even with their multicolored hair, they somehow blended into the landscape around us. I jumped when a red-headed man stepped out from a bush right behind me. Wow, wouldn't want to play a game of hide-and-seek with those guys.

Looking closer at these hide-and-seek masters, their bedraggled, threadbare appearance and colorful locks seemed familiar. They turned to me, and one-by-one began to bow. Heat crept up my face at the humble gratitude of the former prisoners. "What? No. Don't do that," I stuttered, embarrassed, helping a man to his feet. "God freed you, not me." The gentleman hesitated, reluctantly getting to his feet. But it wasn't till Eric leapt down from a tree and landed beside me that I felt true embarrassment.

How often did I imagine that lopsided grin? His face lit up, and I dared to hope the twinkle in his eyes was related to my presence. He jolted forward, reaching both of his arms out to embrace me, but an uncertain frown crossed his face and he stopped mid-hug. Disappointment welled up in me. After the events of last night, all I wanted was the comfort of his arms.

Wait. A few hours ago, I kicked the metaphorical butt of an evil commander, and I didn't die once; that was a big deal. With a surge of bravery and just a bit of zombie-induced giddiness, I sprang forward and wrapped my arms around him in a bear hug. When I clunked against his firm chest and felt his strong arms wrap around me, the world felt right.

His torso rumbled with a whisper just loud enough for me to hear, "I was so worried. I'm glad you're back now…safe and sound. You need to stop this disappearing habit." My heart dropped to my stomach and warm fuzzies took over my body. Maybe there was something there, something that—

Veli cleared his throat loudly. Oops. I blushed and quickly pulled away.

Much to my satisfaction, Eric kept a hand clasped on my shoulder. Our conversation continued but less intimately.

"Thank Him that you're safe. I led the men out, thinking you were with Fletcher, but when we reached our camp and you weren't there," he shook his head, "I imagined the worst. You might have been cornered by a crazy, skillet wielding old lady again."

I tilted my head. "Or roped into a faddish boy band concert?"

He crossed his arms, lips smiling slyly. "I should know better than to trust you'd follow directions; you're quite the troublemaker."

Veli cleared his throat a second time, and Eric's chest puffed out when he noticed his brother. Removing his hand from my shoulder, Eric firmly grasped Veli's forearm. He lowered his voice, but I could still catch the words. "It's been a long time, brother. I see you still remember our old hiding place. The last time I saw you—"

"Let's not speak of that here," Veli cut him off.

Watching the exchange made me glad I was an only child. Wanting to give them privacy, I took a few steps away but couldn't shake an ominous sensation pestering my thoughts. Absentmindedly rubbing the hilt of my sword, I tried to push the impulse away, but it was a deep-seated urging not of myself. A ray of sunlight burrowed through the leafy canopy, bathing the alcove in warm light. My eyes searched upward for answers. What was going on?

The freed prisoners glanced around, shifting back and forth on their feet. A few were pacing the ground, hands clasped together and brows furrowed. They seemed so…out of place. Lost, wondering where to go from here. Now, that was something I could relate to. Despite our vast differences, we both desperately needed reassurance…comfort…purpose.

With a deep breath, words flowed out of me.

"All right, men, listen up. I know we're all very tired, but…well, by now I'm sure the guards have discovered you've flown the coop. You all have done amazingly, and I know you want to get back to your families, but there are two more camps with your brothers and friends. If we don't act now, we may not be able to rescue them. Time is of the essence."

A flash of green hair shifted to my right, and I recognized Beryl's husband taking a step closer to me. "She speaks with wisdom. Lady Nessie, we will follow the plans that you decide on."

Peace settled over me, providing warmth that had nothing to do with the sunlight. Though the fifty pairs of eyes looking to me for direction would normally send me burrowing under covers, everything felt right. "They're not my plans. My sock drawer is a war zone, for crying out loud."

He nodded. "'Many are the plans in a person's heart, but it is the Lord's purpose that prevails.'"

Eric joined me at my side. Part of me wanted to gush in proper girly fashion, but I quickly beat that down with a lead pipe. He probably just didn't want to have to plan a rescue party alone. I was morphing into a psychological nutcase before them all. *He loves me, he loves me not, he loves me, he—*

"So, what's next?" an orange-haired prisoner snapped me out of my thoughts.

"Uhh, everyone take a five minute break and then we'll go over the plan," I managed to get out before stepping out of the circle of prisoners. My muscles protested when I lowered myself to the ground. How could I have such peace taking charge of a rescue operation when the thought of a toaster salesman sent me reeling?

"How did you know?" Eric's voice startled me.

Great, just who I needed to quell my confusing thoughts. "What are you talking about?"

"The password," he answered.

"Oh, you mean the chicken crossing the road thing? That was just the answer to the joke, not a password. Doesn't everyone know that one?"

Eric squatted down. "It doesn't have trans-universal popularity. That's why it's been a safe password, but I guess I'll have to change it now." He paused for a moment, then winked. "You seem to be discovering all of my secrets."

My heart picked up the tempo. Luckily, I didn't have to respond because Beryl's husband called Eric over before the words found their way to my throat. When my five minutes were up, I was even more confused than when I had started.

<h1 style="text-align:center">Chapter 11</h1>

If I didn't know any better, I'd think Veli was a grumpy statue bolted to the grassy incline above the Northern work camp. At least an angry bust of him couldn't make the landscape around us, full of discarded metal and half-constructed welded frames, any less appealing.

What was Veli's deal? His silence for the duration of our journey had forced me to carry on conversations with the former prisoners accompanying us on our mission to the second work camp. That task was not as simple as it sounded, considering Wesley, who had introduced himself right away, talked like a surfer. I didn't care if he had curly blue hair and spent a year in Gulag; there were only so many times I could endure the word "gnarly."

"Want to take a look?" I prodded Veli, pushing one of the mopeds behind an abandoned scrap of metal. He grunted in response and glowered at the less-than-welcoming sight below us.

Who peed in his cheerios? I sighed and nudged Wesley. "Let's get closer for a better view."

But when we crept through the tall grass down to a pile of scrap metal, I wasn't sure I wanted a better view. Framed by ominous puffy clouds in the dusk sky, the single rectangular building housing the inmates seemed menacing, painted obsidian as if decorated for a funeral. There were no trees or homes like the last camp; this one was surrounded on all sides by a blackened field of charred crops. Stacks of cement bricks made for crude walls on the field's edge.

Sheets of tin littered the hill down to the camp. Wesley picked a large sheet to conceal him. "Gnarly," he whispered, peeking behind the edge. Those Sporks and their hide-and-seek skills.

What was that awful smell? The closer we got, the more my nose hairs felt like they were being singed off. The compound reeked of metal and burnt hair. Outside the dark buildings, fires smoldered next to endless piles of iron. Though we were still yards from the site, sweat dripped from my brow. I fanned myself to combat the oncoming heat wave. My mind painted a picture of the men slaving over the fires, perspiration pouring down their dehydrated bodies while guards encouraged productivity with whips.

A small pond just past the edge of the compound could have made the place a little brighter, except for the fact that it was bubbling mysteriously. It definitely wasn't Thomas Kinkade material, unless he was going for a creepy, murky look. Yuck.

At first glance, I didn't see any fences or barriers besides a single iron gate sticking out of the ground. What purpose could a lonely gate serve? Then I noticed, connected to the gate, a thin silver wire hovering inches off the ground and surrounding the camp. Wow, what a fence….if they were trying to keep out midgets. This was going to be a piece of cake.

Thunder crackled and the brewing storm blew more heat across the desolation. Glowing coals in the smoldering fires flickered. A twig snapped behind me, my only indication that still-silent Veli decided to join us.

He stared at the compound, blond hair slicked back like Eric's, lips drawn thin and tight. The man had been mute ever since Eric and I had split the party to simultaneously free both the northern and southern work camps. Lucky me had somehow drawn the short straw, winning hawk-eyed Veli for a companion.

Veli shifted behind the greasy metal sheet to shuffle closer to us. "Wesley, your description of the compound looks accurate, which means the half-breeds should be straight back in the building. We're fortunate you were transferred to the Capitol from this work camp before we arrived."

I clapped a firm hand onto Wesley's back. "Gnarly. So, now we go knock out the guards, step over the wire and bust the prisoners out."

"Not so fast." Veli pointed to the midget defense system. "See that thin string around the camp? That's *traegerwire*. It's best not to go near unless you want second-degree burns."

The Blade of Remiel's hilt dug into my ribs, and I shifted against the cold tin sheet to dislodge the handle. "Can't you just step over?"

He shook his head. "No, it acts as a barrier, like a force field. You don't have to touch the line directly, but if you cross it, you'll suffer." Okay, I was suddenly not so eager to jump over the wire. Veli hesitated before continuing. "…Eric said you had a special sword… one with runes."

I slid the Blade of Remiel out of its sheath and handed it to Veli. The moment his fingers touched the blade, he let out a whistle. "Where did you come across this?"

I twiddled my thumbs. "King Arthur's Shopalot."

Veli raised an eyebrow. "King who? What realm are you from again?" He waved his hands. "Doesn't matter, especially since I couldn't care less. What I do care about is not getting killed, and this will certainly help. I'm not an expert on magical swords, but Eric, who is more well-read on such matters, said this thing is strong enough to cut the wire. I can handle that part, but the guards will blow our cover if they see me. That's where you come in." He motioned towards the hill where the mopeds were stashed. "Your job is to create a diversion. Shouldn't be difficult, seeing as you have a knack for making a mess."

Wrinkling my nose, I pinched his stiff arm, but he carried on, unfazed. "You need to distract them for as long as possible while I handle the guards inside and help the prisoners escape. Wesley, you said there's a door on the east side, which we'll use to lead the prisoners out around the back of the building. Once I give them marching orders, Wesley will make a bird call, and Nessie, you'll need to extricate yourself and join us."

One of the silver-helmed guards in front of the gate wandered closer to the pond, picked up a rock, and skipped it across the murky waters. Hardly menacing. "Why can't you just take them out first?"

Veli rolled his eyes. "If they see a threatening man walking anywhere near them, they're going to blow the whistle and alert more soldiers before we have a chance to get inside. You, on the other hand, have the advantage of looking perpetually lost and confused. It won't be hard for them to believe you're inept."

He was going to get it one day. One day when I didn't need him to help me rescue a bunch of Sporks.

Wesley looked between us, wringing his hands uncomfortably. "I'll go make sure the others are in place." He scurried over to where the other men were hiding, though I suspected his motivations were more to get away from Veli's bad temper.

Veli rubbed his temple thoughtfully, closing his eyes. The brother was usually upbeat after a sarcastic jab; his quietness confused me.

"Is there something wrong?" I frowned. "Besides your incorrigible attit—"

"He's quite taken with you," Veli rumbled, his brows furrowing.

My mouth hung open. I paused, trying to understand his meaning. Wesley? That wouldn't make sense since the depth of our conversations boiled down to the word 'gnarly.' "Uhh…I'm not sure what you mea—"

Veli sighed. "Oh, to be as vacuous as you." He turned to face me, his eyes focused and determined. "I'll do my best to keep you alive. After all, that was the most I've seen him smile in years."

A heavy drop of rain pelted my forearm, and my ears caught the sound of sizzling coals coming from the compound. Veli scrambled towards our team of men to join in the discussion, no doubt. *What was he talking about? The only person he would be that concerned about is… Eric.*

As soon as his name caught my brain waves, my mind ventured into dangerous territory—hope. I wanted to giggle girlishly and point to all of the signs that said we were destined to be together. The truth was that I was really starting to like Eric, and the notion he might be interested was exciting. Instead of squealing with delight, I put a cap over all of my feelings, pushing them back down into a heart crammed with hurt and disappointment.

This romance nonsense always ended up the same way. Blond jock, Steve Honeycutt, running off with my best friend at prom and leaving me to call my mom for a ride home; senior class president, Evan Sanders, breaking up with me in his victory speech at the high school assembly. Matt Castanello, my college beau, serenading me outside my apartment with a beautiful song he'd created… all about how he wanted to see other people.

My best move was to take warning from the mistakes of the past and let whatever chemistry Eric and I had evaporate into the scorching heat. For goodness sake, we were from two different dimensions. Still, the chance at love hovered in my mind like a mosquito. Hope gave me extra incentive to stay alive as I crept towards the prison.

§ § §

The heavens opened up, pelting me with water, adding "drenched sewer rat" to the list of phrases that could be used to describe my appearance. Fortunately, it worked in my favor.

Soaked clothing, matted pixie cut, weary face against the dimly lit dusk sky—I hoped I looked every part of the lost, clueless traveler. Veli had spent a frustratingly long time giving me a lecture on driving his moped, termed a *console*. Normally powered by a specific key card inserted into a slot between the handlebars, my console had been altered with my ingenious pl—Okay, Veli just took out the regular card key and put a fake one in the slot…but still. Sneaky.

With a deep breath, I pushed the "broken" moped towards the pair of silver-helmeted guards. Force field or not, the sentries looked silly standing outside of a lone gate.

See, they were only some silly guards. Nothing to worry ab—"Halt!" the soldiers shouted, snapping to attention, weapons drawn in a heartbeat.

I hoped there was a small vein of chivalry in Spoons. Or macho-ness. A damsel in distress couldn't be picky. "Oh, good sirs, my console won't start and I don't know what to do." The rain served as perfect tears, and I sniffled. "My mother is at home all by herself, and I need to be there for her—"

The first guard put away his sword and removed the silver helmet, allowing raindrops to speckle his curly black hair. Above his lip rested either the sad attempt at a mustache or spilled pepper. The jury was out on that one.

"Don't worry, milady." He bowed pretentiously, offering his hand. Instead of a firm shake, he planted a swift kiss on my knuckles. "My name is Pepe and this is Rolf. We will find out the cause of the trouble so you can see your mother."

The one named Rolf pushed up his visor. His shaven head matched perfectly with his Rottweiler features, which moved his lovability scale down to "tattooed bouncer with knives for fingers." He marched towards us, continuing to hold his sword.

Pepe confidently approached my bike, but then paused, scratching his head in confusion. He kicked the tires a few times and frowned speculatively.

A change shifted in the air. If I strained my ears hard enough, I could have noticed the lack of buzzing that had been there before. The hum of the traegerwire, even. Past Rolf's bald head, a manly silhouette crept towards the west door of the prison. *Please don't look, please don't look.*

"Rolf, what do you think? You look like you might know something about bikes." Yeah, like motorcycles he used to ride away from a scene of a murder.

He snarled, unconvinced. By now, Veli was at the door of the prison, and if the guards turned around they'd want to know why he was there. Probably slice first, ask questions later.

I held my breath as Veli turned to open the door. It slid open, letting out a noticeable squeak. Rolf flinched, and panic took over me.

"Did you know that I'm wanted by Commander Leander?" I blurted.

Pepe tilted his head, a puzzled look on his face, but Rolf snapped up straight, the squeak behind him long forgotten. "What did you say?"

With a sweet wave, I bid my safety goodbye. "I'd love to stay and chat, but I probably need a head start." With that, I jerked the fake key out of the moped. Fumbling for the real key concealed in my sleeve, I jammed it into the slot and launched myself onto the bike.

God, please let that crash course Veli showed me be enough. A quick look over my shoulder earned me a view of Rolf in full pursuit. When I turned back around, the pond that seemed far away just a few minutes ago was right in front of me. With a garbled scream, I hit the brakes. The murky water slammed into my face, stinging my eyes. I rabidly fought to untangle myself from the consode and to get up above the waters. Breaking the surface, my lungs greedily swallowed air, cringing at the water's slimy feel. Sticky sludge brushed against my ankle, and I kicked it away. Did everything have to be disgusting at these work camps?

This is way too much aerobic exercise for me. I thrashed my way to the edge and hoisted myself onto the muddy bank. Just had to keep moving. I jogged away from the figures approaching the pond, pumping my arms and legs as fast as they would take me. A peal of thunder crackled above, kicking up a wind that cooled my wet clothes. Goosebumps raised on my arms. *Veli, be quick.*

My adrenaline-induced marathon propelled me away from the prison and into the black fields. Pieces of dying cornstalks cracked off and were trampled beneath my leather boots. A strong chemical smell emanated from the crops, and my chest tightened, struggling to breathe. Lungs burning, I coughed and sputtered, pushing myself further into the overwhelming miasma.

By now, the rain had started full force, pelting my skin with thick drops of water. My leg muscles felt like lead, and a sharp cramp spread up my side. I ran until the coughing spasms took over. That was going to have to be good enough. Collapsing on the cornstalks, I wheezed and watched the two soldiers close the gap between us.

"Time out," I gasped. "I'm not built for triathlons." Pepe and Rolf didn't seem to appreciate my humor. Tough crowd. Instead, Rolf's rough hands jerked me up from the ground, pushing my arms behind me. Ow. My lungs burned, and I swallowed against my dry throat. If only there was some way to get out of this situation and soothe the pain. *Besides going ahead and dying,* I thought to myself. The notion was tempting, since it looked as if the evening was headed that direction anyway…

But, I couldn't. What would happen to the prisoners and Veli if I just gave up now? What would Eric—My muscles perked up, not quite so hasty to meet their end.

"If you cooperate, you might make it back to Commander Leander's alive," Rolf snarled, prodding me in front of him.

What a jerk. I sunk into a sluggish pace but Rolf's jabs grew more insistent the slower I became. How much time had my fiasco bought Veli and the prisoners? That was the question. My job on the mission was to stall, and I knew how to stall. When I was ten years old, my mother came home early before her surprise party. Aunt Beatrice charged me with the task of occupying my mother while she finished decorating the living room. I raced upstairs, used my mother's makeup to make a nasty scar on my arm, and ran to her car screaming. We made it to the hospital parking lot before she figured out that the gaping wound on my arm was composed of lipstick and blush. I liked to think of it as an extra surprise before the party, but she was not amused. Right then, I had no makeup kit, but hopefully I could use my stalling skills just as easily.

Dragging my feet had been a great tactic in the first encampment, but Rolf nipped my plan in the bud by grabbing me around the waist and dragging me through the trampled crops. Obviously, Rolf was not the one I needed to focus on. Pepe was the sympathetic one, the one who was concerned about—

"What kind of reward do you think we'll get for her?" Pepe inquired excitedly, crushing my fledgling strategy. Rolf grunted in reply, but Pepe carried on, counting on his fingers. "I bet it'll be a lot, especially if Leander wants her."

Bingo.

"What?" I piped up, squirming in Rolf's grip. "Can you believe that? You didn't even do anything to catch me and you want part of the money? The nerve of some people."

Pepe crossed his arms like a defiant child. "I did too help! You'd be long gone if I wasn't here."

Rolf laughed, his grip around my waist getting tighter. "Please! You couldn't have caught her if she was an infectious disease."

I wasn't sure if I wanted to be compared to illnesses, but the conversation was moving in the right direction.

Pepe grabbed the hilt of his sword menacingly. "Maybe we should settle this right now!"

Growling, Rolf dumped me on a pile of decimated cornstalks and drew his blade. He pointed a beefy finger at me. "If you even think of moving, I will sever your legs from your torso. Leander wants you alive, but he didn't say anything about uninjured."

I held up a finger. "Actually, I'm pretty sure that the word 'unharmed' was mentioned somewhere. Maybe I forgot to tell you, but—"

"Shut up!" Rolf shouted and stepped towards Pepe, baring his sharp teeth in a twisted grin. I craned my neck over the trampled crops to check out the prison. If I squinted just right, I could make out dark masses filing out of the side door. Fights took a long time, right?

Wrong. Rolf, sword extended, charged the seemingly-valiant Pepe—who ran screaming, his arms held high in surrender. "Okay, okay; you're right! You did everything. All the money's yours—just don't kill me!" Pepe collapsed onto the crops in fetal position, his dark curls bobbing as he shuddered. Rain drenched his shaking body, and I couldn't help but feel a little bad for him.

Rolf sheathed his sword and spat at Pepe's pitiful form. "You disgust me. You are a disgrace to the army of Spoons."

If Rolf turned around and dragged me back to the camp, it was all over. How could it end like this when we were so close? I looked lovingly at my legs. "If we have to part," I whispered, "know you always carried me beautifully." With that sentiment, I launched from the crumbling crops and headed towards the metal scrap pile that had served as our hiding place, ignoring the protests from my abused muscles.

A monstrous growl tore at Rolf's throat. "You stupid woman!"

He lunged at me, and I swerved out of the way, pumping my arms and legs like an Olympic sprinter. Abandoned metal frames were strewn across the field, but I vaulted over them. My irritated lungs tickled, another coughing fit just over the horizon.

Saliva pooled at the back of my throat, and I was trying to swallow when a rush of air flew past my arm. All righty, someone was swinging weapons.

I twisted around to see the bald guard, drops of rain pouring down his face, within a sword's reach. My stomach clenched. If only Veli would—A sharp pain tore into the side of my torso, burning like a hot iron. I bit my lip to keep from crying out. The tightening in my chest worsened, my lungs constricting. *Have to keep moving,* I thought, careful to avoid the tender stinging at my side when I swung my arms. *Giving up isn't an option.*

Rain obscured my vision. Pure adrenaline vaulted me forward past piles of scrap metal and out of the field, but the sight beyond the dying sheaves of corn crushed my hopes. "Oh. Snap." The words came out as ragged breaths. Six-foot high stacks of iron bricks created a wall around the field. Rolf's angry shouts behind me were drowned in a peal of thunder.

No…My thoughts came in sluggish and weary. *Maybe if I ran along the wall long enough…*But when I leaned forward to keep up the pace, my tired legs slipped on the grass and buckled beneath me.

For a blissful, terrifying moment, I didn't move. Eyes open, I watched thick raindrops fall from the clouds and wash over my aching body. Lightening streaked across the sky and illuminated the gray heavens.

I tried inhaling a deep breath, but it triggered a coughing spell. The pain in my side screamed like a banshee. And suddenly, there it was. Rich and clear, the whistle of a sparrow carried across the field.

I gasped, a wan smile reaching the corners of my lips. Veli's signal. *Thank You.*

The sounds of boots tearing through the field gave my exhausted muscles encouragement to push up. Rolf burst into view, his lips curling upwards when he caught sight of me. That was it. Heart pounding, pulse racing, drenched and tired—was that how I would die? My fingers searched around me for something, anything to protect myself. Rolf's heel crushed the grass beneath him with a heavy step. He edged forward, sword drawn.

I clamped my hands over my face, unwilling to watch. Thunder swallowed my desperate prayers, whispered to a God I hoped had more in store for me than this. "Lord, please let the men escape. If I die, console my parents. If I have no legs, please let me get cool prosthetics so I can be one of those inspirational people who go hike giant mountains."

"Oh, keep praying," Rolf mocked. "Do you want to know what I'm going to do to you?"

"No," I blurted through my hands. Footsteps shuffled and then grew quiet. I was ready for the taunting threats and descriptive torture methods any minute.

"What are you doing?" A voice broke the silence. I peeked through a slit in my fingers. Rolf lay unconscious on the ground next to me. I jerked my hands away, revealing the blond man standing over the fallen guard, my sword hilt in his hand.

"I was praying…and thinking about my legs," I admitted, allowing Veli to help me off of the ground. A wave of dizziness passed over me, and I grabbed onto his wrist for support. Too much exercise. Veli just shook his head. We stepped over Rolf, who didn't look quite as threatening while napping on the ground, and headed through the squashed crops.

"Thanks, Veli." The words seemed to gush out once we reached the edge of the field.

"Don't mention it," he grunted. I opened my mouth, but Veli stopped me. "Seriously, don't mention it."

The sharp throbbing in my tired muscles couldn't keep me from cozying up next to him. "Oh, Veli, I know you try to be a polar bear on the outside, but inside you're just a teddy."

He brushed aside some stalks of blackened corn, covering his mouth to cough. "I have no idea what you just said."

I threw my arms around him in a hug, the sudden movement sending my vision spinning. Whew. Definitely needed some rest when we could afford to slow down. Embracing Veli was good for support but it was like hugging a tree. A tree made of stiff, volatile limbs. "Didn't that feel nice?"

Veli frowned. "You're wet."

Obvious much? "Well, so are you. It's raining and then I sort of fell in a pond, so I think I'd be a little damp."

His hand on my shoulder stopped me from moving away. "And sticky."

In defiance, I went for the hands-on-hips stance, but when my fingers brushed over the slick spot on my side, I cringed. A sharp pang bit into my torso, and I let out a whistle. Examining my hand, I startled at the crimson blood smeared across my skin, heat rushing to my face. At least Eric wasn't here to see this. The last thing I heard before I fainted was Veli's sigh.

Chapter 12

For the second time that day I was carried by a man, but this time by someone not wanting to kill me. At least, that was my hope. It took me a minute after my eyes flitted open to recognize the scurrying shadows as Spork prisoners trekking through hip-length grass. Jail break…work camp…fainting…it all came back to me. The field around us stretched for miles, no compound in sight. No sirens, no shouts, no lights chasing after us in the dim light—we were in the clear.

Veli's strong arm encircled my waist, securing me to his shoulder during the bumpy ride. Good gracious, his shoulder was bony. I twisted away from its pressure on my ribcage. When all this was over, I needed to fatten him up.

A sliver of moonlight peeked out from a cloud and illuminated the wet fields. Haggard, dirty men marched an incline, silent and focused. Veli lifted me to the ground, grumpily offering me an arm for support. His tunic was speckled with red stains that matched the wound at my side. The blood smeared across his wrist made my stomach twinge. *Don't show any sign of pain; he can smell weakness.* I took a careful step onto the damp grass, biting my lip when the movement pulled at my side.

"So, the mission was a success?" I whispered, hiding a grimace and shifting my weight beneath me.

Veli crossed his arms. "Well, it was on *my* part."

For my part, I got sliced with a sword and had to be rescued…again. It wasn't like I signed up for this hero gig. I tried to stand taller but my wobbliness left me reaching for Veli's elbow. "So, where to now? I would think the Spork village is off limits."

Veli pushed a strand of blond hair out of his face and used his used pointer finger to scold me. "You're not going anywhere with us."

"What? I'm as much a part of this as you are!"

A curly blue mop of hair popped up beside us, and I let out a shriek. "Woah, dudes," Wesley whispered. "What's the hang up?"

"Wesley, leave now," Veli ordered, pointing to the line of men marching. Wesley looked me up and down, quickly taking out a piece of jerky from his pockets and handing it to me before falling back into line. Blessed Wesley. He knew the way to my heart. I greedily devoured the dried meat, hoping it would quiet the gnawing in my stomach.

Veli pointed to the red soaking through my tunic and lowered his voice. "Maybe you didn't notice, but you happen to be bleeding. The only place you're going to is a physician and then to rest. I happen to know a doctor nearby, and you seem to be well enough to make it there."

My stubborn temper tantrum was on standby. I stared Veli down, nostrils flaring. What a jerk! Trying to kick me out of the picture already when—

The blood on his tunic caught my attention again. He didn't have to save me from crazy, violent guards or carry my not-so-light body all over the countryside. If he really wanted me out of the picture, he would have left me to die. Which meant his words weren't stemming from annoyance, but…compassion?

Maybe I did need a little patching up. It was true the adrenaline helped me forget that I was exhausted, hungry, and wounded. "Fine. I'll go to the doctor. But after that, I'm coming back with you all."

Veli took two steps toward me and invaded my personal space. Okay, maybe he wasn't feeling compassionate. "Do you have a death wish, Nessie of America? Do you want to undergo torture at the hands of a heartless and powerful man? Because I guarantee if you keep this up, Leander will find you." He mimed a knife across my throat. "You will die, slowly and painfully, while these people look on and see their hopes crushed once again. Is that what you want?" He groaned and started to pace, his arms waving animatedly. "You're a magnet for disaster. I nearly watched a merciless soldier cut you to pieces. It was only by the slimmest chance I was able to save you. If you just played it safe and stayed where you were, you never would have been in danger."

He was right. I had no business being here in the thick of things. Despite my childhood fantasies, I wasn't a spy or a hero, just an overwhelmingly ordinary girl. *But…wait. If I hadn't been there…* "Then you and all your men would have been caught! Would you rather have that?" I snapped, my tantrum revving to flare.

Rows of Sporks walked by, their faces streaked with dirt and scars. A prisoner who couldn't have been more than twenty years old had the haggard wrinkles of an elderly man, and yet, a soft smile touched his lips. They were free, not because I was some amazing savior but because I let myself be used for a bigger purpose. "Look at them, Veli." I stretched my hands out. "Just look at them. We've given them hope."

Veli sneered. "Ah, yes. Hope has a way of buzzing around ears like a dying mosquito."

A light breeze blew across the field, swaying the grass gently. A verse called to mind from what seemed like ages ago in my bedroom. *Do not be discouraged, for the Lord your God will be with you wherever you go.* "Exactly, and that's because hope doesn't die. You should try it out sometime."

"Whatever," he grunted, holding out a hand for support. "Are you ready to get bandaged or would you prefer to bleed to death while you lecture me about hope?"

I shook my head. The day Veli ceased to be incorrigible was the day I started hating carbs. "Let's go find Wesley and let him know we're leaving."

I took his arm, leaning against him while we looked for our gnarly compatriot. "You know," Veli whispered, "this would be faster if you hadn't driven my console into a pond."

Injured or not, I was going to stick my tongue out at him the whole way.

§ § §

If I wasn't an outdoorsy girl, I would be by the time our adventure was over. Six hours of hiking through forest terrain, wild critters, and the wet earth made me long for a bed, any kind of bed. A gnat flew towards my face under the dank forest canopy, and I swatted it away.

A rotting log lay across our path, and I delicately climbed over it, wincing when the new bandage pulled on my torso's tender flesh. My fingertips confirmed my thoughts: the wound was bleeding again.

Rats. I snuck a peek at Veli ahead of me, a half-carved stick in his hand. Maybe he wouldn't notice I was bleeding on what he told me was his favorite tunic. If he didn't detect it, I wasn't going to be the one to break the news. It had taken a lot of convincing to get my sword privileges back.

"Ready to give up yet?" he asked, shaving a strip off of the stick.

"I'm going to sock you in the face," I replied, carefully navigating around a thorn bush on the forest floor.

Luckily the doctor believed my lengthy story involving my blind uncle, a fire poker, and a chicken on the loose. Though Veli had been quiet while the physician bandaged the wound, the taunts returned the minute we met up with Wesley and the freed Sporks (Wesley and the freed Sporks…that would be a good band name). Even when we reached the ex-prisoners' camp—damp leaf beds, snacks of wild berries, dig your own bathroom, definitely not five star accommodations—he was full of quips about my injuries. Somehow, my grandmother's age-old wisdom that when a boy teased you it meant he was trying to be friendly wasn't comforting. No, Nana. When a boy teased you, it just meant he was annoying.

Okay, meet up with Wesley and Sporks, check. Next on the list: reunite with Eric. My heart skipped a beat. Oh, yeah. Fletcher and the gang—they were important, too.

The pale dawn was a welcome sight to my eyes, now lined with dark circles that threatened to become a permanent facial feature. A two hour nap on wet leaves and bumpy roots was not as refreshing as it sounded. One blessing was the leaves didn't complain when I woke up in a puddle of drool.

The monotonous sound of men slogging through wet terrain was disturbed by a squirrel chattering angrily in the trees above us, the only other sign of life I had seen. I grabbed Veli's elbow and pulled him to the side, keeping my voice low. "Are you sure this is where Eric said to meet? There should be some evidence of Fletcher and the others by now."

Veli craned his neck to scan the trees, covered in vibrant red leaves. "We agreed to meet with the other camp in the central clearing before heading to the Northern caves. They've been abandoned for some time. The men should be safe to hide out there until things with Leander settle. We're almost to the spot." He crossed his arms. "Or do you doubt my ability to navigate?"

The chattering squirrel leapt down from his perch and bounded across the forest. "Yeah, pretty much," I shrugged.

He exhaled, balling his fists at his sides. "You irritate my soul."

"You stole the words from my mouth," I snorted. "How can you possibly be related to Eric?"

He gritted his teeth. "His given name is Bran."

Someone was touchy. "Well, it's hard to know when he keeps switching identities. The point is that you two are polar opposites."

Veli's strides slowed until he came to a full stop, his back facing me. "We weren't always that way."

The sarcasm evaporated from his voice, and I felt my forehead for signs of fever. Veli without sarcasm? Surely that had to be some sort of injury-related delusion. No, temperature felt normal, which meant I should probably respond. "What changed?"

He bent down and shifted the leaves aside, tracing the outline of a footprint on the ground. "That seems to be the age-old question, doesn't it?"

"Look, Veli," I crouched beside him. "Life shifts and we shift with it, for better or worse. But—"

The old Veli returned and he snapped out of whatever trance held him.

He jerked his head and stared me down like a savage tiger. "I don't need a counselor, especially one that could use some guidance herself."

Why didn't he tell me how he really felt? I stood up, fully prepared to give him the silent treatment, but something caught my attention. Two trees stretched out above me, their overgrown branches twisting together. The red leaves covering the limbs were radiant, concealing a glowing golden light. I reached my hand out and parted the foliage, stepping into a round clearing. Sunlight washed over the circular glade, nourishing bright orange flowers. "This is the place we agreed to meet." Veli's voice sounded behind me.

A bee flew past my nose and landed on one of the plants nearby. Birds glided above us, playfully chasing each other. But with all the wildlife, there was one major thing missing: Eric. "No one's here." The words came out slowly, and I reached for the hilt of my sword.

"I can see that." Veli stepped past me into the middle of the clearing.

A knot of uneasiness settled like a hard lump in my stomach. "Something's not right," I whispered and took a few cautious steps closer to Veli.

The sound of voices caught my ears right before Fletcher and the rest of the Sporks came into view, bearing victorious smiles. A jolt of electricity ran through me at the sight of Eric's beaming face at the end of the line, but I couldn't shake the ominous feeling. Veli, Eric, and Fletcher embraced each other, but I held back, confused at my premonition. What was going on? Had I eaten some bad berries earlier or something?

The clamor of men talking made my head throb, and I retreated behind the tangled trees to clear my thoughts. I continued walking deeper into the woods, whispering a soothing monologue to myself

"Nothing's wrong, drama queen. All of the men are safe now, and you're just stressed from all of the danger lately." Despite all of my calming tactics, the feeling persisted, especially when growing warmth emanated from my sword. I unsheathed the blade, and hushed whispers drifted into my ears. Voices came from my left, and I crouched low behind a tree.

How was that possib—

Gleaming runes cast a blue glow on my quivering fingers. Okay, so the sword was giving me supersonic hearing, too? I could have used that when I was twelve trying to overhear my mother's phone conversations.

"Leander said they might be around the clearing. Some villagers reported seeing a group of men in these woods the other day."

"So, who are we taking out?"

"There's three men; we can shoot them with the arrows first. The girl—Leander wants her alive, but the rest of the men are half-breed garbage, expendable."

Before the odd voices could continue, I bolted towards the clearing, tripping over a log. My teeth clenched, the fall tearing at my wound, but I pushed myself up and ran into the glade, interrupting Fletcher mid-sentence. "We have to go—now."

Fletcher craned his neck, looking for the unseen threat. "We just got here."

"I don't have time to explain. Let's go!"

The men stood motionless until Veli took charge. For once, he didn't have an insult at the ready. "You heard her. Move out!" his hushed orders sent the Sporks scrambling.

Did Veli stick up for me there? "Push the men back into the thick brush where they can use their hide-and-seek skills," I directed to Eric. "I'm going to watch the clearing."

He reached for my hand. "Fletcher and Veli can move them out. I'll go with you."

No sense in arguing with a cute man holding my hand. Instead, I pulled him down behind the overgrown red trees and waited as minutes passed. Nothing. Was I going crazy? If so, this was going to be pretty awkward. After an eternity, two men with cropped, jet-black hair wearing the uniforms of Spoon soldiers filed into view. Coarse stubble jutted out from their chins. They pushed aside a branch and stalked into the grassy glade, their bows brandished. I watched their lips barely whisper.

"I haven't seen anyone around here," the taller one murmured.

Before his partner could respond, two darts whizzed through the trees. The taller one swatted at his neck, scrambling for the projectile. His companion's knees buckled beneath him. In a matter of seconds, the pair collapsed next to a stalk of orange flowers. One of the soldiers groaned, but it was over; their bodies relaxed, eyelids fluttering closed.

Veli stepped out from behind a nearby tree, gun in hand. He shrugged at my gaping mouth. "What? Tranquilizers come in handy for times such as these. I picked them up from a weapons dealer while you were getting patched up." He stooped down, leaning in close to my torso. "Did you bleed on my favorite tunic?"

Did I have to reiterate what an incorrigible man he was?

Eric grabbed my arm. "You're bleeding?"

I waved my hand while Eric gently inspected the red spot on my shirt. "It's just a little stab wound. Nothing serious."

Eric shook his head, straightening to look at me face to face. "You need to take better care of yourself, Ness."

I could get lost in those shining dark eyes. But no—assassins. Stay focused. My hand reached for Eric's. "I will, but for now we'd better keep moving in case Leander sent anyone else after us."

Eric nodded, pointing to the unconscious soldiers. "What about them?"

"They'll come to eventually," I presumed. "Let's be far away when that happens."

Veli stared at me as if I had told him I ate puppies for breakfast. "You're just going to let them get away so they can try to kill us a second time? In case you didn't realize, lives are on the line here—and not just yours."

He had a point, but I was also ready to get moving. "Fine. Does anyone have some rope?"

"Dude, I totally do!" Wesley' surfer voice piped up from the crowd. Of course he did.

Using the coil from his satchel, we tied the slumping bodies to the overgrown tree.

"What about paper?"

Wesley beamed and pulled out a sheet. I grinned, even offering, "Gnarly." Then, with some quick scribbling, a little folding, and just a bit of fluffing of the unconscious soldiers… "What do you think?"

Veli and Eric regarded the limp men with a hastily-scrawled sign tucked into the rope: *Leander is a doofus.*

Shaking his head, Veli turned away. Before stalking off, he left me with his answer. "You have issues."

Chapter 13

Smells of roasted meat wafted into my nose, awakening a hunger I forgot existed. The Dry Salamander, though not the most upstanding tavern in the northern city of Colander (the geographers of this world were straight out of a Pampered Chef party), at least kept us warm and out of the constant rain. After our three day journey to the abandoned caves to the north, we'd had our fill of the elements. Wesley was left in charge, and we braved the rain once more to look for supplies and lodging. Somehow instead of a cozy bed-and-breakfast, we ended up in the Spoons' equivalent of a biker bar.

The crackling fire in the hearth was enough compensation for the unsavory characters littered about the counter, clanking mugs of mead beside their empty plates. After all, what were some sketchy people when our own heroic trio looked rough—Veli glowering like an angry lumberjack, Eric smiling creepily for some unknown reason, and me resembling an unwashed hobo.

Still, the surrounding diners were a bit special. The burly men at the table beside us communicated by grunt, which was a step up from the hawk-eyed pair in front who sharpened their knives more vigorously whenever they caught me staring. Tricks of the firelight, no doubt.

Flickering shadows danced across the wooden table, stained with wine… or was that blood? I moved my napkin to cover up the red smudge and decided not to think about it.

"So, why did we pick this place again?" I whispered, scooting closer to Eric.

"Because we need food and shelter for the night before we head off, and it's the only tavern within a couple of miles," he said, picking up his fork…or spoon—it was hard to know in this world.

"What did you and Fletcher discuss before we left?"

Veli stabbed his meat more forcefully than needed. "Our next move," he answered. "We need to return to the Capitol to figure out the best way to confront the King about Leander's abuse. Now, stop yammering and fill your mouth with food. It's not wise to talk about these matters in public."

An antisocial man wearing an apron plopped a steaming plate of brown meat and circular grains in front of me, leaving without a smile. Someone wasn't earning their tip tonight. I hesitantly picked up a utensil. Though the food smelled delicious to my deprived stomach, uncertainty held me back. Who knew what kind of meat they ate in alternate universes, especially in creepy taverns? Squid eyeballs? Possum liver?

My stomach let out a long groan. Well, Veli and Eric didn't look like they were dying of food poisoning, so it was probably safe. I cautiously lifted the fork to my mouth and was rewarded with a warm, sweet taste. Ah, beautiful blessed food. The good thing about being among criminals and bums was the standard for manners was pretty low. I shoveled the grains with gusto, lost in a world of delicious food.

"It's not a race, you know." Eric nudged me with a grin, and I glowered at him in return.

Veli impaled bits of meat onto his fork, silent and precise. How those two could be brothers was beyond me. "So, who's older?" I inquired. The pair put down their forks, instantly solemn.

Way to hit a nerve, Nessie. *Change the subject!* My brain screamed. *Restore social tranquility!*

I ruffled my hair nervously. "So, how about those guards of Spoons? Man, can those guys run!"

My optimism was lonely at the table. Lonely, but persistent. "Seen any good movies lately? I just finished watching The Little Mer—"

"He is," Veli spoke, his voice bitter. "Thirteen months. Apparently, thirteen months can tell the difference between an able leader and a second-rate nobody." He raked his knife against the plate, emitting a high scraping noise.

Alert! We were in dangerous territory. The time to retreat was before Veli started throwing knives or food. After going so long without eating, my priority was the latter. "Well, now, I wouldn't—"

Eric slammed his cup onto the table, sending amber cider sloshing over the sides. "Give me a break, Veli! I never asked for my lot in life. I just did what I had to—what anyone would have done in my situation," he argued. "When are you ever going to let it go?"

Veli jumped up, knocking his chair backwards. The grunting men beside us grew quiet to watch the scene. "Why did you even bother coming back?" He saved a special glare for me. "And next time, leave your *heroes* in their own land." With that, he stormed out of the dining area and past the hearth. The fire writhed at his departure long after he'd stomped into the bedroom wing.

Eric cradled his head in his hands. "I think I need some air," he muttered, weaving between a Captain Hook look-alike and the Spoons' version of a drug dealer to get out the door.

And the award for Making Dinner Awkward went to…me. With a sigh, I focused on filing my mouth with food, though my appetite had receded. Mid-bite, the hair on my neck bristled. I slowly raised my head up to see the weapon-sharpeners eyeing me. Under normal circumstances I would never abandon delicious food, but seeing armed men whispering about me was sufficient motivation. I picked up my newly-acquired pack from the floor and left the remaining bites.

The thugs must have decided we were playing a game of Follow the Leader and prowled after me. Just a coincidence? My churning stomach didn't agree.

Increasing my speed, I serpentined through the dining area, eager to reach the corridor Veli disappeared into, but in my peripheral the weapons duo matched my pace.

A muscular hand grabbed my arm before I could reach the hall, and I squealed, attracting the attention of nearby diners. The plump innkeeper released his grip, and my heart rate slipped back into the double digits. "Are you okay, miss?" he asked, pushing a pair of glasses up his nose. Behind me, the men sat down at the hearth.

"Yes, sir. I was just looking for my bedroom." I wrung my hands together. Was I having some kind of PTSD reaction? Someone sliced me with a sword once and suddenly men couldn't move to the other side of the room without me freaking out?

He pointed around the corner to the bedroom wing. "To the right, miss." With a pause, he stroked his gray mustache, scanning my stained and tattered garments. "And if you'd like to freshen up, there's a ladies' bathhouse to the left. Why don't I show you?"

Yep, definitely rocked the hobo look. "Thank you, sir." My breathing settled, and I followed him to a white door, ornately labeled "Ladies Bathhouse." He rapped on the door and swung it open, gesturing into the open room.

"The soap is on the counter." The innkeeper took in a shallow breath. "Feel free to use as much of it as you'd like."

Seriously? My fists balled, but the innkeeper was already making his way into the dining area. If he thought I smelled, he could have just come out and said it. I raised an armpit and took in a whiff. Wow. It was like someone had doused my body in Ode de Garbage Truck. Maybe he had a point. I stepped into the cozy bath house and shut the door behind me, turning the silver lock. Clear vials sat next to the sink on a marble counter, smelling of lilacs and honeysuckle. Warm sconces illuminated the small room, thankfully windowless and with a solid ceiling. My reflection caught in the large mirror on the wall. Ew, was that greasy-haired, dirty vagabond really me?

My cheeks turned red. How long had I tramped around in the forest with Eric like this? Did he get nauseated whenever I walked into a room? This needed to be remedied immediately. My pack and sword were abandoned next to the table holding white towels and a dish of amber liquid. I approached the single porcelain tub in the middle of the room, twisting a silver knob on the faucet. Water bubbled up from a hole at the base. My hand dipped into the forming pool, swishing in the warmth. A few pumps of the golden soap, and I was ready to get clean. Let the scrubbing begin.

I stepped into the basin, slowly sinking into the hot water. After the initial cringe when it hit the still-tender skin under my bandage, I swore I heard my tired, aching muscles singing the Hallelujah chorus. It wasn't a five star hotel, but definitely better than expected in a tavern of rough wannabe criminals. Much cleaner than I'd counted on, considering all of the medieval-esque movies I had seen were lacking methods of personal hygiene.

For a moment, I enjoyed my uninterrupted thoughts. No unexpected glowing swords, no one chasing me, and no breaking into dirty prisons. Only Eric and Veli's fight, the plight of the Sporks, and how I would return home flitted around in my head. Not that my former life beckoned; my porta-potty job wouldn't miss me and friends were not a-dime-a-dozen in my life, but there was part of me that missed normal. The mission impossible stuff had become a little…impossible.

I pumped a few more squirts of the soap into my hand and lathered my hair, carefully working through knots. If I returned home, what would happen with Eric? What was the deal with him? I didn't want to admit there might be more to the butterflies that bounced around in my stomach when we talked. How could I help but smile when I thought about his kindness and compassion, his willingness to risk danger for the innocent, and, best of all, his goofiness?

Knots free, I scoured the dirt encrusting my skin like barnacles. Did I just like Eric because he was my only link to the real world? Was it because he kept me from getting killed? While a great quality to possess, was it one to build a relationship on? My head drifted backwards onto the tub's edge. And why did I ask so many questions that seemed to have no clear answers? Time to jump this train of thought before it could derail. I checked my arm for any residual dirt or blood, satisfied I was clean. Beautiful.

What wasn't beautiful was the shriveled skin on my fingertips, a side effect from thinking too long in the tub. I took my time getting out and drying off, relishing the feeling of a fresh tunic and leggings. Thank you, Eric, for buying new clothes at the market. One last glance in the mirror when I unlocked the door left me assured the bath had been a good choice. I grabbed my sword, attaching the sheath to my waist as I exited the bathhouse. A whole new Nessie emerged from layers of filth beneath, now well-groomed with pack and sword, ready to step out into the corridor knowing that she was not—A hand clamped over my mouth before I could finish the thought. My muffled scream was as futile as my attempt to bite the perpetrator.

"Shh, Ness. We have to get out of here," Eric whispered in my ear.

My racing heart slowed at his voice, but he didn't give me any time to recuperate. We sprinted along the candlelit hallway. Large wooden beams lined the wall, and Eric pulled me behind one, motioning for me to stay silent. A few minutes passed before shadows spread across the carpet, preceding the weapon-sharpeners speed-walking down the corridor and into...the ladies' bathhouse. And those weapons they had been sharpening? The glittering knives and swords firmly grasped in their hands. Not a good sign. My throat went dry, and I tried to swallow.

"Now!" Eric commanded, bolting down the hallway. I didn't need any encouragement to run after him. My legs filled with the warmth of adrenaline, pumping to keep up with Eric's quick pace. I glanced over my shoulder, expecting to see a grimy thug on our heels.

Eric raced down the corridor, twisting around corners until we arrived at a door with the number "38" painted in black. Eric reached for the doorknob and my pulse went into overdrive. What was behind that door? What if more ruffians were lying in wait, crouching with their axes and swords? With a push of encouragement from Eric, I stumbled into the room. The only threat was a still-brooding Veli sitting on a cot. When I saw his stormy look, I considered taking my chances with the weapons-sharpeners. Still, the makeshift beds, sink, and small kitchen table were a lot homier than a coffin. My breathing slowed when Eric twisted the lock into place. I settled onto a cot, looking to him for explanation.

"When I came back in from my walk, I heard those men talking," Eric whispered, his voice shaking. "They were going after you. The innkeeper moved us to this room after I told him. He's going to tell anyone who asks we left and headed north to the mountains, so we should be okay. Still, it's safer if we all stay in the same room and take turns keeping watch."

They were going after you. His words echoed in my head, souring my stomach. More assassins? Oxygen came in shallow breaths, and I lowered myself onto the unoccupied cot. "I'll take the last watch." I tugged a blanket over me and curled into a fetal position. Ladies and gentlemen, the stage counselors referred to as "denial."

Veli harrumphed in the corner and crossed his arms, but Eric tilted his head. "Are you okay, Ness?"

Apathy offered to take over. "Yeah, I'm fine." The words came out monotone and robotic. "People are frequently trying to kill me these days, so what's new?" The room grew silent, and I clutched the pillow. "However, since we have to share this tiny bedroom, you two should probably work out whatever life issues you're having." I rolled over, turning my back to their incredulous glances and let my body shut down.

§ § §

The echo of a bird's call reverberated in my dream. Just ahead of me, a towering castle—no, a fortress—bearing the banner of Spoons rose into the clouds. The details of each stone laid in the walls was crisp and clear. The Capitol of Spoons? How did I get back here?

The morning breeze fluttered the banner, cooling my skin. The comforting smell of bread wafted into my nose. My dream-self headed for the castle while a crowd of nearby villagers stared off vacantly, unresponsive to my waves. The castle's double doors grew in enormity the closer I approached, stretching above for miles and yet somehow still opening with my feeble tug. The massive doors let out a deep groan and swung inward, revealing a throne room with crimson walls and carpet.

Should I go in? There was something I was supposed to remember. Something dangerous. It felt like a pile of lead sat on my chest, but instead of turning around and heading for the hills, I stepped through the doorway. I trudged along the carpet, unable to tell how much time passed before I arrived at a dais. A crowned man sat wearily on a throne, slumping against the chair. His face was wrinkled and drained of energy. A lock of silver hair rested over his closed eyes like a cobweb.

A dead man? What kind of a dream was this? However, with a shuddering breath, he wheezed and coughed, alive but not by much. A shadow fell over his face when an imposing figure approached the throne.

Get out, get out, get out! I tried to run, but found I couldn't move.

Leander, looking as real as real could be, bent to the tired man and whispered in his ear, the hiss of a few words catching my attention: *half-breed, threat, exterminate.* One hand resting on the old man's shoulder, Leander's other hand edged ever-so-slightly towards the crown. A surge of electricity ran through my body, and I bolted forward to stop him, my mouth opening in protest.

Before I could reach the top of the dais, Leander pulled out a gun and shot me. My world faded to red, darker than the crimson staircase I collapsed on. Moisture covered my body, soaking my skin and clothes. My fingers wiped liquid from my face. "Blood," I whispered into the dim light. "Need to get the blood off."

Something touched my shoulder, and I screamed, slapping it away. When the pressure returned, this time forceful, it shook me back and forth, resistant to my fighting until—I shot up from the cot with a gasp, eyes adjusting to the moonlit room. My heartbeat drummed in my ears, and I inspected my body for injury. No gunshot wounds and all my organs were intact. Clear liquid dampened my hands, but my breathing slowed. Not blood, just sweat.

A thin sliver of moon shone through the transparent ceiling, illuminating Veli's form bent over me, his hand hovering above my shoulder. He coughed and stepped back from my cot, casually walking to the counter and getting a glass of water from the sink. "Bad dream?" he asked without turning around. The sincerity in his voice sounded foreign coming from him.

I massaged my temple, trying to make sense of everything. "I'm not sure. I died, so I guess so."

"I can't imagine a death dream being a good omen, but the good thing is that it was only a dream."

I attempted to lie back down, but was doing more tossing and turning than sleeping. With a sigh, I pulled back the covers and stepped beside the cot. "I can take over watch now, Veli." He downed the cup of water and nodded, crossing the room and sitting on the edge of the bed.

I headed for the sink counter and splashed cold water on my face. Why couldn't I shake this paranoid feeling? Eyes closed, I reached for the towel beside the sink and collided with a human torso. "What the heck, Veli?" I shouted, hyperventilating at the stoic man standing beside me. How could he move so quickly and silently?

He said nothing before awkwardly putting a hand on my shoulder. "Um… I wanted to…er…when I was a kid and had nightmares, my mother always told me to think about something positive…like flowers or rainbows. Something of that nature."

Okay, did I somehow fall back asleep? Was that me hallucinating? "…That's really nice, Veli," I ventured. "Did it work?"

His hand retracted and he made his way back to the cot. "Not really. I usually just imagined myself killing whatever I was afraid of."

Of course. Still, I couldn't help but smile. Comforting wasn't exactly his strong suit. "Good night, Veli."

I sunk down by the door, his words echoing in my thoughts. *It was only a dream.* The striking clarity, the crisp details unlike any dream I had before, came back to me, settling in my stomach like a boulder. *Or was it?*

Chapter 14

The rest of the night passed peaceably enough, but remnants of the dream/vision left me pulling at the edges of my new cloak until the ends frayed. Feeling rushed back into my tingling legs when I shifted uncomfortably against the floor. My mind barely registered the newly improved circulation. The Blade of Remiel lay beside me on the ground; hours of staring at its gleaming metal hadn't given the answers I wanted. I pushed myself off the floor, sheathing the sword and moving to a chair at the small table.

Strains of morning light filled the room, and my thoughts argued chaotically. It all made sense: I was going to the castle, confronting the king about Leander's lies, and saving the Sporks; a divine vision, confirming what I needed to do. But what was that last event? Leander shot me? That hardly seemed like vision material.

Did that kind of thing happen in the Bible? My mind blanked, distracted by the reality of this bizarre situation. Not two weeks ago, I was sucked into a parallel universe to save a group of people called Sporks. Why would a death vision be any less odd? Hardly fair, God. After all, the good guys always won; the protagonist triumphant. Even if the hero died, they always came back, just like Gandalf. But what if death found me in this odd world? Did that mean I was dead in my universe too? Did it matter there were multiple universes if there was only one me?

Maybe it was a warning. Maybe God was telling me, "Hey, Nessie, don't do that plan or you'll get shot." But how could that be the case when confronting the king felt like the right plan of action? What good was having a vision if it could be interpreted a million different ways? With a groan, I beat my head against the wall in frustration.

"Knock it off!" a voice yelled from next door. "I'm trying to sleep here!"

"Sorry," I whispered, knowing my apologies didn't make it past the wall. My mind already moved to another question: If this mission cost me my life, was I willing to pay the price?

Lost in my thoughts, I didn't notice Eric wake up and move to the counter where a black box with a hand crank sat. His dark hair was disheveled from sleep, and, tortured as I was, the sight of his hair devoid of wig or cheesy salesman grease gave me warmth even in the drafty room. He yawned, slowly turning the crank of the machine. It rotated and the box hummed with electricity. "You look tired, Ness. Anything troubling you?"

"I can only pick one thing?" I snorted. He lifted the lid of the box and removed a cup of steaming liquid. Wow, talk about convenience. Eric should have sold those instead of toasters.

"*Sertav*, the Spoons' version of coffee," he explained, handing it to me. The sweet, nutty flavor was a pleasant surprise. With a teasing smirk, he pretended to pull out a notepad. "Now that you have a nice hot beverage, it's only natural for you to tell me about your troubles. What seems to be the matter?"

Staring at my rippled reflection in the black liquid, I tried to return the smile, but a sigh escaped my lips. "I had a dream."

He sat down beside me with a cup of his own. "Yeah, it's hard to go back to sleep after one of those. You've been through a lot of trauma. Nightmares are only natural."

My eyes drifted from the steaming liquid to Eric's face. "Well, it wasn't a nightmare."

"No? A dream about me then?" He winked facetiously.

His comment earned a grin, but it was short lived. "It wasn't really even a dream, more like a vision."

Eric lost his joking manner. He rested his cup on the table. "A message, perhaps? Maybe it's to show you what to do."

"Well, I kind of...died at the end."

He rubbed the back of his neck, silent when I launched into the details of the dream—the crispness of the colors and sounds, Leander's crown-itchy fingers, and my untimely death. "Now, what do you make of that? Is it a warning? Instructions? Am I crazy? How do I make the right choice when so much is riding on it?" My head slumped down on the table. Veli's sleeping form muttered unintelligible protests from the cot.

Eric reached over and patted my hair. "I've been there. Well, not with a horribly pessimistic vision-dream, but I do have an odd parallel universe story that you might be interested in, and it involves making difficult decisions."

My head perked up. Eric was finally giving me insight into his shadowy past, a fact that raised my body back into sitting position. "All right, toaster man. What are your deep dark secrets?"

Eric rubbed a hand through his fluffy, black hair and took a sip. "I was born in the kingdom of Spoons at the young age of zero."

"That's quite a young age to be born," I laughed.

Eric stroked his chin. "I think that was the cause of all of my problems." With a cough to clear his throat, his voice took on a more serious tone. "My real name is Bran, as you already know. Eric is my middle name and the one I chose to go by in your world. I am the eldest son of the Duke of Burntbread, hand-picked from birth to be the Commander of the Spoons' army."

Commander? Eric had to be mistaken. "Isn't that position filled by Leander?"

"Well, now it is," Eric leaned forward. "I never wanted to be Commander."

"Let me guess. You wanted to be a toaster salesman in an alternate universe?"

He fiddled with his empty cup. "Not exactly. I was an avid reader. One day, I stumbled upon a dusty old volume in my father's libraries about parallel universes. One of the interesting points concerned the Blades of Remiel used to close the gates between worlds. Fascinating as it was, the book soon passed from my thoughts, but I always wished for a different world—one where I wouldn't have to become some commander for an army."

Eric quickly glanced towards his brother's sleeping form, lowering his voice. "Veli, however, was always marveling about my destiny. He would talk incessantly of it and our games often revolved around my destined role. His jealousy was apparent, admiring what I would get to become."

"And then something changed," I commented, finishing the last sip of my "coffee."

He nodded, pushing back from the table and meandering to the counter. "Everything changed. I was eighteen years old, heavy into my training to become Commander, when I stumbled upon it. It was a warm, sunny day at a yard sale and—"

"They have yard sales here?" Unless a yard sale in Spoons meant someone actually selling the grass in front of their house.

"Of course. Yard sales transcend worlds," he said, turning the crank on the black box. Apparently, Eric was a sertav addict. "Anyway, warm sunny day… yard sale…you get the picture. I was rummaging through a box when I found a sword wrapped in cloth. The weird thing was when I unwrapped the sword and ran my hand across the blade, there was this…strange sensation—a tingling. It could have been a trick of the light, but when I traced the engravings on the side, it seemed to…glow." Steaming cup in hand, Eric leaned against the counter, stirring the liquid.

"The man seemed confused when I asked about the price and said he had never seen the sword in his life. In the end, he told me I could have it. A few weeks later, I remembered the book about the Blades of Remiel and the words etched on the side of the sword: 'Eethi andre canasi'"

Finally, something I recognized! I withdrew the sword from its sheath and placed it on the table. "'Enter with Him.'"

"Indeed." Eric turned off the black box and returned to the table. "My first instinct was to find the book in my father's library and read it again. It seemed like fate, an out to the predestined life I'd rejected. My father was skeptical when I tried convincing him I could serve the kingdom better as a trans-universal diplomat, an explorer."

I nodded. It was hard to imagine Eric the war-hungry commander, running around on horseback, shouting orders to soldiers.

"Veli, on the other hand, was furious. He'd obsessed for years about my future role of commander and couldn't understand why I would be willing to throw that away. What he didn't know was that I hated the idea. Veli was always the one who came up with the great battle plans and strategies in our games. He had to help me in my training, even completing some of my exercises for me. Becoming commander was his dream, not mine." Eric carefully pulled out his chair to sit down, but the legs scraped across the floor.

A loud snore escaped from Veli's sleeping form, and I craned my neck to peek at him. Memories of our first meeting, him barking orders at me, his blade at my throat, came to mind. He was definitely the feistier of the pair.

Eric eyed his brother and placed his cup on the table before sitting down. "Unfortunately, our society is built upon the privilege of the eldest, and I was given a privilege I never wanted. For weeks, I pleaded with my father and, when that failed, the king. They were hesitant at first since rejecting one's social destiny is unheard of in Spoons. They wouldn't have relented but for one thing: they saw I wasn't cut out to be the commander. History and politics bore me to tears. I wasn't the one meant to lead an army." My mind considered his gentle friendliness, his warm concern compared to Leander's fierce, calculating heart.

"All of this considered, the king and my father consented to let me scope out whatever unknown world the sword led to. Leander, second in the class, assumed training to be the commander."

Eric shook his head slowly. "Veli was absolutely livid with me. Not only denied the privilege to fulfill his dream because of his birth rank, he was also denied the chance to live it out through me." He waved his arms, nearly knocking over the half-full cup of sertav. "But what was I supposed to do? Be something I didn't want to be for the rest of my life? Send young men to their deaths on the whim of a king? I couldn't live with that.

"I bid farewell to my family, but Veli said nothing to me when I took the Blade of Remiel with me into a field at dusk. The runes' words barely left my tongue when my eyes opened to the front door of Ferdinand's Toaster Emporium." Wow, that store was just across the street from my apartment complex. Small world…or parallel universe. Whatever. The image of a tunic-clad Eric in the middle of the city made me snicker, but he kept going.

"Unsure what a toaster was, I wandered into the store. The man behind the counter assumed I was from a Renaissance Fair, since there was apparently one in town. It didn't take long for him to hook me with his spiel." Eric's voice changed to a deep baritone. "My name is Ferdinand and this is my emporium. You look like a worthy fellow. Come, embark with me on a life-changing mission."

My laughter made Veli stir again, and I quickly clamped a hand over my mouth. Poor Eric, sitting outside the Toaster Emporium. The one time my car had broken down beside the store and I'd had to use their phone, Ferdinand had almost convinced *me* to quit my day job to sell toasters.

"You can imagine my excitement. Only being in the world a few minutes and already appointed an important task." Eric rubbed his chin thoughtfully. "Unfortunately, he was talking about an employment opportunity selling toasters. Let's just say, hindsight is twenty-twenty. I ecstatically accepted his offer and when he handed me a bunch of toasters and told me to go sell them, I was clueless."

"That's why you ended up at my apartment complex!" All the pieces of the puzzle clicked together. "It's right across from Ferdinand's. No wonder you looked so confused every time I opened the door." I patted his shoulder. "Aww, poor Eric. You visited my apartment every day for…I don't even know how long."

He counted the months on his fingers. "A year. I didn't know where to go or even what a toaster was. The first door I knocked on, an old lady appeared, and I said, 'Madam, may I interest you in a…toaster?' She refused, but I was undaunted. I kept looking at the box for any kind of clue as to what I was actually selling. 'But, milady, you can put your…bread in it. Yes, behold, a bread holder!' She bought one, but only because I called her 'milady.'"

Ah, Eric. Charming as always.

"My first couple of weeks were less-than-stellar. Unfamiliar with the customs of your world, I also had no housing, no steady source of food, and no friends. A pastor found me in my 'Renaissance costume,' looking hungry and forlorn. He thought I was either on drugs or crazy, but he took me under his wing. Concluding I was simply an eccentric foreigner, he helped me get on my feet."

I frowned. "But why did you keep coming back to the same apartment complex every week to sell your toasters? Didn't you know that the tenants probably hadn't changed their minds from the week before?"

Eric peered into his sertav, running his finger around the rim of the cup. "Well, I branched out after the first couple of weeks. The pastor taught me the city's layout, sending me down different streets, but when the day was done, I always found myself coming back to your apartment complex. Really, just to your apartment. Your door was the only one I knocked on every week." He blushed. "That's stupid, isn't it? I don't know why, but I felt drawn to you for some reason. You never slammed the door in my face and even bought two toasters from me! But I think it was more than that." He combed a hand through his fluffy hair. "Our lives were intertwined in ways I hadn't yet discovered."

"No, that isn't stupid at all," I said. "A little creepy, but not stupid. I'll even let you have 'sweet.'"

"Well, that's all the secrets I'll let you have from my toaster rounds." He winked. "After living with the pastor for a few weeks, the topic of God came up. In my universe, we learned about God, but our churches are diluted and serve as social centers for the villagers."

"God had become just another story to me, like the Santa Claus of your world. When I talked with the pastor, it started changing me. Jesus was so much more than just a fairy-tale spirit of good; He loved me just as I was. I couldn't earn His love or approval because He graciously given it to me already. After accepting His gift, I was a new creation, able to see myself and my situation through a different perspective. It changed everything for me, and I began thinking of going back to my world to share this good news with the people of Spoons."

Eric's eyes shifted to the clear ceiling where the sunlight began to take over the sky. "While I don't understand the entire reason God put me in your world, towards the end of my time there I knew I had to return. King Arthur's Shopalot was a frequent destination of mine because the wares made me think of home. When I saw you there with the sword, I recognized it as another Blade of Remiel. After we left, I ran to the pastor's home, said goodbye, and used my sword to return here."

My hand wandered towards the hilt of my blade. "I've been meaning to ask you how that works."

His brow wrinkled. "The Blades of Remiel can be a little…finicky. You can't just pop in and out of worlds. The swords come to the bearers for a reason, and that reason has to be fulfilled before it will let you leave." He held up an empty sheath. "After I returned here, my sword vanished. I guess that means I'm not the one meant to carry it anymore. But you're not leaving just yet, are you?"

My face earned an academy award for Best Performance of Not Being Freaked

Out as I shook my head. "No, no rush." Especially since, according to him, my sword might never let me leave. What was it my mother used to tell me? "Cross that bridge when you get to it?" Refocusing on his words, the story distracted me from my fearful thoughts.

"When I got back to Spoons, everything was in an uproar. Leander had, for all intents and purposes, taken over for the king and was oppressing the half-breeds, murdering their leaders. A lot can happen in a year."

"So, time doesn't pass differently in other worlds?" There went my theory for a free six-week vacation away from work.

He shook his head. "No, a day spent here is a day passed there."

Oh, well. Having no friends had the upside of no one caring if you disappeared. My boss probably fired me already, but maybe that was a blessing.

"As soon as I got here, I started making a plan to foil Leander's plots, starting with rescuing Atalanta. That's when you showed up." The morning light glinted off my sword on the table. "Sorry for pretending I didn't know you at first. I wasn't sure how to get into all of that without you thinking I was crazy. I didn't expect you to recognize me, especially with my disguise on, and when you did, it caught me off guard. But now, you know everything. Any questions?"

Pursing my lips, I thought for a while. "Just one. When you first sold toasters a year ago, your hair was fluffy, like it is now. Not too long after that, you started slicking it back. Why?"

He blushed. "All the salesmen in the commercials did it, made me think it was standard procedure. It became a habit after that."

I assessed his soft, gel-free hair. "I like it better now, fluffy."

"Your suggestion has been duly noted," he laughed. "Anything else?"

"Well…since you've already opened up, it's time for me to confess. I felt a connection too when we first met. I wouldn't have bought two toasters from you if I didn't." Okay, yes. I did want to make double the toast in half the time. That was a small perk. "And now that I'm getting to know you, I'm glad that you knocked on my door a year ago trying to sell me a bread holder. I also want to point out the fact," I continued, pointing my finger at him, "this back story is only partially related to my original problem and hasn't pointed me to a decision."

Eric held up his hands in surrender. "You're right. I'm really just an attention hog trying to distract you from your problems and tell you about me at the same time. Aren't I clever?"

"Since I saw through it, I guess not."

"But, Nessie," Eric leaned his elbows on the table, "discussing your options would have been pointless. We both already know what decision you'll make."

"Really, now?"

His voice was soft and gentle. "I don't know why your vision had such a violent ending, but I do know that you're going to march up to King Kermit's castle and tell him about the injustice against the half-breeds. You're not going to let Leander stop you because you know that's why God brought you here."

Why did he have to be so right? I crossed my arms. After all of my overthinking, I was no closer to a clear answer, but that didn't change the facts. Confronting the king was the right thing to do, regardless of weird dream-visions.

Eric poked my shoulder. "And if you die after all this is over, at least you get to know some cool stuff about me."

"That's not funny!" I shouted, punching him in the ribs, but we were both laughing when Veli groggily walked over to the counter.

"I'm not sure why you all are so mirthful when we might be dead before the week is done," he muttered.

"That's more likely for some of us than others," Eric teased.

"Stop it!" I giggled and punched again.

"Oh, how I despise love," Veli sighed.

With my funny, kind, sweet toaster salesman sitting across from me, a million Disney romance scenes flooded into my brain. "Me, too," I replied to Veli. "But I guess we're stuck with it now."

Eric beamed at me, taking my fingers in his. It was just as magical as Disney, except for Veli's comments about finding a place to vomit. Oh, well. Good enough for me.

Chapter 15

Fallen leaves crunched under my leather boots, the noise launching roosting birds into the sky. The recently evacuated bush quivered from the sudden movement. Trees, birds, and squirrels were all I had seen for the past day, so much so I even dreamt about them in the few hours of sleep I'd snatched behind a log. The forest was fidgety as if the animals sensed our nervousness.

Bushes and thickets lined the dirt path we traveled, lending us secrecy we desperately needed. The cold morning breeze raised goosebumps on my skin, and I rubbed my forearms to keep warm. I appreciated Veli wanted to get moving before dawn to stay out of sight of soldiers, but there were certain disadvantages to waking up before the sun did.

Far off to the south, the outline of the Capitol of Spoons was gray and hazy. While only the size of my thumbnail, it would only be a matter of days before its gates loomed in front of us. What happened then…well, we would just have to see.

I thought of Wesley and hoped he was doing well back at the caves to the North. Despite his unique mannerisms, he had manned up to the challenge of protecting the freed Sporks while they hid in the caves, waiting for things to blow over. "Will the prisoners ever get to go back to their families?" I asked Veli who was marching ahead of Eric and me. After being apart for so long, the former inmates had to be itching to return.

"Still can't get them out of your head, huh?" He took a sip of water from the canteen in his hand. "Fletcher mentioned sneaking them back into the village soon. Their families have been notified and are working on creating crawlspaces and places for them to hide. Besides, Leander isn't so much concerned about them right now as he is about you."

"That's comforting." Sarcasm was becoming a second language to me.

Veli shrugged. "You asked for it, and it's too late to change your mind. We can only plan and try not to get killed."

"I would especially appreciate that," Eric piped up.

Okay, butterflies. Stop running around in my stomach. I had an important epiphany to share. "I think our best option is to take the offensive and go straight for the king." My throat was dry when I spoke.

Veli held up his hands, stopping in his tracks. "Let's hold on a second. I thought I said we should try not to die. Maybe my brain malfunctioned and what actually came out was, 'Hey, Leander is trying to kill you; why don't we go knock on his front door and see what happens?'" If sarcasm was a second language for me, Veli was fluent.

Halting next to a green thicket that rustled with quarreling squirrels, I marveled at my ability to restrain myself from punching people. "You don't have to come if you don't want to. Your presence would be useful, but I'm not going to beg you."

He kicked a pile of leaves on the ground, sending a shower of colors fluttering in the air. "Just because I think it's a stupid idea doesn't mean I'm not coming. I'm up for a good suicide mission any day."

My attempt to boot him in the shin was more like assaulting a wall. "That was for your poor attitude," I growled, but his laughter was hardly the response I desired.

"Well, if that's all you're going to do to Leander, I'd better come along."

Eric's raised his hand. "You can count me in since someone has to keep Veli in check."

Uh-oh. Things were still not completely smoothed over with the brothers. Veli crossed his arms. "Glad to know you're sticking around for that now."

Maybe I would be safer if stepped out from in between them. I lifted my foot forward, but Eric stopped me. "No, Ness. You don't need to move just because my *brother*," he craned his neck to look over me at Veli, "is being a jerk. Look, Veli, I'm sorry I left, but I can't change what happened. I didn't want to be Commander. I went to explore a new land. That's it; it's over. Now stop sulking and move on with it."

Veli's fists balled at his sides. If they were going to solve their problems the manly way, I didn't want to get caught in the crossfire. "I'm just gonna be over here..."

I leaned out of the way, but Veli stomped his foot. "Eric says you're fine, so obviously it's okay. By all means, Nessie, stay where you are." He gestured to his brother. "Aren't we so lucky that Eric knows everything? What would we do without him here? Oh. Well, I have the answer to that question, because he already abandoned me once."

Ouch.

His voice grew low and husky. "You weren't here, Eric. Can you really come to me after you've seen what Leander's done in your absence and tell me it's over?" He shook his head. "It's *not* over. You left, and your decision made an impact; the kingdom went to crap while you were selling bread on your little vacation. Don't come back here and pretend like everything is peachy keen."

All right, no more. I bowed down and darted out of the brother sandwich. Luckily, no one tried to stop me that time. I stood ready to hide behind the thicket next to me in case they started duking it out with swords or fists.

Eric stared at the ground, his lips drawn in a tight line. When he finally spoke, the words were soft. "I'm sorry." He combed a hand through his dark hair. "I ran away. I knew I didn't want to be Commander, but I had no clue what to do. I'm at least in part to blame for this mess that Leander made." Eric took a step forward, lifting a hand to Veli's shoulder. "I didn't think about you having to stay here and clean up after me. I really am sorry," his voice was barely audible, "brother."

Veli regarded him, his stern features like stone. He stood quietly, looking down at the ground, minutes passing in silence. Finally, his eyes clenched shut and he pulled Eric into a tight embrace. "Brother," Veli affirmed.

Whew. I needed some popcorn if I was going to be watching a real-life movie from the Hallmark channel.

"All better?" I ventured, ready to dart behind the bush if they turned on me.

The pair faced me. "We will help you clean up Leander's mess," Veli drew out slowly, as if testing the words.

Eric nodded. "Do you think we'll need more manpower?"

Yeah, because I needed more testosterone in my life. "No. Our mission requires the stealth of few rather than a large group of—"

A crash came from the thicket beside me, and I leapt backwards, almost tripping over myself. Guards! Thieves! Dinosaurs! It didn't matter what it was, but something large was coming to eat me. My trembling hands found the hilt of my sword and unsheathed it, cautiously waving it at the offending bush… the bush that was emitting yelps and way-too-familiar cries of "Oh, goodness me!" If there was a time I wanted to use expletives, it was then. Veli and Eric had their weapons drawn at the tuft of pink peeping through the foliage.

Whispered prayers poured from my lips. "Oh, Lord, please let this not be who I think it is."

"Peace, my friends," the bush voiced. She came out of the foliage, looking similar to the last time I had seen her, except wearing a brown riding tunic—as if that would make her fit into this drab medieval-ish world when cheetah print tights graced her legs.

"Mystical Unicorn? What are you doing here?" My surprise hid my chagrin.

She flashed her brilliantly white teeth at me and dodged the weaponry to envelope me in a bear-sized hug. "NESSIE! My house companion! I was so sad you were gone." Her pouty face was short-lived, quickly shifting into wide-eyed excitement. The words came out so fast that I had trouble distinguishing one from the other. "So, I used the solar fusion capacity of the toaster to create a portal to this world. I mean, you were already here, and I thought I could join you! I hope you don't mind. I figured since the toaster was broken anyway—"

"You know her?" Eric asked, mouth agape, his sword balanced dangerously close to her bubbly form. And Veli…let's just say Veli's eyebrows could not get any higher.

Glancing at the bouncy girl, images of a hyper Pomeranian came to mind. Oh, how I would have loved to deny this, but her beaming face framed by leaf-littered hair convicted me. I reluctantly sheathed my sword. "Hey, guys. This is Mystical Unicorn."

Veli scrutinized her, squinting at her cheetah print leggings. "Is that fashion normal where you come from?"

"Ummm…Mystical Unicorn is…one-of-a-kind," I replied carefully.

"Yes, she is!" Mystical Unicorn squealed, bowing low with a curtsey. "And now, she is at your service."

How the heck—I closed my eyes and counted down from ten, trying to keep my voice even and calm. "So…how did you find me exactly…roomie?" The last word was squeezed out with some effort.

Her fingers spread out into jazz hands. "Boy, was I lucky! The solar flares had linked up with the energy that the Blade of Remiel gave off and the toaster portal sent me right to your doorstep. Just think—if the energy fields hadn't been properly aligned, I could have been miles and miles away from you. It could have been months before I found out where you were. But we're lucky you can't get away from me that easily!" She mimed a punch to my shoulder.

My well of enthusiasm was found lacking. "Oh, yay…" I stroked my fore-head, trying to massage out the forming wrinkles. *God, I don't know if you're trying to be funny, but radiant pink hair is not usually a good characteristic for someone on a stealth mission.* Out of all the people in all the worlds, why had God sent this one crashing through a bush in a parallel universe to meet me? Couldn't He have picked someone with more muscles and less gab?

Mystical Unicorn wrapped me in a crushing embrace. "I was so worried. All I could think was to come find you! I'm so glad we can share this journey."

That made one of us. Okay, that was unkind, Nessie. It was time to put on my big girl panties and be nice. Her Cheshire-cat grin softened, and I smiled (a real one, this time) back. "I'm glad, too." *I think.*

Chapter 16

The luxurious comfort of the castle's study was inappropriate for the storming emotions raging inside. Leander crushed the letter in his hand and cast it into the fire. The paper collapsed on itself and blackened to ash. Leander leaned back into his padded armchair, wishing all problems could be eliminated so easily.

He stared at the portrait of himself over the mantle, so regal and noble, framed by royal tapestries that depicted the lineage of Spoons. That was the face of a champion. Sure, some might call him militant with his cropped black hair, and others might say the scar running down his cheek was unsightly, but no one would dare say it to his face.

Never one for failure, Leander tended to handle it poorly. The words of the letter branded themselves onto his mind. *Your men were incapacitated at the clearing. Assumed cause: mystery girl and entourage. Sign posted at site: Leander is a doofus.* The commander slammed his fist onto the mahogany table, over-turning his tea and knocking over the stack of military papers on his desk. The pile of paperwork launched onto the floor with a thud before scattering in a flurry of white.

He didn't even know what a "doofus" was, although he was sure it wasn't a compliment. Who was this girl? The first time Leander met her he knew she would cause problems but tried to convince himself she was just another crazy person. More curiously, her presumed "husband" seemed familiar. If only he'd ended it then. Just a quick slice and his problems could have been eliminated.

Leander sighed, wiping up the brown puddle on his desk. Everything had been going so well. He was close to convincing King Kermit to declare Leander his heir, which would have been followed by a convenient accident for the aging king. Taking control wouldn't be too difficult for Leander. Already he acted in the king's stead. It was all falling into place, but then Nessie had to come and rip it all back up.

"I have legions of men at my fingertips," he muttered, "the best weapons in the kingdom, and gloriously raw power. So, what does this girl have that I don't?"

A knock sounded on the door to his study. "This had better be good,"

Leander yelled and grimaced when he saw a frightened, lanky soldier peek in, the pock marks of adolescence dotting his face.

The soldier cleared his throat, his voice cracking with signs of puberty. "Maybe I should return at a better time," he offered, cowering at the sight of Leander's scowl.

"Out with it, boy," Leander ordered. "What went wrong this time?"

"Your men…at the inn." His eyes darted wildly around the room. "They lost her and her companions."

Leander reached for the nearest breakable object—an antique vase—and hurled it to the ground with a thunderous growl. "One girl," he seethed. "One measly girl, and she evades us still." Rage pounded through his veins. "Tell your troop leader to double his efforts. Take the tranquilizers and shoot them on sight. I want her alive." His nails bit into the flesh of his palm, pale with tension. "At least until I'm through with her."

The soldier fled the room and Leander chuckled at the sound of scurrying footsteps fading down the hallway. He may not have known the word, but Leander was no doofus.

Chapter 17

"You know what else I love?" Mystical Unicorn chirped like one of the many birds fluttering in the trees above us. "Rainbows."

Veli twitched, but he played it off by combing through his blond hair and coughing. Eric glanced at me with a weary expression, miming a gun to his head.

Join the club, buddy.

It all seemed repetitive—the thick bushes rustling with wildlife, dim light filtering through the leaf canopy, the same eternally chatting roommate. If Veli wasn't such a good tracker, I would have wondered if we were circling the same road. At least our packs were light—the blessings of being poor fugitives. "Uhh… Mystical Unicorn," I whispered, batting Eric's hand down. My arms gestured to the towering trees surrounding the dirt path we had been traveling for miles. "We have to be quiet because…thieves! Yes, the thieves are prowling around and can hear you. So…quiet…is needed."

She leaned in close, lowering her voice to a whisper. "Oh! Thanks for warning me."

Blessed wonderful silence. I could have traveled like that for hours, listening only to the sound of twittering birds and crickets, but our reprieve was short-lived. Out of the corner of my eye, I saw Mystical Unicorn swinging her arms. She tilted her head back and gazed up at the red and orange leaves above us, casually lifting a hand to drum on her collarbone. Oh, goodness. It was coming.

With a bounce in her step, Mystical Unicorn started humming a jaunty rendition of "Walkin' On Sunshine."

This was going to be a very long journey.

Veli pulled his hair in anguish. "Unicorn…lady! Thieves can hear humming, so…let's be quiet," he blurted.

"Oh, really?" Mystical Unicorn gasped. "I didn't know that."

Eric shot me an anguished look and motioned me over beside him. "How do you find the strength to go on living with her? Earplugs?" His smirking face was briefly lit by a patch of sunlight. "Did she say that she made a toaster portal?"

I waved my hand. "I have no idea what she's saying half the time. You sold toasters—do you know anything about that?"

We rounded a curve in the dirt road, and a wooden bridge came into view. Thank heavens! At last, the monotonous forest road had some kind of variance, a sign we were on the right track. The only thing worse than traveling with an ADHD a cappella singer was being lost in the woods with one.

Eric readjusted the straps of his pack. "Well, the book I read discussed how to create a portal, but I've never understood how to do it. How does she know?"

Mystical Unicorn squinted in concentration, her thin lips pursed. Who knew what level of strength she had to be summoning to stay quiet? "She just knows a lot, I guess."

"Eric!" Veli whispered and waved him to the front.

The ex-toaster salesman jogged to Veli's side. Since their oh-so-therapeutic chat, the two had been getting along like best buds. "Are you guys friends now?" I shouted to them, and Mystical Unicorn whipped around, holding her finger to her lips. The leafy bushes lining the path to the bridge rustled and another squirrel rocketed across the trail.

"Shh, Nessie. The thieves could hear you."

Those eyes, all watery and innocent, made it impossible for me to keep lying. How could I when she was so genuine? "Well, I should probably tell you that there aren't really any—"

Arms shot out from the bushes and wrapped around my waist, pinning me to the muscular body it was attached to. The edge of something sharp tickled my throat.

"Let go! Who are you?" I growled, wriggling against my attacker's grasp.

A throaty voice chuckled in my ear. "Why, we are your friendly neighborhood thieves."

Go figure.

§ § §

Either the chattering birds had flew off or flight-or-fight was taking over. Regardless, the only sounds I processed were the thump of my own heart beat and heavy breathing in my ear.

What was the point of having an awesome sword if I was always detained before I could use it? A rough hand dug in my pockets in search for coins. "Watch your hands, buddy!" I snapped, jabbing my elbow into my attacker's sternum.

Eric lunged forward, but Veli clamped a hand on his shoulder, pointing to the weapon at my neck.

"And what if I don't, sweetheart?" the voice laughed.

The hairs on the back of my neck stiffened. *Nessie* I thought to myself, *don't forget all your training from those* Sixty Minutes *episodes.* "Then I'll rip your arms off and beat you with them!" I shouted, squirming in his grip. *Sixty Minutes* talked about threatening your attackers, right?

A coarse cackle, fit for any proper villain, erupted from his mouth, but the roving hands stopped. "All righty, boys. Put on your best manners. We've got us a stern one!"

With deft skill, fifteen scraggly thieves dropped from the trees above us and encircled our party, brandishing ornate knives and bows. Luckily for my sense of smell, they were not the homeless kind, but well-to-do, snazzily-dressed robbers. The crew sported brown cloaks and vests, their trousers clean despite hiding in trees. No tattoos or ghastly scars. Glittering jewels from scabbards and hilts flickered in patches of sunlight, but it couldn't compare to the countless rings decorating my captor's fingers. Looked like times were good for the criminally-employed.

Veli and Eric held their swords steady, but Mystical Unicorn, my less-than-helpful roommate, stared agape at the robbers before turning to me. "Nessie. Thieves!"

Yeah, kinda noticed, Unicorn.

Eric twisted away from Veli and moved towards me, causing the circle of thieves to flinch. "Let her go, unless you want to part with your hands, you fiend!"

The grip around my stomach tightened. "Ah, this must be your beau."

Beau? My eyes evaluated the tall, dark, and handsome man in front of me, wielding a sword in my defense. "Well, our relationship status is not clearly defined at the moment, but that's a statement I wouldn't regret if it were valid."

Eric's eyebrows shot up and he lowered the sword. "Really? I feel the same way!"

I stopped wriggling in the thief's grip and let the words sink in. Did this mean…?

The knife at my neck kept me from jumping up and down, but it didn't stop the girlish squeal from rising in my throat. Eric liked me! If I sent him a note that said "Circle yes or no," he would have circled yes! "Eric, you are the sweetest, most—"

My captor coughed, snapping Eric back to attention. "I'm glad I could be here for this touching moment, but we really ought to be robbing you now."

The circle of thieves constricted, reaching for the packs on Eric and Veli's shoulders. If you disregarded the weapons, they looked like gentlemen wanting to help out heavy-laden travelers. A redhead with a goatee taking the bag from Eric reminded me of the nice barista at my Starbucks back home. I couldn't imagine the guy who always gave me an extra shot of espresso impaling me with a dagger. Then again, maybe I shouldn't stake my life on half-baked judgments, especially when the man beside him was so burly and could have snapped me in two. Time to come clean and hope for the best.

"Good luck," I scoffed. "We should be robbing *you*. All of my worldly belongings consist of a leftover waffle from yesterday's breakfast." Despite popular belief, waffles extended across universes. The cosmos would be a sad place indeed if they did not.

The redhead held up the knapsack and groaned. "You mean we waited in these bushes for nothing?" He pointed back to the thicket. "Man, I got attacked by a frog. I hate frogs. They've got those beady eyes, and they're all slimy." He waved his knife at my captor. "Robert Hood, I can't believe you dragged us into this."

You've got to be kidding me. "Are you related to a Robin Hood?" I asked, eliciting a growl from behind me.

"Yes, unfortunately."

"I thought he stole from the rich and gave to the poor." Couldn't believe I was arguing with the brother of a man who I once thought was fictional. Wait…or was Robin Hood a fox? My Disney habit was really starting to mess me up.

"*He* does," Robert retorted with a huff, shaking his shaggy blond hair. "I, however, don't. I'm very nondiscriminatory in whom I rob."

"Well," I nodded to Eric's pack, "you can't really rob someone who doesn't have anything to take." Unfortunately, I learned this lesson the hard way in elementary school during my brief stint as a child criminal. A week of trying to take the lunch money from kids whose moms packed bratwurst sandwiches for them was not only fruitless, but earned me a trip to the guidance counselor's office.

He released me and pushed me forward, pointing to my knapsack. "Prove it. Your pockets might be empty, but that pack sure looks full." I rubbed my neck gingerly, finally getting a good look at the robber—a tall man with shaggy blond hair, the beginnings of a beard, and…a lip ring? The smug look on his face screamed "arrogant jerk." Well, I'd show him.

With a sense of triumph, I displayed my belongings: an extra tunic, my cloak, a canteen, a postage stamp from home (how did that get in there?), some soap from the inn, and a fistful of waffle crumbs.

Horror washed over me. "I was gonna eat that!"

"Well, that's just pathetic," Robert moped, crossing his arms and poking out his lip ring.

The redhead dropped Eric's pack on the ground. "Geez, times are tough when you can't get a single coin from a robbery. This economy, I'm telling you."

"We could take the sword," the burly man suggested, pointing to the sheath at my waist.

Okay, God could step in anytime now.

The sound of approaching hoof beats alerted the muggers before they entertained the idea any further. "Could be Leander's men," Robert sighed. "It's not worth it. We'd better get out of here and head to the castle. The ladies of the court have been deprived of my handsome face too long, and at least people at the ball will be wearing fancy jewelry we can snag."

The robbers blended back into the woods as easily as they had emerged. I knelt on the ground, gathering waffle crumbs into my hand.

Eric bounded over to me and leaned down, delicately inspecting my neck where the blade had been. "If those are Leander's men, we should probably hide, too."

"I'm coming." I picked up the largest of the crumbs and poured them into my pack. Eric, wise man that he was, didn't comment.

Mystical Unicorn ran behind the bushes where Robert disappeared, and we followed suit until the road was clear once more.

"That was a great trick you pulled on the robbers," Veli patted my back. Was that the first compliment ever uttered from his mouth?

"What trick?" I asked, pushing myself off the ground to reassemble the rest of my pack.

"The one about being poor."

There was an awkward silence for a couple of minutes before my hesitant voice broke it. "We're not really poor?"

Veli laughed. "We're the sons of Dukes! You think they just cut us off as soon as we're old enough to leave? We're loaded."

"And you carry it all around with you? That's just asking to get robbed!"

Eric brushed strands of hair away from my face. "We'll be all right, as long as you're around to scare them off with our poverty."

Veli snorted. "Yeah. Right. We're not stupid enough to carry loads of money, but how do you think we've been paying for food and supplies?"

Argh. Even practical when he was being a jerk.

"Shall we continue our journey?" Mystical Unicorn suggested. A helpful comment from the pink-haired eccentric? Maybe that encounter sobered her bubbliness.

"But this time, keep your mouth shut, Nessie." Veli shook a fist at me, but I saw him wink before he turned around and marched down the road.

I knew that man was really a teddy bear.

§ § §

The beady eyes of my dinner glinted in the firelight, staring at me with a vacant, accusing look. Hopefully the obsidian shadows of the forest concealed my frown at the dead fish. I didn't mind getting muddy or wrestling bears like the rest of them, but butchering my dinner while it watched me was another thing entirely.

That's not to say I wasn't grateful for the gurgling stream beside our make-shift camp or the meal it provided. Veli had given us the okay for a fire to cook our food, though the way he hurried us along indicated his nervousness.

My hesitance at dinner clearly put a damper on his schedule. I turned to Eric, handsome in the glow of the fire, and wrinkled my nose. "Is there some-thing less…in need of cutting its head off to eat?"

"It's not such a big deal, Nessie." He held out an open palm. "I'll do it for you if you're that worried about it."

With a sigh of relief, I handed my fishy friend over. Thank you, God, for chivalry. "You can't expect me to believe a Duke's son is an expert butcher. I bet you'd be eating a four course meal if you were at King Kermit's ball right now."

Eric shrugged and grabbed a knife from his pack. "You spend a lot of time living off the land when you're learning battle tactics in the wilderness."

A strand of hair fell into my eyes, but the strong odor on my fingers de-terred me from brushing it away. "I still wouldn't mind a four course meal right now."

"Hurry up. I'm sure this chit-chat will be fondly remembered when you're sitting in a dungeon because Leander's men saw the fire," Veli harrumphed, pacing around the fallen logs that marked the edge of our camp.

Eric's hands moved faster to scale the fish. "You just want me to take you to the ball," he smirked.

Excitement bubbled up in me. Never mind the fact Eric had dead fish parts on his hands. Not too long ago I woke up in Disney Princess footie pajamas;

going to a semi-medieval ball with a dark, handsome (in my opinion) Duke was kind of a big deal for me.

"Let me guess," Veli leaned forward and tossed another stick into the fire. "It's a masquerade."

"Aren't they always?" Eric reached for the canteen at his feet and poured its contents over the fish.

A masquerade! How mysterious and intriguing—it felt so secretive. I imagined me wearing an extravagant costume, running up to Leander undetected. Even King Kermit wouldn't—"That's it!" I shouted, grabbing Eric's fishy forearm and sloshing water out of the canteen. "We can talk to King Kermit at the ball!"

Veli snorted. "You're going to prance up to the king in front of hundreds of people, tell him his right hand man is murdering an innocent race, and then finish dancing the night away?"

"We'll be in disguise." I stood up from the log. "It'll be perfect."

"No, it's stupid. But this whole mission is stupid, so at least it's consistent."

Eric scratched his nose with the back of his wrist. "It would take a lot of planning, but I see the benefits of going during the masquerade. Leander will be too preoccupied with the ball to notice us immediately, and our disguises would blend in without being questioned. Better yet, Veli and I could use our connections to easily procure invitations."

"I guess it could work," Veli said. Despite the skepticism in his voice, he had already started sketching out a map of the castle with his sword on the ground. "If we plan it carefully, we might not fail as miserably as expected. Still, we need to figure out how we'll distract Leander and speak to the king, where the confrontation will occur, and what the message will be. Then there's the question of—"

The giddiness was too much for me. A fit of girlish giggles took over. "What will I wear?" I blurted, taking stock of my travel-weary tunic, leggings, and boots. Those would hardly do. Maybe the sword had magic makeover powers. After all, that was for the mission.

Eric handed the finished filet to Veli for roasting and turned to face me. "You could wear a trash bag and still look amazing."

Oh, the lies infatuation produced, but the sweetness of it made me gush. At that comment, Veli had a seizure of hysterics as if Eric said something hilarious.

"Hey, Nessie?" Mystical Unicorn's distant voice interrupted the laughing fit. She pushed a low branch out of her way and stepped over a fallen log into our camp. "I was looking for some food in the woods and I found these berries, but now that I've eaten some I'm thinking they might be poisonous…"

Veli pushed himself off the log, and rubbed his hands together. "Looks like we're going to have to induce vomiting."

All I wanted was one romantic moment. Was that too much to ask for? Oh, well. That was as good as it got when the love interest was butchering a fish. Story of my life.

Chapter 18

Leander thrust his sword through the chest of the practice dummy, relishing the thrill of victory when his blade tore through the canvas. Noon sunlight bathed the well-stocked armory, glinting off metal swords, bows, and guns. He pushed his blade further into the human-like targets in front of him. *Now if only I could switch out the dummy for that stupid girl messing up my plans.*

He withdrew the blade and roughly slammed it into its empty wire frame on the wall, letting the resounding clang echo in the large room. Once upon a time, Leander would have been shocked at the thoughts now freely flowing from his mind, but that was a lifetime ago. Back when everyone thought some Duke's son was going to be Commander and Leander would be a common soldier marching under the king's banner. These days Leander was all too eager to imagine sending a volley of shots into that girl, Nessie, and her friends.

Inspired by the thought, he grabbed a bow and quiver off the armory wall and headed back to the unfortunate practice dummy. Its shiny button eyes seemed to plead with him, drawing a smirk from his lips. He readied the weapon, loosed the string, and watched an arrow sprout from the target's chest.

Perfect.

After ripping the dummy to shreds, Leander let out a content sigh. One day. He walked back to the bow's resting place, ready to hang it back up on the wall, but hesitated. His fingers traced the Spoon's emblem engraved into the wood.

Standard issue training bow for the military. He'd used it in archery practice, back when he barely knew how to aim.

His first practice felt like a lifetime ago. Arrow after arrow soaring over the target and into the grove of trees behind him. The joking comments of his fellow soldiers turning his cheeks red.

Leander shook his head, finally hanging the bow back into place, but the memories remained. The first day of archery practice was the day he met *her*. It was his seventh or eighth time chasing after his stray ammo when he saw that beautiful forest nymph with radiant hair, walking in the woods, his missing arrows grasped in her hand.

Leander strolled over to the target, hoping to clear his head, but it wouldn't stop the replay. He remembered the wave of shyness that had washed over him, and when he'd bowed awkwardly, how her tinkling laughter filling the air. The rest was a blur, but somehow through all of his blubbering, he managed to have a conversation with the beauty. Her long name, Taika Epona, betrayed her birthplace of Forks before she even spoke of it. Such a mysterious title sounded so foreign to his ears. She proved equally as enigmatic in personality and nature. Leander had been too infatuated to care about her birthplace then; she was fun, exotic even. Ironic, considering he now spat at the name of Forks, systematically eradicating the world of their very presence.

Leander peered through a hole in the practice dummy's chest where a heart might have been. What a metaphor.

Those summer days passed so quickly, his favorite times stealing moments with the girl from Forks. Their relationship blossomed, as did his efforts in training until his strength and prestige were unmatched among his peers. When winter came and went, it was undeniable: he loved her.

Despite this, his marriage proposal was sweetly rejected. *"You've gotten too prideful, Leander…You treat me like a possession."*

"But, Taika, you're my world. I want you at my side."

"As a trophy, Leander? Or as a wife? You're not the same man you used to be. I can't marry you."

Well, leave then, wretched woman. Go back to your stupid kingdom of Forks with the rest of your cursed people. Who needed her anyway? With the Duke's son out of the picture, Leander could slide into place as the Commander and attain the most precious commodity: power. With power, any woman was his for the taking. With power, he could get revenge on his former sweetheart and the people she had forsaken him for. With power, no one could ever again refuse him.

Even after years of tormenting the remnants of the Forkish people, he needed revenge, deeper and sweeter. And this Nessie girl, well, she was asking for it.

He plucked his arrows from the target's chest. The memories stirred fresh rage. He'd been so weak before, but time had passed and his mistakes taught him the only way to succeed was to take what he wanted. Well, he wanted to be king, and no hero-wannabe or half-breed trash was going to get in his way.

Leander just needed to watch and bide his time. It wouldn't be long before Nessie was in his grasp. Who knew why she made it her own personal mission to save all the little half-breeds or why she felt it necessary to interfere with his plans?

The arrow snapped in his hand, bending under the pressure of his iron grip.

It didn't matter, because soon she would either be bowing to his will or dead. He didn't care which. These days, it didn't pay to be picky.

Chapter 19

My senses heightened at the sight of my prey. The smell of sweat blended with freshly cooked meat spread across the village market-place, but I didn't let it tear my concentration away. She was a beauty sitting behind the glass. Hunkering down, I studied the environment, waiting and watching—

"You have a crazy look in your eyes," Eric commented, walking up beside me.

"Shh!" I reprimanded and swatted him away. "That's the one," I said, pointing with awe.

He followed my finger to the tailor's shop where a simple but elegant emerald dress hung in the window display. The one-shoulder number looked gorgeous, with a glittering brooch cinching the fabric at the waist. I'd never been much for material possessions. I was the kid wearing hand-me-downs to prom, so don't think that I was some fancy-pants dresser, but the words "masquerade ball" sent my blood pressure sky-rocketing. Disney footie pajamas, remember?

Eric laughed. "Okay, I'll get it for you if that's what you want to wear to the ball. Just don't rip anyone apart to get it."

Good man. Preventing shop-lifting and murder in one sentence.

I slid the door open and stepped inside the shop, taken aback by the hundreds of reams of colorful fabrics lining the walls. Silky sapphires and muted yellows tempted my eyes away from the gorgeous jade dress until the tailor, a petite woman with large, round glasses and chopsticks in her auburn hair, stepped out from behind the counter. Her choice of attire—a smock made out of scraps of patterned fabric—gave me a headache if I stared too long. How could the maker of such beautiful garments clothe herself like a frequent thrift store shopper? And I meant a poorly-stocked thrift store.

Eric inquired about the dress, and she pushed her glasses down her nose laughing. "You want to buy that dress? That dress? Oh, you must be pulling my leg!" She turned her back to us, wistfully looking at the display case. "Oh, no. That dress is like a child to me. Have a look at these other dresses by the wall," she indicated rich gowns of violet and maroon. "That dress is not for sale."

My heart sank. The others were pretty enough. I reached out and stroked the skirt of a velvet ball gown. Sparkling rhinestones, bunched taffeta, crinoline skirts—they were gorgeous, but none had the simple elegance of the emerald dress.

Eric tilted his head, regarding me. After a few moments of watching me halfheartedly examine fabric and bodices, he nodded to the tailor. "I'll pay twice what it would sell for, plus extra if you deliver it to the Cornerstone Inn in town."

Her posture straightened, her hands clasped together. "Well, everyone must let their children go sometime. Let me set everything out for you to try on." She adjusted the chopsticks in her hair and crossed to the back of the room, pushing aside curtains and disappearing.

My high-pitched squeal echoed in the small store. I crushed Eric in a bear hug. "You're the best!"

Seriously. Any guy that could survive a shopping trip with a masquerade-crazed girl was a keeper.

He beamed and started to follow me to the back, but I shook my finger at him. "It's bad luck to see the date before the ball."

He rubbed his chin. "I thought that was just for weddings."

Memories of my first moments in Spoons, of Eric passing me off as his spouse to get away from Leander, flooded my mind. "Well, seeing as I don't remember our first 'wedding,' this will have to do."

He reached over and ruffled my dark hair. "You were in quite a lot of trouble as I recall. The ceremony had to be expedited."

All of the silliness fled from me, and I stepped closer, resting my head on his shoulder. "You saved my life that day. I never thanked you for stepping in to protect me."

He paused for a moment, letting the words sink in. With a slight tilt of the head he brought up his fingers to brush my cheek. "The rewards far outweighed the risk."

"You pay extra for time flirting," the tailor bellowed from the other room. I jerked my head up, catching a glimpse of my pink cheeks in the mirror on the wall.

"I'll be waiting out here," Eric said and slid the door open.

Happiness bubbled up inside. I was so lucky to have a guy like—

"Insolent girl!" a scratchy voice hissed behind me.

I whipped around to see an unfortunately familiar face: wrinkly skin, toothy scowl, and gray hair sticking out in all directions. That old lady who had tried to marry me off to her son.

"How dare you?" Ferny seethed. "I've been watching you, gallivanting around with some greasy slime ball, while my darling boy sits at home reeling from your rejection."

Watching me? A shiver ran up my back. What a creep. I glanced at the front door, wondering if I should get Eric.

"Are you coming or not?" the tailor called from the back, and I didn't need any more encouragement.

"You and your son need help," I said, starting for the back of the dress shop.

"This isn't the last you've seen of me!" Ferny insisted, but I was already behind the curtains. No reason to let her ruin a perfectly good dress-buying experience.

After a little bit of squeezing and sucking in, I made it into the most beautiful dress in the world, a dress that I would wear to a masquerade ball. *Calm the breathing, Nessie.* Angels sang the hallelujah chorus when I looked in the full-length mirror in front of me. The soft, silky material draped elegantly down my torso and reached to the floor. A slit from the knee down would allow me to move gracefully if that ability were in my genes. Sadly, it wasn't, but at least I had the option. I could have swished around in the smooth fabric forever, but the tailor poked me with a pin before I could get too comfortable in my daydreams.

"I said, 'Do you need a mask?'" she repeated, shoving a row of pins in the fabric.

"Oh, yes. That would be lovely."

She stood back, tapping her chin while she sized me up. "That'll do quite nicely. Now get dressed so I can start working on this."

I managed to clothe myself and wandered to the front door, periodically squealing with happiness. Yes, I would possibly be heading to my death in an effort to save the lives of the Sporks, but I was going to look darn good doing it. A woman who worked at a porta-potty company didn't get to be a princess very often, but my Cinderella moment was unfolding before my eyes. If I ignored the whole crazy-lady-threatening-me part, it was a perfect day.

The door chimed and my head perked up, wondering if Ferny had returned to make trouble. "What in King Kermit's name are you wearing, child?" the tailor exclaimed to the newcomer.

The quivering voice froze me behind the curtains. "I don't know where I am or what I'm doing here. I was just sitting in my apartment when—" No. No…couldn't be.

I lifted the partition and poked my face out, instantly recognizing the panicked blonde in front of me, sporting a ponytail, T-shirt from some seafood restaurant, a pair of faded jeans, and Reebok sneakers. Her face was puffy and red, tears streaming down behind black-rimmed glasses.

"Nessie!" she screamed and enfolded me in a bone-crushing embrace, sobbing into my shoulder. Her muffled cries were unintelligible, but I patted her back in what I hoped was a soothing manner.

It was that feeling when I saw someone I knew but in a completely different setting than I was used to, like when I ran into my principal at the swimming pool or my lazy cousin at his important office job. That's what it felt like to see my next door neighbor in a parallel universe.

"Felicia!" I replied with surprise.

It's a small world after all.

Chapter 20

"P lease," Felicia's chin quivered. Her fingers squeezed my arms like blood pressure cuffs. "Please just tell me that I'm dreaming. Tell me that I've gone crazy…or that my kids put wild mushrooms in my coffee this morning. I don't care what you say, but just help me understand that none of this," she lifted the hem of a dress beside her, "is real."

Oh, goodness. Our conversation was not going to go well. I gently removed her hands and pulled out a stool behind the counter. "Why don't you take a seat?"

She complied but was chewing on her pinky nail like it was a chocolate chip cookie. Yeah, I would be a nail-biter, too, if I was a single mother of four kids.

The front door chimed, signaling the entrance of my compatriots. Just what I needed. Eric, Veli, and Unicorn paused at the entrance, attention riveted on the frazzled blonde before me. I shook my head at them, and Eric quietly closed the door behind.

Here went nothing. I leaned back onto the counter. "I'm not quite sure how you got here, Felicia, but unfortunately, this *is* real. This isn't a dream or a hallucination. You're in what some would call a 'parallel universe.'"

A nervous laugh escaped her. She paused, devouring her half-chewed fingernail. "I'm sorry. My hearing must be going. I thought you said 'parallel universe,' but that can't be right. That would be crazy."

I looked over my shoulder at the tailor who was pretending to pin up a garment on a mannequin. Guess the cat was out of the bag now, though I was less concerned about rumors of parallel universes and more about Felicia. If my memory served me correctly, my transition into Spoons had been a lot smoother. Then again, Unicorn's speech and my own gravitation towards science fiction and fantasy prepped me for it in a way.

Felicia was clearly a lover of all things non-fiction. From what little I knew about my neighbor, the only kind of adventure she wanted was keeping her four kids alive and well. Not a traveler, read only biographies, drank her coffee black— a very no-nonsense kind of girl. And a parallel universe sounded like a lot of nonsense.

She went back to full nail-biting mode, her free hand tapping on the counter.

"It's going to be okay, Felicia. I promise," I tried patting her back.

She jerked out of my reach, her wild eyes reminding me of a tiger ready to lunge for the jugular. "Okay? Okay! How can you tell me I'm going to be okay when my kids are in a whole other universe? Who's going to tell them everything's okay when I don't pick them up from my Mom's house on Monday? Do you think my job will think it's okay that I just don't show up? Are you going to write a note to excuse me because I'm in a freaking parallel universe!" She curled in on herself, cradling her head in her hands and sobbing with abandonment. I really could have used a book on how to counsel someone who just world-jumped.

The floor creaked beside me, and I turned to see Veli's softened face. "I'll take it from here." Really, now? Mr. Sarcasm himself was going to offer comfort?

I held up my hands and backed away. "Suit yourself." Eric waved me over to the entrance. Better there than in the middle of crazy-mom-meets-Veli cross-fire.

I stepped around dresses and bolts of fabric to get to the front door, but Mystical Unicorn waylaid me before I could reach Eric. She chewed on her bottom lip, tears welling in her eyes. "It's all my fault," she whispered.

"Oh, don't say that. It's nobody's fault." Maybe if I gave her a hug, she would calm down. I wrapped my arms around her, praying it was enough to stop the tears.

She rested her head on me, creating a damp spot on my shoulder. "You don't understand," she wailed. "When I rewired your toaster to reflect the solar flare and open a portal to this world, I must have created a mini vortex."

The sound of her crying faded away into the background. I stood frozen, not realizing my mouth dropped open until Unicorn nudged me. "A mini vortex," I repeated, unwilling to let my brain register what she had said. Please, God. Not that.

"It must have sucked Felicia in when she got close to your apartment door," Mystical Unicorn reasoned, wringing her hands.

"A mini vortex." So…that meant…what? Every delivery man, tenant, and visitor to my apartment would be whisked into a parallel universe? Lovely. "In that case, it probably is your fault."

Mystical Unicorn's blubbering intensified. She fell forward into my limp arms, depositing tears and snot onto my tunic. In full-fledged denial mode, I stared off into the tailor's shop, vaguely registering that Felicia was calmly talking to Veli after his pep talk.

Man. If Veli could pacify a hysterical mother from another planet, things were messed up. I tried not to think about the wet spot forming on my arm as the reality set in: things were *seriously* messed up.

§ § §

One day. The thought was intrusive. Once the dying sun finally set over the hill, there would be only one day between me and dancing the night away with Eric. Oh, and informing the king about genocide in his realm. Secretly. Without getting killed by Leander.

Sitting on the grassy bank where the Blade of Remiel first dumped me in Spoons, I pulled at a weed and twisted it. Twilight settled over the city below, and further down the slope children scurried around trying to finish their games. King Kermit's castle loomed in the distance, towering above the city square. It seemed much larger now I knew the fate that awaited me inside.

Funny how the span of a Saturday normally filled with chick flick marathons and popcorn was also the amount of time that could change my life forever. If the vision proved true, I might not have any more Saturdays left.

Absorbed in my somber mood, I didn't notice Eric sat beside me until his voice momentarily interrupted the crickets chirping.

"Looks intimidating, doesn't it?"

I rested my head on his shoulder. "I was hoping you were going to say something more encouraging."

Squeals from the children playing resonated down the hill from us. Through the dim evening light, I could make out their forms tossing a ball back and forth.

He held up his hands. "Hey now. Just because I'm not going to give you a fluff pep talk doesn't mean I'm negative. There's some wisdom in being realistic."

"Realistic! Now there's an idea," I scoffed, pushing myself off his shoulder to sit up. "I'm looking at a castle we're going to infiltrate in less than twenty-four hours in some parallel universe wearing medieval garb. My life is in danger. There's a girl with pink hair named Mystical Unicorn in our entourage and people are getting sucked into toaster portals. I don't even know what real is anymore." With a huff, I collapsed onto the ground, the stubby pokes of grass against my back.

"I've been where you are, Nessie. Listen: Parallel universe or not, you can still trust God."

Such a familiar, worn-out concept. Trusting in a higher power I couldn't see or feel—was it faith or just naiveté? "Well, right now, I think God is messing with me."

The last of the sun's light faded, but people still wandered the streets. Guess the city people were night owls. "C'mon. You can't see even a little bit that God had a purpose for bringing you here?"

My bitter laugh scared the crickets off for good "Maybe some divine comedy. I mean, I guess I can see my purpose in this whole 'save-the-Sporks' campaign, but why did God pick me? Why now? Why couldn't He have chosen someone from this universe?" I stared up at the diamond stars scattered across the sky like spilled glitter around the moon. "Why would an infinite, all-knowing God want to have a relationship with a screw-up like me?"

Eric's voice was soft and gentle. "We don't know all of God's plan, but sometimes He lets us see little glimpses."

A sigh escaped my lips. "I know. I just don't see why God would need me here when there are plenty of people who could do the same job, and probably a lot better."

He paused for a moment, thinking. We watched the people scurrying in and out of the castle. "Maybe," he said after a few minutes, "maybe God didn't need you. You needed Him, and maybe here was the best place to show you that. Yeah, it's a pretty crazy situation, but look at everything He's done for you: keeping you safe from Leander, freeing the half-breeds from horrible torture camps, rescuing you from old women." He nudged my arm playfully. "Despite all the crazy things we've been through, you're still safe. No one else has been able to get as far as you have in helping these people. That's not just a fluke."

"*...For the Lord your God will be with you wherever you go.*" Why did that verse keep coming up?

And how could this toaster salesman make so much sense when nothing else seemed to? That was part of why I loved him. Woah, where did that come from? I stole a glance of Eric who was still contemplating the stars and my predicament. Did I love him? Sure, we had known each other for a while, but for most of that he'd only been my friendly, slightly awkward toaster salesman. Only recently had he shown himself to be a thoughtful, compassionate, brave man.

Real love came with commitment and time—a hurdle we had yet to arrive at. On the other hand, we endured trials many couples never faced, such as trying to rescue oppressed people, escaping death a couple of times, and having to put up with Mystical Unicorn and her undying cheerfulness.

He caught my stare. "What? Is there something hanging out of my nose?"

Typical. I was thinking about love and he was thinking about boogers. My hand reached over to give him a noogie and then rested on his palm, our fingers entwining. "No. I was just thinking of another reason why I might have come here."

His lips shifted into a lopsided smile. "What?"

"You, silly. Now, let's shut up and watch the stars."

We sat as the breeze slipped through our hair. I leaned my head against his, relishing his warmth in the cool night. My efforts at connecting constellations proved futile (parallel universe, duh), but I enjoyed trying to make some sense of the scattered heavenly bodies. After a few minutes, Eric turned back to look at me.

"Man, I really hope we don't die soon, because this is pretty perfect."

I, too, was a fan of this whole not-dying-right-now idea, but the memory of my unfortunate dream/vision resurfaced.

A speck of white appeared in the sky and I pulled a reverse-Cinderella, wishing upon a star that my dream *wouldn't* come true. The speck started moving. I tugged on Eric's shirt, pointing to the heavens. "Look, a shooting star!" Shooting stars were a good omen for wishes, right? My finger was still extended at the white object when it started to grow in size.

"Do shooting stars do that?" Eric wondered aloud.

Did they have airplanes in this world…or UFOs? Were wishes null and void if they were based on an alien spacecraft? That's when it hit me.

A white ball bounced off my head into a patch of weeds beside me. "Woah, you threw that one out of the park, Pancho!" a boy exclaimed.

A herd of children ran up the hill and chattered excitedly as they chased after the ball. I rubbed my bruised head and gazed back up at the sparkling sky. Was that a *no*?

Parents shouted from further down the bank, calling children home for the night. The herd whined, slowly making their way down.

"Is this all going to end?" My croaky whisper seemed a pathetic interruption of the beautiful silence between us.

"One day," Eric replied. "Maybe tomorrow, maybe in fifty years. We're never guaranteed anything. All we can do is make the best of what we have. It's no different in your world, driving to your job every day. Any moment, it could all come crashing down. It just feels more real when there's a price on your head."

The hoot of an owl carried behind us, and I perked up. "Is there really a price on my head?"

"Yeah," Eric admitted. "I saw a poster today in the village. Pretty lucky since it's the first one I've seen so far."

"Do we need to worry about staying low then?"

"Away from soldiers, yes," Eric replied. "The villagers, not so much. The people in these parts are sympathetic to our cause. Even if someone sees the reward poster, they're not going to turn us in."

That was good news. "How much is the reward?"

"In your world, it would be about five thousand dollars."

Well, it wasn't a million, but it was more than I'd ever had before. "Was there a picture?"

"I guess you could call it that. It looked like a stick figure with hair."

"Quick," I exclaimed. "Shave my head, and they'll never recognize me!"

We both giggled and for a moment, the weight of the next day dissolved. The danger and the consequences if we failed were forgotten and replaced with thoughts of my home and the life I led there—my mundane, purposeless existence. I went to church, but basically told God I could handle my own life. Here, in this foreign world, I found friends and possibly love. Laughed and cried, been kidnapped and almost killed, and yet, I still had a hard time trusting God. When would I learn?

Maybe Eric was right; maybe I needed this place after all.

My view of the moon was suddenly obscured by a looming shadow. My heart raced, and I clambered for my sword, but the silhouette switched on a light. I caught my breath. Just Veli. "Geez. You scared me half to death!"

He swung the flashlight and glanced at the ground before raising his head. Was he biting his lip? "We need to talk," he barked.

Eric stood up and stepped towards his brother. "Okay, go ahead."

Shifting his weight back and forth, Veli nodded at me. "I was hoping we could talk…privately."

"Well, why don't you just come out and tell me to scram?" With a grunt, I pushed myself off the grass. "Okay, I'll leave so you all can discuss manly th—"

Veli sighed. "You, Nessie. I want to talk to you. Alone." Clearing his throat, he looked at his feet. "Please."

Clearly, this was some Veli doppelganger sent by Leander to kill us. With my hand on the hilt of my sword, Veli led me further up the hill. "What's going on?" I inquired as soon as he halted. Below, Eric settled himself back down on the grass.

The paranoid Veli clone craned his neck around, peering into the darkness. "What do you know about Felicia?"

"She's my neighbor from my world," I explained, brow furrowed. "You don't have to worry about her being some enemy spy from Leander. I've lived next to her for two years. She's legitimate."

Veli pursed his lips. "I…what else do you know about her?"

"I don't know. She has four kids. Her husband left her a while ago. She's a nice lady but usually overwhelmed? Why the inquisition?"

"Because I—" He cut himself off to lean into my face, shooting me a death glare. "I swear, Nessie, if you tell anyone else I will punch you so hard—"

"Veli," I snapped. "I'm not going to tell anyone. Get it out; what is wrong with you?"

His left hand fiddled with the edge of his tunic. "I have…feelings…"

The smirk was an immediate reaction. "That's a first." Snarkiness was a serious medical condition that had no cure. "I apologize. Please continue."

"She seems nice and her appearance is pleasing." The words came more fluidly. "She was reasonable and rational after I started talking to her in the tailor's shop. And when I saw her, I didn't immediately hate her, which is unusual. Her smile is aesthetically—"

Oh. My. Goodness. I couldn't help clapping excitedly. "You *like* her!"

Veli drew his sword. "Don't say that!"

"Just relax, Veli." I delicately nudged the weapon down and he sheathed it with a sigh. "It's not a bad thing to be interested in someone."

He paced, treading a path of trampled grass. "But I don't know what to do. What if I say the wrong thing? What if she doesn't like me? I've always hated everyone, so this was never a problem, but she seems…different."

I cautiously put my hand on Veli's shoulder. "Just keep talking and getting to know her. You're not asking her to marry you by chatting."

"I guess, but this girl stuff is too confusing. Plus, she has kids, and children don't normally like me." Veli rubbed his temple. "I'm going to go back to the camp and try to get some sleep."

After traveling a few paces, he turned around. "Remember, if you tell anyone I will make life *unpleasant* for you."

"Cross my heart," I promised and watched him trudge down the hill.

Who would have guessed that stern, sarcastic Veli would fall in love?

Chapter 21

The Cornerstone Inn. Best inn before we reached the city square, the toaster salesman had said. Might as well enjoy it if we were going to be pushing up daisies soon.

Fireflies flickered around the entrance, twinkling like Christmas lights. The warm glow from the open door revealed happy townsfolk chatting inside, buzzing with excitement.

I entered beside Eric and let the sounds of mingled chatter wash over me.

The innkeepers, an amiable couple with gray hair, spoke with Eric about our arrangements at a small bar to the side. Men at the counter were telling hunting stories animatedly while women and children sat in cozy wooden booths eating dinner.

A stack of glass jars lined the front door, and patrons, both young and old, grabbed the clear containers, holding on to them at their tables. I waited for a waitress to fill the jars with drink or food, but when no one arrived, I conceded this was some weird other-world ritual. Had Eric brought us to some strange Jar Cult? Fascination with glassware aside, the people seemed normal enough. Happy. Full of life.

Their weightless enthusiasm was far from contagious. To me, every inch closer to the castle was another move in this tangled dance, where a false step might prove fatal. For once, I was glad there were no windows in the wall looking out to King Kermit's fortress. The thought wouldn't leave my head that by this time tomorrow night, I would be standing on the castle stairs, the fate of a couple hundred lives weighing on my shoulders. Even remembering the beautiful dress Eric bought did little to ease those images.

A young man with dark curls settled on the stone hearth and pulled out a fiddle. He drew his bow across the strings, an energetic song filling the warm room. Couples abandoned their dinner to dance in the open space in front of the fire, while other travelers clapped along. Their jovial faces assaulted me with an overwhelming sense of life.

How could they afford to be so happy in times like these? Why was I so jealous of their joy? I watched Eric finish his discussion with the innkeeper before navigating the minefield of waltzing couples to reach me. What was it that handsome man said to me the night before? *It was all going to end one day, but why spend my time moping around until it did?*

Eric reached the booth and attempted to sit down, but I grabbed his hand. Sucking up my feelings of depression, I playfully pulled him into the dancing crowd. Worrying wouldn't add extra time to my life.

The fiddler finished his song and couples bowed to each other.

"Milady." Eric bent low to the ground, waving his free arm dramatically. What a dork.

I curtsied awkwardly, laughing when I bumped into the couple beside me. He closed the gap between us, resting a hand on my waist. "Ready?" his voice tickled my ear.

There went those butterflies in my stomach. The curly-haired musician raised his bow, and Eric swept me along with the music, spinning through the crowd. Bystanders clapped on the edge of the dance floor, singing along with the melody. People blurred into blobs of color the more that we twirled, but Eric's strong arms kept me stable.

The music slowed and the spinning stopped, Eric releasing me to clap along with the other dancers. "C'mon," he nudged. "Clap!"

I may not have been a good dancer, but clapping I could do. Eric scooted close to me, his shoulder rubbing against mine.

A middle-aged woman dancing nearby with her husband stopped to regard us. Her proximity was the only reason I could make out the words amidst the raucous dancers. "Aww, look, Henry. Do you remember when we were like that?"

The crow's feet at his eyes crinkled. "Like what? Able to dance without joint pain?"

She smacked him playfully. "No, silly. Young and in love."

"I don't know about the first one," he admitted, a smile on his lips, "but I don't think much has changed about the last." He kissed her, as if to prove the truth behind his words.

Okay, that was a Nicholas Sparks moment. Must not tear up.

The woman beamed and then turned to Eric. "You must be here for the Firefly Festival."

I opened my mouth to contradict her, but Eric jumped in. "The Firefly Festival is tonight? I completely forgot about it!"

She pointed at the entrance. "There're some extra jars by the door. You'd better grab one before they're all snatched up."

Oh good. Time to join the Jar Cult. We thanked the couple and made our way to the stack of jars by the door. In transit, I caught a glimpse of Veli and Felicia laughing and swaying on the dance floor.

"I must be really tired," Eric remarked, rubbing his eyes. "For a second there, it looked like Veli was happy." Pausing, he tapped his chin. "He's been awfully protective of her since she got here, and they've been talking quite a bit. It kind of makes you wonder."

Snarky comments regarding Veli's romantic interest bubbled up in my throat, but I remembered the *unpleasantness* he threatened me with. "Who knows?" Eric dragged me out of the door and snagged a glass jar, joining the other villagers under the dusky sky. "So, is this Firefly Festival pretty self-explanatory?"

A tiny golden sphere illuminated the space between Eric and me. He cupped his hands to catch the firefly. "Yeah, but it's still just as amazing every year." He deposited the bug into the jar and loosely draped the lid over the opening. "Except I usually don't have such a sweet bug-catching companion. Would you like to go for a stroll with our firefly?"

Let me see, did I want to go on a walk with a gorgeous, amazing, toaster-selling dancer? Yes.

We wandered past benches and fountains, having to rely on the occasional spark of fireflies for light as the darkness grew.

I poked his side. "Bet you get stuck with Veli every year, don't you?"

"Only when I was younger." He pinched my arm. "The Firefly Festival happens at the end of summer when fall is starting. Spoons has seen some pretty awful winters, and the villagers aren't eager to face more blistering cold. The celebration is a way to remember summer, to enjoy life and the good days we do have. I quickly learned spending the Firefly Festival with your brother was not as magical as spending it with a girl."

The weight of his words hit me. Eric was the son of a Duke; surely he had been destined to marry some refined, delicate China doll of a woman. Someone with a negative-size waist and hair meant for shampoo commercials. At the very least, someone who knew how to cook.

I turned away from Eric and shivered, the chill returning in the night air. Clearly, my brain was stuck in some fairly tale mode to think that the secretary of a portable toilet company would run off into the sunset with the handsome nobleman. For Pete's sake, I was dressed in some purple tunic with lime green leggings. Tall, lanky, dark pixie cut. How could I think he'd find me attractive?

Eric closed the gap between us. "Nessie, I've been to two different worlds and seen plenty of extraordinary women."

Wow. Thanks for rubbing it in there, Eric.

He set the jar down next to a rose bush and took my hands in his. There was only the dim glow of his firefly and the feel of his warm hands shielding mine from the night air. "Out of all the women I've seen in every world, you surpass them all."

Instantly redeemed.

The moment was perfect. *He* was perfect. It would have been a shame to let the romantic atmosphere go to waste.

I wanted to kiss him. Still, I held back. What if I ruined the mood with being too forward? Then again, we could both be dead tomorrow night, so the bar was pretty low. Feeling a surge of adrenaline I leaned in to kiss him, but the lack of light foiled my aim. The tender peck was bestowed upon his eye instead. Good grief. I couldn't even kiss correctly. We laughed at the mistake, though I'd never been more thankful for the night hiding my red cheeks. Hugging was a much safer activity.

The wind stirred, making the chilly night air uncomfortable. Eric stepped towards the garden's entrance but grasped my hand. "Let's go back inside."

"I'll be there in a minute," I assured, shifting my weight. "I just want to…think a little bit before I go to bed."

He frowned, craning his neck to peer around the garden. "I guess it's okay. There are still some other villagers nearby, but don't wander too far from the inn."

"You have my word," I said, holding my hand up. "Scout's honor."

A lightning bug illuminated his sassy eye roll. "You were never a Scout."

"Who told?" I growled. Our jokes faded and the more pressing questions weighed on my mind. "What time are we leaving tomorrow?" My voice was little more than a whisper, as if voicing the thought made it real.

"We'll probably go over our plans during the day here," he replied. "Then we'll get ready for the ball and take a carriage to the castle at sunset."

"Well, if we're not in a hurry," I sighed, "I'm probably going to sleep in. I'll only fret when I'm awake tomorrow. Who knows how long I'll be sitting out here thinking and praying. Don't wait up for me."

"Are you sure?" he asked. "I really don't mind." He fought back a yawn.

I noted his slumping outline. "You'll need your beauty rest for the ball tomorrow."

He reluctantly exited the garden, giving me the copy of the rune key design to my room before he stepped outside.

The stars held little answers for me, though I had more than enough questions to go around. Instead of giving me peace, restlessness grew with the passing time. How long did I have to shiver under the stars to know the heavens were not going to morph into a fortune-telling widescreen? *Just a little bit longer*, I thought, *but not without my cloak.*

Leaving my firefly by the rose bush, I retreated back into the lamp-lit inn, walking past the hearth and across the crimson carpet to hallways of numbered doors. The wing that held our rooms was just around the corner, but the mention of my name in hushed whispers left me frozen.

I glanced over my shoulder. No one. *Nessie, you're hearing things.* The thought made me shake my head. It was probably just someone down the hall talking about their cow "Bessie." How vain of me to insert myself into other people's conversations.

"…She's outside right now…" Snippets of the continued dialogue perked up my ears. I scooted closer to the edge of the corner, and pressed my ear against the cool wall.

"…And I just don't know what to do." Eric? No need to conceal myself then. I lifted my foot, ready to step out. "I tried giving Nessie a pep talk, but it felt forced, like I had to convince myself. The more I think about it, the less sure I am that this is going to end well."

My leg hovered inches from the floor, a knot forming in the pit of my stomach. "You knew this was foolhardy from the start." Veli's gruff voice was easily recognizable. "Why did you wait until now to have second thoughts?"

Eric's heavy sigh carried through the door. "I can't reconcile the fact that she's way out of her league. What does she know about confronting kings and rescuing people? She's just a girl from some other universe that happened to accidentally come here."

Just some girl? My face flushed with heat. *I'm going to punch him.*

"What if we've misconstrued this whole thing? I think it would be better to send her back before tomorrow evening."

The world slowed down. Thoughts of moving registered on some other plane of consciousness. My body drifted back down the hallways and outside into the now-welcome chilly air.

My mind stammered, unable to complete full sentences. Words repeated over and over in my head while my body moved like a wraith towards the dark garden.

Out of my league? Just some girl? My fists clenched and unclenched. Was it just earlier this night that he had been out here among the flowers, all lovey-dovey and intimate? Traitor. What a two-faced lying traitor. One minute cheering me on, the next saying that…that he didn't believe in me? That he didn't think

I should be here? Looking up to the inky sky, I finally found my words, spitting out of me with bitter force.

"God, what are you doing?" I shouted to the stars, shaking my fists in protest "Do You think it's funny to mess with me, to mess with my life? I just wanted to follow the purpose You had for me, and now I'm facing danger and death while my friends…even Eric…" my voice dropped to a whisper, "want to get rid of me." I wished tears would come and drench my face, that I would curl into a ball and forget the world—anything to get those blasted feelings out of me, but there was nothing.

Memories of Sunday schools past, full of countless smiling affirmations of "God loves you, sweetheart," played in my mind. I set my face hard and cold, trampling a bed of flowers with my pacing.

"Well, if You love me, You sure have a funny way of showing it."

The anger-infused adrenaline crashed. I felt empty and cold. Who was I kidding? Arguing with the sky was getting me nowhere.

I turned on my heels, my foot accidentally making contact with the glass jar Eric left by the rose bush. It fell over, dumping the lid a few inches away. In desperate haste, the firefly soared in freedom. Ruined…just like Eric and me.

"No!" I shouted, unwilling to part with him so quickly. Seeing the flickering light fade was like watching my last hope slip away. I jumped up and sifted the darkness for his tiny body, straining my arms upwards. Instead of finding the insect, a fierce pressure clamped onto my forearm and twisted it behind me.

Screams burst from my throat and echoed in the night. No one rushed to my defense. *This can't be happening*, I thought, writhing against an iron grip. Pulse in overdrive, I searched for help. No one. I was left alone.

Well, not quite alone.

Hot breath tickled my ear, "Why, you're a better catch than a firefly." A damp cloth smothered my face, the sharp scent stinging my lungs. My screams turned into hyperventilation, each shallow breath sucking more chemicals and burning my chest.

No. It was too soon. I wasn't supposed to die until tomorrow night. Reality sank in like a boulder catapulted into a pool: the voice of my attacker belonged to Leander. Every warning Veli threatened poured into my mind like ghost stories to haunt me before going to sleep.

Unconsciousness tried to overwhelm me, but I fought it.

If I gave up, I was dead.

The last thing I saw before passing out was the soft glowing blink of a firefly as it lost itself in the night sky.

Chapter 22

I woke up with a gasp, clawing at ropes bound tight against my chest. Had to get out, had to escape. My bleary eyes cleared and darted around the room. An orange fire crackled below an ostentatious portrait of a man in soldier's uniform. He wore a silver pendant, his raven hair shorn close in military style, and a long scar ran down his cheek. Leander! I squirmed in the hard chair I was attached to, searching in vain for my sword. The scratchy ropes burned against my skin. I tried shouting, but a gag muffled the noise. It was useless. Whoever tied the ropes didn't want me to escape. Better to use my energy on forming a different plan.

To my right was the largest mahogany desk I'd ever seen, littered with papers and a pile of weapons. The leather armchair behind it was vacant…for now. Bookshelves stretched across the stone walls on either side of the desk, packed with old volumes. On my left, a large map was spread out over a round table, dotted with figurines of soldiers and tents.

A thin, long window—guess Leander didn't want transparent ceilings in his study—at the top of the stone wall let in dawn's muted light. If only I were skinnier and taller.

How long had I been there? More importantly, how could anyone sleep with the yelling in the hallway? The door burst open. Ferny and Leander entered, angrily shouting in tones that should have woken anyone in a five mile radius.

"I led you to the girl, didn't I?" Ferny's mass of wild gray hair bounced when she shook her fists. "We had a deal! When you're through with her, she's mine."

Leander's lips curved into a cruel smile, contorting the scar on his cheek. He wore a purple and lime green military uniform—where were the fashion police when you needed them—and at his side, a leather scabbard held my sword. My mouth went dry. That was a problem.

"When I'm through with her, there won't be anything left for you to keep." When he noticed that I was awake, he put on a mock frown, running a hand through his cropped black hair. "Rats, I was hoping to surprise you. Oh, well." He crouched down, leaning in close. "I'm still toying with a couple different endings for your pitiful life: there's torture and public execution. Which of those do you prefer? I, for one, would probably go for public execution since it sounds less painful, but I'm sure that would be more demoralizing for those little half-breeds you've been working so hard to save."

"As much as I love seeing you humiliate her," Ferny's scratchy voice interrupted, "we have a deal to discuss here."

Leander pushed himself up and scoffed. "Whatever favors you think you're owed for turning in a conspirator against the state have already been paid. Retreat from this castle before I make room for you in the dungeon."

Ferny snarled at him, revealing a row of sharp teeth. "We had a deal, Leander! You will regret this." Her voice trailed off, but she backed through the entrance and disappeared.

Leander turned his gaze upon me and licked his lips. The hairs on my arm stood on end. "No, I don't think I will."

Time to tap into my inner James Bond and escape, except Bond had a lot more to work with in his situations. Leander's study was fresh out of jet packs and grappling hooks. There was little use in the conceited portrait over the fire, the desk scattered with papers and clay army figurines, and candles lit on the walls like tiny fireflies—Ugh. Fireflies. I remembered wandering the dark garden with Eric, foolishly attempting to kiss him.

On second thought, what was the point of escaping? Eric had lost all hope in me, ready to drop me like nothing ever happened. Leander was going to be king, the half-breeds were as good as dead, and God—

Leander hummed to himself, shifting through the weapons on his desk.

God was, for all intents and purposes, determined to mess up my life. Well, there you go, God; it was all messed up. Congratulations. As if to make matters worse, a fly landed on my leg. I shook it off, cursing the bug in my head; couldn't the world just let me be angry in peace?

You said You would be with me, Father, I prayed. *Well, if You're with me, why am I tied up by some maniac getting ready to die? None of this makes sense.*

My insect companion came around for another visit, this time tickling my arm when it perched. "Stop it!" I shouted, but the noise was muffled. Surely, Leander released the fly for the ultimate form of torture. My annoyance would be his greatest form of entertainment. The hum of the fly whizzed past my ear, grating on my last nerve. Please, Leander, just shoot me. The thought brought back memories of my dream/vision. Would it come true after all? Did it really matter now? Our plans, our relationships, all falling apart like—

The fly landed on my nose and even the most severe nose scrunches would not shake him. Wiggling against my restraints did nothing to dislodge my unwelcome visitor. Stubbornly, the fly dug his heels in, refusing to be intimidated even when I shook like one possessed. Unfortunately, the constant quaking lifted up the chair and gravity crashed the both of us to the floor.

The fly launched off my face and exited the narrow window at the top of the wall. Leander's snide laugh echoed in the room, coinciding with the stomp of his boots. He approached my fallen form, his shadow stretching across the floor. I closed my eyes, bracing myself. The thud of his footfalls ceased and the room grew quiet.

His laughter ceased, cut off as if someone pressed the mute button on his voice. The floor shook beside me, and I peeked to see his face, deceptively restful in unconsciousness, level with mine. The ropes binding me went slack, and I pushed myself off the floor, rubbing my wrists. Feeling flooded back into my hands and feet with the sensation of pins-and-needles.

The toothy grin of my rescuer made me wonder if Leander would have been a better option. Ferny formed an iron grip around my chapped wrist with her bony fingers. "Come, child. I may still be able to fetch a priest while the day is young."

Not this again. I pushed against her. "No, thanks."

She waved her free arm at the heap of swords and knives next to Leander's desk. "Would you rather suffer whatever pain Leander has cooked up for you?"

I had to say it was tempting when I glanced at the peacefully-snoozing Commander. Still, gauging from Ferny's hurried actions, whatever sedative she used on him was temporary. When he woke up, I would be at his nonexistent mercy. "I'm going to say 'no' to that one."

Her sharp teeth beamed in triumph. "Come, then. The daylight is burning."

I jerked out of her grip, taking a step backwards. "Look, Ferny. I appreciate you saving me—really, I do, even though you were the one that got me here in the first place. However, I'm getting tired of everyone telling me what to do. I'm going to follow this novel idea and do whatever I want now."

I reached out to slide the door open. "So, I'm not going to get tortured by Leander. I'm also not going to marry your son, because I've been busy trying to prevent genocide in your country which has left me tired and bitter. To make matters worse, if that's possible, I already had a man interested in me, but now I'm thinking I might not date for another fifty years because it's just too emotionally complicated." The speech left me flushed and out of breath.

Ferny's wrinkled face turned beet red, her gray hair bouncing with every step she took towards me. "You ungrateful child!" she boomed.

"Yes, I'm super ungrateful," I affirmed, brushing frizzed, cropped hair out of my face. "You don't want this kind of girl marrying your innocent son and corrupting his ways." It was time to bring out the big guns. "And I supposed it's time you knew the truth: I can't cook."

The gasp that erupted from her open mouth could have taken a person's breath away. "What? How do you ever expect to be married if you can't cook?"

Yay for self-esteem builders. Was she related to the Martha Stewart wanna-be that tried to be my roommate? I held my hands up in surrender. "You got me, Ferny. Guess you'll just have to let me go now you know what a poor match I am for your son."

Her bony fingers curled into a fist. "I don't think so. You broke his heart, you little cretin. Nobody hurts my son without feeling pain themselves. Luckily, Leander will probably punish you enough for the both of us, and he'll be waking up angry in a few minutes to finish what he started." Her clenched hand swung at my head, but I dodged out of the way. Whew. That was a close one.

Was this lady on steroids? She grabbed onto my shoulders, whipping me around and shoving me onto the ground. I kicked at her shins, straining to reach my sword on Leander's fallen body. Too short.

What to do when you have no weapons? My thoughts traversed back to the second grade where I'd survived many a playground tussle with Ron Gardner because of my sharp incisors. Bingo. I bit her hand, but her skin was as hard as granite and tasted like baby powder. Okay, so Ron Gardner wasn't a crazy, bionic mother from another world. Time for a different tactic. With all my strength summoned, I jabbed my feet into her stomach and watched her go limp, joining Leander on the floor.

Wow, I wasted my battling talents all these years when I could have been enjoying an illustrious leg wrestling career. Or maybe Ferny's demise was more related to the flash of pink at the front door, belonging to an armed Mystical Unicorn, her radiant hair gleaming behind her. She had one hand on a gun and the other resting on her hip, posing like some Joan of Arc avenger.

"I took out the guards in the halls," she informed me, marching through the doorway. She made a beeline for Leander's desk and rifled through the pile of weapons.

My jaw dropped. Surely this was some kind of delusion from my addled brain. "Took out? Like the Mafia kind of 'took out?'"

She sighed, picking up a scary-looking gun and opening its chamber. "Don't be so juvenile, Nessie. No, I just used the tranquilizers. Now, we'd better get out of here before everyone comes to."

She had a point. The room was filled with two temporarily unconscious bodies. "Maybe it's just better if I stay—" I tiptoed over to Leander's body and gingerly untied the sheath from his belt.

Mystical Unicorn snapped the chamber closed and discarded the gun onto Leander's desk. "I didn't track you all the way here to hear a 'thanks, but no thanks.' You have ten seconds to get your butt in gear before I shoot you and drag your body behind me."

Wow. Where was the 'hippy-go-lucky', cheetah-print wearing Mystical Unicorn I knew? Not seeing any other options, I strapped the sheath around my waist and sprinted behind this strange version of Mystical Unicorn.

Well, that was weird. But considering the fact I was in a parallel universe trying to save Sporks in a kingdom run by a monarch named after a Muppet… at least it was consistent.

<h1 style="text-align:center">Chapter 23</h1>

Mystical Unicorn and I crouched behind the swan-shaped shrubbery of the courtyard, the morning daylight obscured by the shadow of Kermit's castle. Someone with a serious animal obsession had designed the garden between the castle and the entry gate. A stone path ran between hedges crafted like chickens and ducks. To top everything off, the fountain in the middle of the courtyard was a sculpted dolphin spitting water out of its mouth.

Mystical Unicorn waved me closer to her and peeked out from behind the shrub, tranquilizer gun in hand. The sight made me smile. Maybe someone still believed in me. We crept along the empty courtyard, staying low to the ground. Our game of hide-and-seek catered to my childhood dreams of being an army man.

Sword at my side, I snaked behind her, weaving in and out of the fowl-themed bushes. Further up the paw-print path, I caught sight of the steel entry gate, swung open. Villagers walked past the opening, carrying goods to market.

"Look, Unicorn!" I rose from the ground and pointed.

She snatched my arm and wrenched me behind the fountain, putting a finger to her lips. A shrill voice rang out around the hedge. So much for my dreams of being an army man.

"Let me go, you swine!" a woman shrieked.

Oh, no. Anything but that.

"If you don't release me right this instance, I swear I'll scream so loud any police officer within a fifty mile radius will come running and—"

A gruff voice joined the conversation. "Look, lady, I don't know what you're talking about, but you need to come with me."

Unicorn pushed me behind a goose shrub just before the soldier dragged a fuming woman towards the fountain. A quick peek confirmed my worst fears: Betty Crocker lady, in the flesh. She writhed against the bodybuilder of a soldier carting her away. *Stay low. Avoid eye conta—*

Her gaze locked with mine, and I cursed under my breath. A grating screech pierced the tranquility of the early morning. "You! I know you! Agatha? Ag… Agnes!" She dug her heels into the ground, struggling against the guard. "I came back to your apartment out of the goodness of my heart to give you some recipes, and suddenly I'm here in this crazy land with all these people wearing forks on their clothes. For the love of all that is good, tell this man to release me."

Unicorn groaned. The guard backpedaled, swatting a meaty hand at the bush that concealed us. His thick fingers met my ear and twisted. Ow! No wonder little old ladies did that to trouble-makers. "Weren't you the prisoner that Leander brought in earlier?"

I shook my head emphatically, a poor choice for my twisted ear. "Don't think so. You heard the woman; my name is Agatha. Agatha… Christie."

A frown crossed his face, and the vein on his neck pulsed. "What are you doing hiding in the bushes?"

"Hiding? What makes you think I'm hiding? I was just squatting over here. Can't a girl squat once in a while without being questioned of her motives?" I waved my arms. "Just forget it. I'm leaving." With a grimace, I jerked my head forward, hoping to break his grip. Searing pain burned my cartilage, but I wasn't any closer to getting out of the guard's pinch.

Another soldier ran up, this one a much skinnier teenager with freckles across his panicked face. "Leander's in his room out cold and the prisoner is gone!" His nose scrunched when he saw me. "Never mind the second part; why are you out here?"

Here went nothing. "I was released for good behavior."

"I don't think so," the first guard growled, wringing my ear tighter.

"Okay, how about I went for some fresh air while he was taking a nap?" He drew his sword and advanced. "All right, here's what happened…" I licked my lips. Forget excuses. Bribery. "Do you like brownies?"

Betty snorted. "Well, if you do, don't take any from her. She can't cook."

The teenager's brow furrowed, a mixture of pity and revulsion washing over his face. "I don't know what a brownie is, but I don't understand how you'll ever get married if you can't cook."

That was the last straw. A war cry bellowed from my lungs. I lunged from the bodybuilder's death grip and launched myself at the teen, beating him with my fists. My clenched fingers pounded his chest, his back, and his head. Mystical Unicorn used her newfound ninja skills to take out Guard Number One.

"You're crazy, lady!" my victim extricated himself from my fury and ran as fast as his little stick legs could take him, weaving in and out of shrubs before making it into the castle. My breathing came in thick snorts, and I shook my fist at the dust he'd kicked up.

Sorry, I blacked out there. When my brain came back to its senses, it registered two things:

First, the first guard lay unconscious at Unicorn's feet.

Second, Betty, probably in search of the ingredients for lemon meringue pie, disappeared in the fray. Not that I was sad to see her go, but a shiver ran up my spine. The population of Spoons was not prepared for this Martha Stewart monstrosity to be unleashed upon the unsuspecting townspeople.

Unicorn made a beeline for the steel gate. "We'd better get out of here before the entire Spoon army comes to get us. But I have to ask…who was that crazy lady?"

How does one explain Ms. Betty Crocker? "First, tell me where you learned your ninja moves."

"Touché." She flipped long pink hair over her shoulder. "Well, let's get a move on. There's a ball to get ready for. I also didn't have time to tell Eric and Veli about your disappearance. We don't want them to find both of us missing."

Warmth and doubt filled me at once, causing a tornado of emotion. Unicorn still wanted me to confront the king, but did I? If Eric and Veli didn't believe in me, why should I believe in myself?

Something tugged in my heart, drawing my eyes upward. No. God and I weren't exactly on speaking terms. I may have gotten out of Leander's grasp, but He was the one who had put me in this mess. Still, the sight of my pink-haired companion humming while she carried her tranquilizer gun out of the open gate softened my bitterness. "Hey, I don't think I said it before, but," I patted her on the back, "thanks. What you did back there was really cool."

"No problem, Nessie. That's what roommates are for."

Images of Ninja Unicorn crossed my mind like a movie on repeat. "Actually, I *was* kind of wondering how you pulled off all of that stuff when—"

She shook her head. I could have sworn I saw a drop of moisture run down her cheek. "Not right now. One day, we'll talk about it. Right now, we can just…" She looked around at the trees lining the road. I watched her transform from crazy-spy-samurai lady to my tree-hugging Unicorn. "We can just commune with nature," she chirped, forcing a cardboard smile.

Allowing the ambiance of the forest road to serve as our radio, we walked back to the inn, my trusty Unicorn and I.

156

Chapter 24

"No, no, no, no. Never in a million years."

Our return to Eric and Veli's cramped room at the inn was not going as anticipated. To start off with, the space was much too small to fit two cots, a vanity, and a fireplace. Add four people to the mix, and claustrophobia started to set in. We were fortunate that Felicia took a nap in her room or it would have been unbearable.

"C'mon, Eric," I plopped myself onto the hard cot by the door, careful to dodge the sharp edge of a nightstand. Sunlight poured through the transparent ceiling, and I wiped the sweat off my brow. How could all of this still hurt when I was well aware of his opinions on my competence?

His posture was rigid, a far cry from his normal easygoing self. "Nope. Too dangerous." He stepped in front of the mantle of the fireplace, full of burnt coals, and crossed his arms.

"Veli, talk some sense into your brother," I appealed, but Veli shook his head. He stretched out on the white cot by the vanity, leaning against the decorative crimson curtains on the wall.

"I don't know, Nessie. Unless you want to get shot by Leander, it might not be a great idea."

Really, Veli?

"Unicorn rescued me so that I could finish this!" I objected passionately, my arms waving at the pink-haired ninja perched on the table of the vanity. She scooted closer to the edge of the mahogany and dangled her feet off the side, jiggling her leg nervously.

"Actually, Nessie," Unicorn looked at her toes, "My goal was just to get you away from Leander." Her voice grew quiet. "I don't think it's a good idea for you to go back."

All heads were down. The trio concentrated on the paisley carpet as if they were going to be tested on the design later. I swallowed to moisten my dry throat. "Et tu, Unicorn?"

It was official: my friends and my life sucked. Who were Eric and Veli to tell me I couldn't go to the ball when they hadn't even realized I'd been kidnapped until after I came back? It was a good thing my roommate had been going out for fresh air when Leander nabbed me.

Growling in frustration, I slammed my hands onto the nightstand, rattling the lamp sitting atop. "Why did you even come to rescue me, Unicorn?" She looked away, clasping her hands together. "We've come so far and you're going to just let it all go to waste? What about the Sporks or half-breeds or whatever you call them? You're just going to let them suffer because you're scared?"

Mystical Unicorn's leg stopped shaking, and the three conspirators froze. If I looked closely it was hard to tell that they were even breathing. Just three sneaky backstabbing statues sitting in a bedroom. "No," Eric's voice slowly filled the room. "We're still going ahead with the plan."

"Oh," the words from my lips were barely audible.

My noble companions were just going to leave me behind while they saved the world. Hot, bitter tears made their way down my face. "That's fine. I mean, I've spent my whole life waiting to be useful; what're a few years more? I'll just be sitting here staring at the wall while you risk your lives. Have a great time."

"Don't be like that, Ness," Eric sighed, uncrossing his arms. "I just can't risk—"

My feet jumped up from the cot and closed the gap between us. "Eric, one time you said I was here for a reason, that I was the sea monster in your dream defeating Leander. You've always told me, time and time again, to trust God had gone through the trouble of bringing me to this parallel universe so I could make a difference. Why won't you trust Him for me?"

Okay, so it stung a little to hear the words coming from my mouth, especially having my own trust issues earlier that morning. If I had been a little closer to the mirror of the vanity, I would have checked to see if the word "hypocrite" was written on my forehead.

My face was uncomfortably close to his, invading his personal space. He turned away from me. "I…"

Enough excuses. I spun on my heels and headed for the door, but he caught the edge of my tunic before I could make it through. "Nessie, I was so close to losing you," he whispered, eyes pleading. "I know I'm being a hypocrite. The words I've been encouraging you with are ones I know I should say, but it's hard to actually live them out. How can I watch you head out on the battlefield not knowing if you'll come back?"

His fingers released my clothes and reached for my hand. "We read stories about conquering heroes with their happy endings, but sometimes the good guys get stuck full of swords before they even have a chance to change anything. How could I live with myself if something happened to you and I had been the one pushing you to Leander? I want to trust," his eyes implored mine, "I really do, but every time I think of someone hurting you, I just can't let go."

Ugh. His words melted me a little. "Eric, I'm just as scared as you, but if I don't face Leander tonight, he wins. I need to know that he's no longer a threat to the half-breeds or you or me or anyone."

He brushed my hand and pulled away, shaking his head sadly. "I can't let you do that. I understand Leander is a threat to you, so I think the best thing would be…" He paused, reaching for the hilt of my Remiel blade. "The best thing for everyone," he repeated, "would be for you to just go home. We can figure out a way for you to take Felicia back before her kids start to worry."

So, he was serious about sending me home. He really didn't believe in me.

Veli twiddled his thumbs when Felicia was mentioned, but she was off enjoying her nap, unable to hear the exciting news she might be returning to normality. Oddly enough, according to Unicorn, my next door neighbor had grown quite fond of the long chats with Veli. The concept of having an enjoyable discussion with Veli baffled me.

Eric cleared his throat, the words coming out flat. "For the record, you really have done a remarkable thing here. I was too cowardly to step up to Leander before. I thought I had to run away from my home if I wanted to be anyone different, but you've given us all courage and passion to accomplish what we should have banded together to do long ago."

"Well, aren't I just a dandy little cheerleader?" I smiled sarcastically, grabbing my sword from his hands and slamming it into the sheath. "Let me know next time you need me to travel to another world so I can give you a pep talk."

The room was uncomfortably silent. I spun on my heels, one mission in mind: to lock myself in my room for the rest of the night…or at least until everyone left for the ball.

§ § §

Stiffly marching down the carpeted hallways, past decorative statues and urns that shone in the morning sunlight, I clenched and unclenched my fists. Eric, Veli, and Unicorn didn't know what storm they'd unleashed; my wrath would manifest in the form of toilet-papering their rooms later.

I paused in front of my door, rifling in my pockets. My copy of the rune key design was in there somewhere. Why a society would want to operate on locks without physical keys was beyond me.

"Are you okay, Nessie?" spoke a soft voice.

159

Was I *okay?* A few choice words rushed to the forefront of my mind before recognizing Felicia, still sporting her ponytail, T-shirt, and jeans. She clearly had not embraced the fashion of this world, but the look suited her.

"I'm *fine.*" The bitter syllable forced out of my mouth.

She crossed her arms and opened the door next to mine. "No, you're not. Come into my room and we'll chat over some coffee—or sertav—whatever." She shrugged. "I haven't found the equivalent of a pint of ice cream in this world yet, so if you see anything, let me know."

A wan smile begrudgingly settled on my lips. I followed her into a room similar to Eric's, but with a sertav machine where the fireplace had been. She walked to the counter where the black box sat, and I leaned against the wall. "What's going on?" Felicia asked. The hum of the machine filled the room when she turned the crank, waiting for the water to heat up.

My shoulders lifted in a half-hearted shrug. "Nothing, really. Just," I sighed, "we're supposed to be talking to the king to save these people, but everyone's decided it's too dangerous for me. They all agreed I need to go back home as if my role in this never happened. I'm just so angry."

Felicia poured the hot drink into mugs with the competence of a caffeine-addicted mother of four. "At…?"

It may have been faster to point out who I *wasn't* mad at. I counted on my fingers. "Eric, for trying to get rid of me. I really thought we might be able to have something, but he's just trying to push me away. I'm angry at him for leading me on this far to drop me now. At Veli and Unicorn for going along with his 'this-is-too-dangerous' speech, when they're all planning to take the risks and leave me behind. At God for bringing me to this stupid world and letting all these stupid things happen." Time to come full circle. "At me, for being so angry."

She nodded and placed a mug in my hands. "What are you going to do?"

"I guess I'm going to go home and try to forget about everything. Maybe consume a few gallons of cookie dough. What else can I do?"

Her voice was low. "I was angry, too."

"At Eric?" My brow contorted. If he was in some kind of love triangle with my next door neighbor, he was in for—

"No," she wrinkled her nose. "I had four children and my husband just walked away from everything, leaving me to deal with the fallout—no goodbye, nothing." She took a sip and stared at the paisley design of the carpet. "Don't get me wrong—I love my kids—but it's hard raising them by myself. I was a wreck the first year, angry at God, angry at the world.

"You don't know why it happened, why you're in such a rough place, and you're constantly trying to deduce the reasons. I'd like to tell you that you'll find out all the answers, but it doesn't work that way. Part of faith is trusting something bigger even when we don't know what's going on, even when it seems like everything is crumbling around us."

She put her mug down onto the nightstand and sat on the cot, patting the empty spot beside her. Oh, what the heck. I plopped down beside her on the springy bunk. "The feelings don't go away overnight. Every day is a new battle. Coming to…this place…has not been easy." She nudged her glasses up. "You saw me when I first got here. I couldn't understand why my kids were left without a mother. I'm still trying to figure out what I believe and why I'm here. Who knows? Maybe I'm here to talk to you." She was smiling gently. "And Veli seems nice."

Wow, overstatement of the century. "That's not something I thought I'd ever hear." Deep down I knew she was right, a thought that loosened the tightness in my chest ever-so-slightly. Now if I could just get my stubborn anger to ease. A feeble prayer emerged from my tangled thoughts. *God, I am clueless about what's going on, but here's me trusting that You've got this.*

She stood up from the cot and crossed over the counter to pour more sertav. "So, what are you going to do?"

Good question. Toilet-papering my companions' rooms seemed out of the picture, but a better idea entered my mind. The trio didn't believed in me, and I couldn't look in a crystal ball and predict my future. However, I hadn't been transported to some parallel universe for nothing. It was go big or go home, and I was *not* going home. At least, not yet. "I have a ball to get ready for." With a sneaky grin on my lips, I pushed myself to my feet and headed for the door. Girl talk…who would have thought it would make such a difference? I paused before exiting. "Thanks, Felicia."

She raised her mug in salute. "Don't mention it. Save the Sporks or whatever so I can get back to my kids, and we'll call it even."

If only it were as easy as she implied. "I'll see what I can do." With that, I slipped out of her room and into mine. It was time for a makeover.

Chapter 25

The vanity mirror certainly lived up to its name. Not to toot my own horn, but since my friends didn't know my plan to attend the ball, the task of beefing up my ego fell to me. It wasn't too difficult. The one-strapped emerald dress flowed like silky water to the floor. An oval brooch, glittering with crystals, bunched the fabric at my left hip, pulling the material so my leg peeked cautiously from behind the knee-length slit. The tailor had thrown in a matching green handbag and mask with her delivery, tying the ensemble together. My hair was the only thing not cooperating. Traumatized pieces stuck out at odd angles. Curse my unruly follicles! Oh, well. I couldn't be completely perfect.

I practiced moving around the small room, mock-dancing past my bed.

A knock sounded on the door. Let's just say when you're dressed in a ballroom gown, your options for hide and seek are limited. The door flung open without my consent, and I wrapped myself in the rose-colored drapes hanging on the wall. Very inconspicuous, I know.

"Am I interrupting anythi—?" Veli trailed off when he noticed my use of the curtains as a cloak.

Well, look what the cat dragged in: one of the traitors coming to spy on me. "What?" I huffed, rolling my eyes. "I'm cold."

"Uh huh," he muttered incredulously, his muscled bulk easily filling the door frame. "Yeah, I always cover myself in the curtains when I'm cold." He motioned towards the fluffy cover on the cot. "Blankets are just so…old-fashioned, you know?"

"Are you going to make fun of me or did you actually come in to do something productive?" I snapped. *Please, just think I'm PMS-ing and go away.*

He rubbed his arms. "Actually, I'm getting a little chilly myself. Do you think you could spare a panel?"

"What do you want, Veli? I'm busy."

He closed the door behind him and sat down on the cot, examining the lines on his palm. "Yeah, I'd be pretty busy too if I were trying to secretly get ready for a ball and sneak into a castle without invitations, transportation, back-up, or a plan."

Just needed to play it cool. "What would make you think that? I was getting ready to pack all my things for home."

"I'm not stupid," Veli said, slowly rising from the cot. "I knew as soon as you huffed off to your room that you were planning on going to the ball."

Curse that man and his keen insight. "Well, that would just be foolish." I forced a laugh. My hands fidgeted with the edge of the curtain. "Like you said, I have no way to get into the castle and no help if I did decide to attend."

"Yeah, that's why I came in here." Veli waved his hand in my direction. "You can come out of the curtains now because I know you're wearing the dress. I may have agreed with Eric that it's dangerous for you to come, but if you're going to come anyway, it would be more harmful for you to go in blind."

A frustrated sigh escaped my lips. He had a point, and if I wanted to make it through the night with all of my organs intact, I should take all the help I could get, even if it was from an incorrigible man. I let the red drapes fall. Maybe I could be friends with the surly blond man…like the kind of friends that don't talk for years and barely know each other's names. "For the record, these curtains are really warm."

"Very nice," he complimented with an approving smile. He stepped back and squinted. "Eric may have paid for that dress, but I doubt he'd remember what it looks like. He used to wear the same tunic for months at a time when we were kids; the guy just isn't that observant about clothes. Hopefully, your mask will do most of your disguising work, but it won't hurt to change up your appearance." He grabbed the brush from my nightstand. "Have a seat."

Was this the part where he beat me with a hairbrush for trying to sneak out? "Why? What are you planning to do with that?"

"I'm going to fix your hair so you look nice and don't die. Welcome to Salon D'Veli. Now, sit down and shut up."

"I don't think that's a very inviting slogan," I muttered but was secretly pleased with his assistance. Getting ready for a ball was hard work, particularly when I had to account for the possibility of getting murdered.

When Veli was done teaching my hair to obey, he snatched a box of makeup out of his pocket and went to town. "A gift from Felicia. Now, wipe that surprised look off of your face, unless you want to end up going to the masquerade ball as a clown." My eyebrows refused to lower, and he got defensive. "Look, my mother used to make me help her get ready for important events at the palace when I was misbehaving. I guess I picked up some things."

His painted my eyelashes with mascara, his hand possessing the steadiness of a surgeon. I held my eyelids open, trying not to blink. "You must have been in trouble a lot."

He pursed his lips, gently pulling up on my eyelashes with the wand. "She has the patience of a saint," he said softly. "I don't get to see her that much anymore. I'm always running off, trying to right the wrongs in this messed-up kingdom."

Veli may have been a jerk on the outside, but he was definitely a softie deep down. If I needed further evidence of his sensitive side, I only needed to look in the vanity. Not only did I look stunning, but his touch-ups caused me to do a double-take. Pixie cut stylishly in place, makeup accentuating my eyes and lips; I barely recognized myself. "Thank you, Veli." I smiled, but he held up a hand.

"I'm not done." He reached into his pocket again, this time pulling out a golden oval hair clip with a delicate engraving of a flower etched into the side. A single ruby was set into the middle of the flower.

"It's beautiful," I gasped.

"Deadly, too." He smiled and pressed the ruby on top. The clip sprang open revealing a small dagger.

Hold on. He didn't wear hairclips. "Veli…why do you have this?" Knowing him, it probably belonged to an ex-girlfriend. I could imagine her now: tall, muscular, and proficient at killing. Xena Warrior Princess, maybe?

He put his hands in his pockets. "I don't know. I saw it in the village market when you were trying on your dress. I originally bought it for Felicia so she could protect herself against all the guys that must hit on her all the time, but when I thought about how defenseless and incompetent you were…" He reached for my mask on the edge of the vanity.

Tender moment over. I waved my hand. "You don't need to finish that train of thought."

After tying on my emerald mask, lined with pearls, he stepped back to survey his handiwork. "Well, Nessie, if you die tonight, at least no one can say you looked bad. Though it's probably a good idea to try to stay alive since my brother likes you a lot, even though he's too scared to trust it." He sighed and rubbed his neck thoughtfully. "I've kind of gotten used to you being around, so not dying is preferable."

My eyes teared up. I attempted to pull the brute into a big hug, but he grabbed my chin in his hand. "Do. Not. Cry. If you mess up your makeup with tears, I will do Leander a favor and stab you myself."

Okay, moisture evaporated. However, his stern demeanor didn't keep me from wrapping my arms around him. "Aww, Veli. You're the best fairy god-father I've ever had."

"Well, it took a few miracles just to hide the bags underneath your eyes," his expression softened. "But, if you manage to stay alive tonight and tell every-one that I helped you play dress-up, you can bet that I will personally go out of my way to kill you."

Ignoring his hopefully-empty threats, I grinned up at him. "So, were you serious about this Salon D'Veli? I think it sounds kind of catchy."

Another knock pounded at the door, and I pointed Veli to the curtains. "Who is it?" I called, my nervous voice raising an octave. My fingers unlaced the mask and yanked it off my head. The curtains looked a bit lumpy, but other than that, Veli was safely concealed.

The knocker hesitated. "It's Eric." Well, in that case, he could have waited out there all night. "I wanted to say good-bye."

"Okay, bye," I snipped.

The thick door didn't conceal his deep cough. "I was just thinking that after all the danger is over, maybe we could…I don't know…"

Every sarcastic impulse inside bubbled to the top when I made my way to the door, spitting the words out like something sour. "We can get dinner. I'll make a couple batches of toast and we can chat about old times. Just stop by my apartment, since you know where I live."

Eric's groan came out muffled through wood. "Nessie, what do you want me to do? I'm being torn in two here! I don't want you to leave me, but I can't bear the thought of you getting killed. I wish," he trailed off. "I wish things were different. I wish I never let Leander come into power. I wish I asked you out the first time I knocked on your door instead of trying to sell you the same toaster every day. And sometimes I wish when I saw you in King Arthur's Shopalot, I would have convinced you to put down the sword and walk away from a world that could cause you so much pain and danger."

Complicated man. How could someone make me so angry and then soften me a few breaths later? "But, Eric, if I didn't have the pain and danger, I never would have found the thrill of adventure and purpose." Deep breath. Let the anger go. "I never would have started loving you."

His silence dragged on until he tapped outside. "Can you open the door? I need to see your face," Eric pleaded.

The curtains rustled, and Veli peeped out of the curtains to shake his head no, even making slicing motions by his neck. I certainly couldn't let Eric see me dressed like this, but his voice was too adorable.

"Later, when you come back from the ball," I blurted. "I'll wait for you. I won't leave until morning."

"And what if I don't come back?"

The thought jolted me into action, and I flung open the door. I grabbed the lapel of his tunic and pulled him in close. His lips were warm and sweet on mine, and I felt his fingers come up to brush my cheek. In an instant, my tense muscles relaxed and I leaned into him. *If only we could stay here forev—* Eric's fingertips withdrew and he pulled back. *Quick, before he registers that I'm too dolled up for a night in!*

I slammed the door in his face, panting for air. His reaction seemed to take hours. "If that was a farewell kiss," he said at last, an underlying tone of dazed cheer in his voice, "we should be apart more often."

My fingers massaged my temple. Good, he was as oblivious as Veli said. "I'll see you tonight," I chirped. Sneaky Nessie, with my double-meaning words.

When he left, Veli untangled himself from the curtains and chastised me with the tube of mascara in his hand. "I can't keep doing your makeup if you're going to run around kissing everybody. Look, your lipstick is smudged now."

But I was too busy smiling to notice.

Chapter 26

First stop: buffet. My mother would have judged me for meandering over to the long tables stretched out across the side of the expansive ballroom, filled with more meat, drinks, and snacks than I imagined possible, but I just reminded myself of my situation. Post-betrayal grumpiness affected my appetite for dinner, and with my survival questionable, I was going to eat anything my stomach ordered.

Even through the peripheral-impaired vision of my mask, it was clear Leander spared no expense for the ball, decorating even the cream-colored tablecloths with gold trim. Sparkling chandeliers glittered over the buffet line. Were those diamonds? Sheesh.

Unashamedly, I grabbed handfuls of fruit, cheese, and crackers delicately arranged on ornate silver platters.

"Geez, save some for the rest of us!" a man snipped at me rudely, swatting my hand that was already loaded with a piece of cheese. I whipped around and glared daggers at the man in a black horse mask. A man who apparently had a death wish.

Just as I was about to unleash a verbal assault, his hand lifted the mask for a brief instant. Oh, just Veli. Smiling, I threw a nonfatal punch to his arm. "Princess Rainbow Sprinkles from the neighboring kingdom of Knives?" I hissed. "I thought you were trying to help me get into the ball, but the invitation you forged proved me wrong."

He laughed, stealing a grape from my plate. "Well, you're here, aren't you? Besides, I knew they would be more uneasy about denying a royal figure entry."

"Veli, they saw me ride up on a console. I hardly think that looks royal."

"You'd be surprised at some of the royalty around here."

Blaring trumpets interrupted our conversation and drew my attention to the rest of the ballroom packed with men and women in masks. I took in the extravagance of the marble floor, the towering ivory pillars decorated with strings of glowing white lights. At the entrance, finely-dressed guests traversed the lush carpet of the grand staircase to mingle with others located on the second floor overlook. A magnificent chandelier, much larger than the diamond one over the buffet, hung from the ceiling like a fountain of glowing crystals, shedding light on the painted gold lace designs on the ceiling. Rich, rouge drapes graced the walls, reaching from the ceiling all the way to the floor.

A balcony set off to the side overlooked the gardens, but my attention was drawn to the dais on the far side of the room. There Leander stood beside the throne where an older man with a neatly trimmed white beard and a golden crown sat. The king slumped in the chair, his lifeless eyes staring off into the crowd. Leander was decked out in purple and lime military regalia and decorated with medals. I didn't know they gave medals for being a jerk.

"Ladies and lords, I speak for the King and the rest of Spoons when I say welcome to the Semi-Annual Ball." I scanned the crowed in vain for Eric or Mystical Unicorn while Leander, too cool for a mask, went on. "Tonight is an especially unique event, as King Kermit will be naming his successor. Please make sure you do not leave before the big announcement at midnight. Until then, enjoy yourselves."

The packed room erupted into hundreds of cheers. Leander waved and took his seat beside the king. Well, that complicated things. So much for easy access to Kermit.

I patted my side, searching for the Blade of Remiel before remembering that I'd had to hand it over to Veli for safekeeping. The missing weight was uncomfortable, but there was no way I could have concealed it under the silky dress. Veli's hairclip dagger would have to do. Well, that and the extra knife I managed to fit into my green handbag.

"Two hours until the big reveal," Veli whispered. "As if we all don't know who King Kermit will name as his successor. Anyway, I suggest you make your move before the proclamation is made. I'm going to get in a few dances with Felicia while I eavesdrop on the other government officials, but I'll find you if it looks like you need help."

So Felicia was with them, too. How was it I was the only one the ball was too dangerous for?

"Oh, and by the way," Veli added, stuffing a piece of cheese under his mask. "I think Eric is planning on confronting Leander in a more aggressive approach, as in 'with a knife,' which probably won't work out too well for him. I'll try to stall if I find him in this crowd, but if you see Eric, you should probably occupy him until you go through with your own plan."

"But once he knows I'm here, he's going to go psycho," I hissed.

"Then you better not let him know that it's you. I would start working on that voice of yours." Veli craned his neck over the crowds of people. "I think I see him over there." He pointed Eric out in the crowd, sporting a simple black mask and tux. This night was turning out to be more complicated as time went on. Better shove some cheese cubes and crackers in my handbag before leaving the safety of the buffet, just in case I needed my strength.

Before I could make a beeline for Eric, who was enthralled in a discussion with a group of masked partygoers, I was intercepted by a tall man with an ornately jeweled mask. "This dance, milady?" he offered a hand.

Why was that pompous voice familiar? The shaggy blond hair and lip ring also rang a bell. "I don't dance." I excused myself and tried to push past him.

He smiled arrogantly, rubbing the stubble on his chin. "What you mean to say is that you *didn't* dance. My presence has changed everything."

I stopped my fervent departure and stared him down. His cocky mouth, beady eyes, and stocky legs reminded me of a jerk I had met before. He tapped his foot impatiently, but when I didn't fall into his arms, he lunged forward and snatched my handbag, bolting off into the thick crowd.

Ah, the ever-lovely Robert Hood, whose wonderful idea it was to come to the ball in the first place. I should have remembered. Well, all he got was my extra knife and a bag of crackers and cheese. Maybe he would let it sit outside in the heat a while before deciding to look through his treasures. In the meantime, there were bigger fish to fry. I weaved in and out of the crowd, Eric in my crosshairs. After all, if I was at a ball, I was going to dance with the dark, handsome, stubborn, and sweet duke whom I loved.

But a crisis occurred within arm's length of him. What was I supposed to say? He was engaged in a serious discussion with burly middle-aged men. Was I going to waltz up to him and demand a dance? Should I hide my identity like Veli suggested or come clean from the start? Did my voice need disguising, and could I hold up the charade if needed?

One of the stout men witnessed the abrupt halt of my determined trek and waved at me. As if in slow motion, the sharply-dressed duke pivoted to face me, which gave me time to absorb the sight of his dark tux and black superhero-like mask. And his hair. His glorious hair was no longer slicked back like a greasy toaster salesmen. No, it was fluffy and wonderful.

The minutes passed with me silently staring at him. A touch of color tinged his cheeks and he broke the circle to step towards me. "Would you like to dance?" he finally broke the silence.

Did I ever!

With one hand warmly resting against my back and the other holding my wrist, he twirled me around the room like an expert ballroom dancer. Guess that was part of courtly training for a duke. His smooth movements across the floor counteracted my awkward missteps. Just when I thought he was going to collide with a nearby servant or swaying couple, he twirled past them.

I ignored my racing pulse, taking in the sights and sounds around me. A young couple held hands, making their way to the balcony. The image shifted when I spun and saw King Kermit looking bored out of his mind; was he asleep? It was so hard to tell from the distance, but one thing I did notice: Leander disappeared from his vigil, leaving the king fair game.

"You're not much for conversation, huh?" Eric interrupted my trance with a smile.

I stared into his twinkling eyes and felt the deceit melt away. How could I pretend with him? My lips parted to tell him the truth, but another's voice came out.

"May I cut in?" a man addressed Eric.

My stomach clenched, and I clung a little too tightly to Eric's hand when my body pivoted to Leander in his purple and green military garb. That was it. Leander was going to shoot me.

Instead, Leander leaned closer to Eric, rubbing his chin. "Do I know you?"

Even worse than I imagined; Leander was going to kill Eric!

My fingers fumbled for the hairclip but halted when Eric stuck out a hand. "Bran, son of the Duke of Burntbread. We trained together."

Leander smirked and returned the shake. "Ah, you're the chump who was too scared to be Commander. It's unfortunate you have so much trouble holding onto the good things that fall into your lap." He took hold of my free hand.

Great news: Leander didn't recognize me, which meant that he wouldn't kill us on sight. Bad news: The Veli-spruced-up version of me was attractive to Leander. Was there an urn nearby I could barf in?

The room seemed to grow hotter. The men didn't say anything for a moment, locked in a fierce staring contest. I remembered watching a similar scene on the nature channel when alpha giraffes lobbed their necks at each other over a female. Leander caressed my fingers possessively. Eww! If I survived the night, I would need to burn off my hand.

Eric finally stepped back and crossed his arms. "I agree," he quipped sarcastically. "Every time I see corruption and oppression in the kingdom, I think, 'Why can't I be more like Leander?'"

The crush of Leander's grip was proportional to his anger level. "Watch yourself, son of Burntbread," he growled. "Those who whisper treason often conveniently disappear." Eric opened his mouth, a vein in his neck pulsing. My plate was already full tonight; there was no reason to add "Breaking Eric Out of the Dungeon" to the list.

"I love this song," I blurted with what ended up as a German-British accent (don't ask) and fed Leander a coy smile.

The commander was too caught up in his own arrogant world to connect the dots of my identity, but Eric spent enough time around me to recognize my oddly-disguised voice. The anger softened and he reached out a hand. Before he could do anything rash, I dragged Leander into the crowd of dancers.

"Aren't you an eager one?" he laughed with a wink and pulled me into a suffocating embrace even though there was plenty of space around us. Sweat gathered on my back. Any minute Leander was going pull out a knife to stab me. He spun me to the point of nausea, and I wasn't sure what would upset him more: finding out who I was or being thrown up on.

I could have kissed the orchestra when the song ended, freeing me from his death grip. "It was a pleasure," I said with a polite curtsey, sucking in deep breaths of oxygen. Just when I had turned to maneuver my way back into the crowd, his hand caught my wrist.

"Not so fast," he chuckled.

Why was the Psycho theme playing in my head? The next four songs played out like a horror movie, Leander humming and leading me without showing signs of letting up. Sweat drenched my brow from both exertion and anxiety. How was I ever going to talk with the king? Maybe that was his big plan: lure me to the masquerade ball and dance me to death. When the clock struck twelve, Leander would announce his new role as heir and then shoot me just like in my dream, laughing the whole time because he cleverly outwitted me by playing the dance card.

We were mid-song when an idea came to me, so brilliant I didn't know why I never thought of it before. I pushed back from his stifling presence, one glorious word on my tongue. "Bathroom!" He opened his mouth to speak, but I cut him off, clearing my German-British voice. "I have to…you know…go. Where's the bathroom?"

Frowning, he pointed to the far wall but left me with the reassurance he would find me later. Couldn't wait. The image of Leander watching me kept me from turning around. What if he saw the sweat pooling in my armpits and got suspicious?

Staying close to the walls of the ballroom, I snuck past decorative crimson curtains when someone grabbed my wrist and jerked me behind the drapes. Everything went black, and a hand clamped over my mouth before I could scream.

"Eric is on the rampage," Veli, my curtain companion, hissed into my ear. He slowly released his grip on me, and I leaned my forehead against the cool wall, hoping my heart rate would settle back into the double digits.

"Thank you for scaring me half to death, Veli. I'll just tell my chest to stop having a heart attack now." I whispered. Why was it a bad idea to hide in a curtain when I thought of it earlier? "And I was going to tell him, but I didn't have time because—"

The drapes rustled, revealing a sliver of light before everything went dark again. A different voice entered the mix, the voice of a very angry toaster salesman. "You were going to tell me what?" Eric growled.

Fabulous. Forget Leander; Eric might be the one to shoot me before the night was over. "That I made it here safely?" Something told me the answer wasn't going to mollify him.

"You are in so much trouble," Eric snarled. "I can't believe you, sneaking behind my back!"

The fabric shifted and a higher voice joined. "Guys, why are we hiding in the drapes?" Mystical Unicorn whispered. "I brought Felicia in case we were having a meeting."

"Okay, how many people are in this curtain?" I asked the darkness.

When I took roll, it was Veli, Eric, Mystical Unicorn, Felicia, me, and some servant trying to escape having to dish out hors d'oeuvres. Once we got rid of the servant and established Felicia was on the lookout for other intruders, the conversation resumed.

Eric was the first to pipe up. "You lied to me."

My anger made it difficult to whisper. I clenched my fists. "What choice did I have? You would have locked me in a closet if you had even imagined I would come."

"That's a pretty good idea. Is there a closet around?" Veli commented. I had to remember to punch him later.

Eric's voice lost its hard edge. "He had you, Nessie! When I saw Leander pull you into the crowd and I realized who you were, I thought I was going to hyperventilate. There wasn't anything I could do without drawing attention to your identity." His pitiful sigh tugged on my heart strings. "And I just stared at the crowd feeling… so helpless."

It was impossible to stay mad at that man, something I blamed on the fluffy hair. My hand reached out in the darkness for his fingers. "If you would think back, I was the one pulling Leander away. Eric, I'm not as vulnerable as you think. You're just going to have to trust that I'll be okay."

The orchestra struck up a jaunty waltz. Partygoers walked past the curtain, conversing loudly and laughing. Eric finally huffed in defeat. "I guess I'll just have to get used to it. If I tied you up somewhere, you'd just gnaw through the restraints. At least I can keep a better eye on you if we're together."

A smile touched my lips and my fingers rubbed his hand gently.

"Veli, are you stroking my hand?" Mystical Unicorn gasped. "That wouldn't be cool since you and Felicia seem to have something going on over there."

Oops. I was wondering why Eric's skin was so…feminine. I jerked my hand away.

"I'm nowhere near your hand," Veli protested. "And who said anything about Felicia and me? We are very…amicable—"

"You don't need to say anything," Unicorn giggled. "Anyone with functioning eyes can see that you guys like each other."

"Shut up!" Veli whined, but I could hear Felicia's gentle laughter near the edge of the curtain.

"As much as I care about Veli's love life, and I do care very much, I think we should probably get a move on with our plan," I refereed. "And before you have an aneurism, Eric, I'm going to be the one talking to King Kermit."

"You mean, *we're* going to talk to King Kermit," he corrected.

Incorrigible man, forcing me to compromise. "All right; Felicia can be our lookout and Veli our backup. Mystical Unicorn, you'll distract Leander. Sound good?"

"No," Unicorn blurted. Since when did my easygoing roomie refuse orders? "I'll be your backup. Veli can distract Leander."

Well, she did have ninja moves. "All right. In fifteen minutes when the clock strikes eleven o'clock, we'll get into position."

Apparently all this lying about needing the bathroom struck my conscience… or my bladder. After making a pit stop at my original destination, the toilet, I paid the cheese and cracker table a second visit. After all, Robert Hood made off with the stash in my bag, and I was a nervous eater.

My cheeks properly stuffed, I scanned the crowd for Eric. How would—

"Crackers and cheese? The nerve." Oh, no. That shrill voice again.

"I feel the same way! At the very least, they could have made some salmon filets on beds of seasoned rice or sautéed foie gras with parmesan popovers." Ew, that one wasn't much better.

Positioning myself behind a tall vase of flowers, I examined the scene. The scraggly brown blindfold with eye slits cut out couldn't conceal Ferny's identity, not with her wild gray hair sticking out like Einstein. I also didn't need to be a rocket scientist to link the other woman's meticulously bejeweled mask and handmade dress to the perfectly-curled Betty Crocker.

How did Betty get an invitation to the ball? Was there some article about that in *Martha Stewart?* Regardless, I pulled up a front row seat to the fist fight, knowing there was no way two of the world's most annoying people could coexist. But to my astonishment, the women were chatting like two peas in a pod. "It's so nice to see young people like you who appreciate the joys of cooking. My name is Ferny," she beamed, revealing a snaggletooth grin.

"Betty," the blonde curtseyed, offering a dainty hand.

Elbert appeared on the scene, decked out in a grey suit and fedora, sans mask. His eyes lit up when he caught sight of Betty.

Ew. The thought made me watch with eager interest. Elbert, no longer sniveling, stepped out of his mother's shadow and took hold of Betty's hand. Come to think of it, the out-of-date bedazzler couldn't be much older than him, though she carried on like she was in a "Leave It to Beaver" rerun. Elbert planted a firm kiss on Betty's hand. "Enchanté, mademoiselle. Might you happen to be single?"

Her giggle came out like a hyperventilating wheeze. If he was still attracted to her after that, props to him. "Actually, I am."

Ferny gasped, raising a hand to her mouth. "How is that possible? You sound like a phenomenal cook!"

All right, I got it, Ferny. Women need to cook.

Elbert held on to Betty's hand, wiggling his eyebrows. "We could make beautiful cupcakes together."

What a strange world this was proving to be. A hand brushed my shoulder. I whirled around expecting Eric, the one person in all universes who didn't care if I could only make a bowl of cereal.

Leander's grin made his scar stretch. "If I didn't know better, I'd think you were trying to get away from me."

If he knew any better, I'd be dead.

Now, what accent was I using before? Portuguese-Australian?

No…German-British. "I got a little hungry."

"Well, now that you're refreshed, I'm not letting you go for the rest of the night."

Oh, joy.

Chapter 27

The golden lights of the ballroom revolved in circles above me. The next two songs passed in torturous slow motion with Leander spinning me to the point of exhaustion. To make my nausea worse, the band struck up a romantic song. The sweet melody wafting from their fiddles would have been beautiful, if it weren't for Leander's mummifying grip and the ever-moving hands of the clock slipping closer to eleven.

How was I going to extract myself from my pompous dance partner?

"Commander," a man in military uniform approached us and saluted. In a blessed, glorious moment, Leander released me to address the soldier whose hand was resting under his dark buzz cut.

"Captain. At ease."

The man stared at us, his blue eyes unblinking. "Commander, you were dancing, sir."

Leander expelled a frustrated sigh, shifting his weight. "Thank you, Captain Obvious. Do you have anything further to report?"

"A servant discovered people hiding in the curtains," Captain Obvious informed. "That sounds suspicious."

I made sure to push my mask up and glanced over my shoulder for the exit. Hopefully, this Captain Obvious fellow hadn't gotten any descriptions.

"No duh," Leander snapped. "Look into it."

"Some guests have complained of missing valuables and reported seeing a local thief. Also, the old lady that knocked you out earlier is by the cheese table with her son and the woman sighted in the garden."

Leander perked up. I felt a lump form in my throat when he whispered, "Nessie?" Obvious shook his head, and Leander scowled. "Just keep an eye on them for now, and we'll deal with them later—when I'm king."

Captain Obvious frowned, lifting his finger in the air. "But Kermit is the king, not you."

Shouts carried across the ballroom from the buffet table, and I turned my head to see Veli punching Robert Hood in the face. Ha! Good job, Veli! Bundling revenge and distraction into one package.

Captain Obvious bolted towards the confusion with Leander following suit.

Free at last! Without a second thought, I forced my way through guests who stopped dancing to gape at the fight and headed towards King Kermit. My eyes caught a wink from my black-masked toaster salesman loitering at the far end of the dais' steps.

Now, Eric and I were free to run up to the throne and talk to the king about Leander, but all of the guests would be watching. What if Leander saw us? Veli's fight would only occupy him for so long. Goosebumps prickled my skin. I scanned the room for a better option. The guards on either side of the dais craned their necks to see the brawl better. A servant peeked out from behind a pair of red curtains behind the king, strolling over to refill the king's glass and watch the fuss.

King Kermit picked up the cup and sipped the purple liquid dully. With one last glance towards the scuffle, the servant disappeared behind the curtain once more.

"This man assaulted me for no reason!" Robert Hood yelled, but the guards had already discovered the stolen jewelry in his coat pockets. They latched onto his arms and began dragging him towards the door. Guests began to go back to their conversations.

Not good. If the fight was no longer a distraction—Leander pivoted in the crowd and locked eyes with mine. Even from the distance, I made out his cocky smile. Maybe it was the lateness of the hour or the stress building up. Maybe it was the thought of having to dance with Leander again. Either way, something in me snapped.

"Now!" I shouted to Eric. My heart felt like it was going to beat out of my chest. I leapt onto the dais and grabbed Kermit's wrinkled wrist. Eric lunged forward, flanking the king. With a yank, I jerked Kermit to his feet and dragged him behind.

Someone would probably call Adult Protective Services on me, but I reminded myself that I had the greater good in mind when I kidnapped the aging king. He ran surprisingly fast for an old man, and I was able to pull him behind the red curtain and into the servant's quarters before the guards interpreted Leander's frantic shouts.

The stone hallway spread out before us, a network of drab walls full of bustling servants. Or should I say formerly-bustling servants. Everyone stopped their tasks and froze in place, riveted on us: two elegantly-dressed masked figures hauling the king behind them.

Yeah, we looked crazy. A young man at a sink let water overflow the pitcher he'd been filling. The running faucet echoed in the hallway. Right beside us, an older woman gawked next to her serving cart, loaded with mugs and wine glasses. Was that sertav steaming inside?

It was a shame to waste any caffeinated beverage, but desperate times—you know. My arm swiped the glasses off the top and sent the porcelain flying onto the stone floor. The sound of shattering glass broke the silent spell on the servants, and they flinched, hunkering down to protect themselves.

"Calm down, everyone," I panted, stepping around the mess of liquid and shards. "We're not going to hurt anyone. Just trying to…uhh…"

Eric, decked out in his black cape and superhero mask, made it look easy when he hoisted the flailing Kermit onto the cart. "No time," he blurted, pushing the cart in front of him. "Let's go."

He broke into a sprint and I tried to follow, something that wasn't easy in a satin evening gown. Boy, was I glad for that knee slit now. We bolted down the main hallway and veered off at the first intersection, continuing to twist and turn in the stone labyrinth. A woman carrying a pile of laundry jumped aside when the cart barreled past.

"Sorry!" I gasped, huffing and puffing to keep up with Eric. Was he in track? Former champion in the Spoons Marathon?

Before I could ponder the question, Eric halted in front of me, too late for my brain to get the message. I slammed into the back of him, bumping him and the cart forward with a less-than-delicate "oomph." Kermit grumbled curses under his breath and tried to hoist himself onto the ground, but Eric kept a firm hand on the aging king.

My shaggy-haired companion rubbed the back of his neck and let out a low whistle. "What now?" The stone wall ahead of him meant one thing: dead end. A thin red drape hanging next to me was the only decoration in the gray masonry.

"They went this way!" a masculine voice echoed down the corridor behind us. We were running out of options and time.

I swallowed nervously. "What's behind curtain number one?" I whispered and snatched the red drape aside, revealing a small alcove holding mops, detergent, and the largest laundry bin I'd seen in my life.

Bingo.

The dumpster-sized hamper must have had a hundred towels and sheets in it. I rifled a pile of towels aside and faced the king. "Please, get in."

Eric released his grip, but the monarch refused to move. The crow's feet at his eyes crinkled with a glare, and he crossed his frail arms. Was this going to be it? Was this how all our hard work would end? Tears gathered in my eyes, and I took off my mask to see him better. "Please, King Kermit. We're trying to save your life. If Leander has his way, you'll be dead within a week."

The soldiers' shouts reverberated in the small space. "Try this direction!"

I folded my hands together, merely mouthing the words now. "Please."

With a harrumph, he lowered himself off the cart, easing his feet onto the floor with a groan. His bony fingers grasped my hand for a boost into the hamper. Eric moved more towels aside and got in next to the king. I hoisted my leg over, the slit sliding up dangerously. Oops, better keep that down. A girl had to have her modesty, even when kidnapping the king.

Careful to mind the dress, I crouched in the laundry bin, burrowing until I was covered. Believe it or not, in all of my crazy childhood adventures, I never once burrowed in a hamper, and I found I didn't enjoy the experience. The darkness, the muffled noises outside, the hot air warming my face whenever I exhaled—it wasn't exactly a tea party. Add that to the beads of sweat dripping down my face, and it was taking a lot of willpower to pop out of the scratchy towels and suck in the cool oxygen outside.

"Over here, sir." The soldier's voice was loud even through the towels, which meant he was close.

Why was my heart beating so noisily? I held my breath. Seconds passed in agony until a deeper voice answered. "It's a dead end. They must have continued on foot with the king. Let's head out." The sound of rapid marching echoed in the alcove before fading.

I let out the air I'd been holding, squirming against the rough towels. I jumped to my feet in an explosion of white terry cloth. Sweet blessed air.

Eric's masked face and Kermit's wrinkled head emerged from the sea of towels. King Kermit, though still wearing a serious frown, sprung over the side of the laundry bin. Hello? What happened to the half-dead corpse that had been sipping prune juice on the throne?

"I promise I'll explain everything, but we need to get to a safer place," I whispered to the king.

He said nothing, marching out of the alcove and backtracking down the empty corridor. I pivoted to Eric, but he shrugged helplessly. Guess we didn't have a choice but to follow. King Kermit navigated the hallways with ease, never pausing or looking back. How he kept the identical gray walls apart was a mystery to me, but he guided us through the labyrinth until we reached a winding staircase. With my luck, the staircase would lead to a room of soldiers ready to execute us.

I shot an arrow prayer. *God, help us out here. We just need ten minutes alone with him.*

Sweat came in full force now, drenching my lovely emerald dress. Guess Eric would be regretting that purchase. Without much of a choice, we trailed after the king's purple-robed figure like ducklings. I hoisted myself up, step after step, but the stairs seemed unending. My legs burned, dragging like weights beneath me. Still the circular staircase went on. Just when I thought Eric would have to leave my out-of-shape body behind on the steps, we reached a door.

Unlike King Kermit, I was wheezing when he slid the door open and went through. My vision adjusted to the torch-lit room when I peeked inside. Swords, bows, guns, maces, and other sharp metal things I didn't recognize glowed orange from the light of the fireplace. A skewered practice dummy stared at me with button eyes. Did Kermit lead us here so he could deliver our punishment himself? Pick a weapon, any weapon.

However, when we filed into the violent-looking room, the king merely turned around and crossed his arms. Silence permeated the open space. I shifted back and forth on my feet, awaiting our punishment, but Kermit broke into a grin. "Before we begin, I have to tell you what you did back there was the most fun that I've had in six years, hands down." The frown lines quickly settled back into place. He reached his gnarled fingers up and stroked his white beard. "Now, to business. Tell me what all of this is about. Be warned that, no matter how exciting that was, if you're trying to ransom or overthrow me or something," he pulled a sword off of the wall, "I'm going to have to kill you."

Wow, the king had spunk.

Eric noticed my bare face and removed his mask, bowing low to the ground. "Bran, son of the Duke of Burntbread, at your service, my liege."

Oh, crap. Did that mean I had to curtsey, too? My thighs were not much for supporting me but I bent my knees and lowered myself, pulling the satin material of my dress tight. "Nessie, daughter of Frank and Lucy Burgh of America. Also at your service."

The king waved his arms in dismissal. "All right, all right. Get up now. I want to know why you're risking death to kidnap me."

Crickets chirped in my head. Was this really happening? Here was my moment, what I had been planning and waiting for, and I couldn't think of what to say. Whispering a prayer, I took a breath and let the words come.

Chapter 28

The fireplace crackled, consuming a fresh log with vigor. Moonlight filtered in through the ceiling, washing the fluffy-haired toaster salesman and the wizened king in pale luminescence.

They stared at me, waiting for me to begin. Any day, brain. I wiped my sweaty palms onto the satin fabric of my dress and cleared my throat.

King Kermit didn't need to hear about my roommate drama, so my story began when I arrived in Spoons, a visitor from the land Eric set out to explore. Recounting Atalanta's public execution attempt and how I learned of Leander's attacks on the half-breeds, I continued with the deplorable conditions the Sporks lived in and the horrible work camps.

When I divulged the account of rescuing the men from the camps, King Kermit crossed his arms. "Ah, so this isn't your first run in with taking the law into your own hands."

I threw my arms in the air. "Well, what do you expect me to do? All the guards are under Leander's thumb!" Eric to put a hand on my shoulder, the warmth relaxing the tension in my muscles.

Kermit sighed, pacing the armory. "He always showed such promise in training. Then one day, he changed. At first it was subtle, but now I don't even recognize the boy. I always knew the day would come when I would have to discipline him, but I never knew it would be something like this. Forks and Spoons have shared a rivalry for generations, but this is," he shook his head, "unthinkable. I'll have to deal with this immediately."

Success! We had done it! Time to party because the mission was complete. The king would restore the half-breeds and Leander would get—

"Don't you know that it's rude to talk about someone behind their back?" a voice chuckled from the open door.

My heart thumped like the percussion section of a marching band. Leander stepped into the doorway, cropped black hair askew, arms behind his back.

King Kermit maintained his serious frown, unfazed. "Is it true what they're saying? Have you really imprisoned all of these men? What's next? Were you going to kill them one by one?"

Leander smirked, his voice coming out like smooth butter. "Kermit, you know you can't believe everything you hear." His boots clanked against the stone when he walked closer. He brought his arms out from behind his back, lifting a gun in front of him and holding it level at us.

Just in case that wasn't clear, there was a freakishly large, metal, deadly gun in his trigger happy grip. Not like a water gun or anything, lest anyone secretly think, *Oh, she's just over exaggerating.* Nope, I could tell by looking it was a million caliber. If fired, you were there one minute and gone the next, without a trace of blood, guts, hair, or clothing.

Raising the behemoth of a weapon, Leander shrugged. Cue villainous monologue. "But in this case, you should probably believe what you hear." His sneer pulled at the scar on his cheek. "And might I just say at first I was really bummed. I worked hard planning all of this so you would name me your heir and then 'mysteriously' die in a matter of weeks. Oh well. I have learned to make a happy mistake.

"You see, all the subjects will be upset you were kidnapped and killed by these half-breed radicals." Leander poked his lip out. "However, they're going to feel much better when I let them know you named me your heir with your dying breath." He slowly circled us, keeping the gun level. "Their eyes will just light up to hear that I avenged the king by killing his kidnappers, especially when I assure them I won't rest until every savage, blood-thirsty half-breed is dead. They'll be so awed, I'll probably get my picture on a postage stamp."

A bitter laugh exited my throat. "Leander, I always figured one of these days you'd go postal." If I was only going to live for the next few minutes, I planned on fitting in as many puns as possible.

He paused circling, nudging the muzzle of the gun at my back. "And you, you little cretin." Leander leaned his face close, tickling my ear with his whisper. "Wasting my precious time, trying to steal my moment. You think you're so smart, fooling me with your pretty little disguise?" He pinched my cheek, rubbing the skin between his fingers. "I bet this isn't even your real face."

Hello? My face had feelings, too. And thanks for letting me know I was so ugly on a day-to-day basis that no one recognized me when I looked nice.

He stepped backwards, waving the gun nonchalantly. "My only dilemma now is who to kill first." A smile lit up his face. "But before I decide, do you have any last words?"

King Kermit craned his neck to look at the moon outside. The words came out softly. "Why," he rasped. "Why are there so many songs about rainbows?"

Seriously?

Leander's fingers inched closer to the trigger. "I'm not sure. I guess rainbows are…pretty? Next."

Eric's reached for my hand, his sweaty grip surprisingly comforting. "Nessie, I hoped it wouldn't end this way, but I don't regret any of it."

Leander gagged, and I squeezed my eyes shut. It was all so surreal. Surrounded by a serial killer, a king named after a Muppet, and a toaster salesman that I had desperately come to love. What should I say? What words could possibly summarize twenty-four years of life? Should I try to say something to stall—something like 'Hey, guess what?' or "I hid a million dollars under the—" so he wouldn't kill me out of curiosity? It just seemed so futile, and I was tired of running around trying to stay alive. Maybe it was easier to give up.

"You win," I sighed, tears blurring my vision. What a waste of last words. They'd never make a movie of me now.

"Well, these are my last words to you. King Kermit, you were a great king. Too bad you're old now." Leander stroked the barrel of the gun. "Eric, you're a nice guy, but unfortunately, nice guys get killed by people like me a lot."

He stepped closer to me and lifted my chin. "Aww, don't cry, Nessie. You have been a worthy opponent. You even tricked me into thinking you were some hot chick. Just think of all the wonderful moments you got to spend dancing with me. That way, you'll see that your life wasn't totally wasted."

I jerked back from his grasp to look at Eric and squeezed the toaster's salesman hand like no tomorrow—ironic, right? "No, my life wasn't wasted at all."

Leander chuckled. "Really, Nessie? What kind of future do you have? You think anyone would want to marry you when rumor is that you can't cook?"

Heat rushed to my cheeks. My fingers clenched together tightly, balling into a fist. "What. Did. You. Say?" I seethed.

"What? You can't cook or hear?" the trigger-happy commander smirked.

Oh, it was on. I ripped the ruby dagger clip from my hair and threw it at him…or attempted to throw it at him. While my hopes of fatally wounding Leander weren't realized, the blade sunk into the snarling gunman's leg. Good enough. With a Xena Warrior Princess battle cry, I kneed him in the groin and clamped down on his gun hand, biting his fingers.

His high-pitched scream was music to my ears. The release of the firearm in his hand…not so much. The world slipped into slow-motion, and the clatter of the gun meeting the floor echoed in surround sound. More passionate than any tennis player, I dove while Leander writhed on the floor. I latched onto the weapon, wrapping my fingers around the barrel.

"Eric, I got it," I shouted but, with an angry growl, Leander ripped the dagger from his leg and tossed it aside like a steroid-pumped hulk.

Good grief. Talk about an adrenaline high. Leander's chest pumped up and down with every panting breath. He lowered his chin and lunged at me, releasing a ghastly roar into the armory. The impact of his muscular body knocked me off balance, but I caught myself before falling to the ground. I wrapped both my hands around the weapon, wrestling him for possession of the freaking-huge gun.

"It's mine, you psycho Doctor-Seuss-sounding character!" I shrieked, holding on to the slick metal for dear life.

He jerked back, but I clung to the weapon. "No way, you normally-homely, cooking-deficient weirdo!"

Everything passed around me in blurs. King Kermit sprinted to the doorway, cupping his hands and calling for help. Eric rushed to the wall and wrenched a gun from its stand, fumbling to lift the bulky firearm.

"Shoot him!" I yelled.

"I don't want to hit you!" Eric shouted, circling our scuffle. "You guys are too close!" He ran towards us, reaching out an arm to push me to the side.

But he was too late. My hands were slippery from all the sweat. When Leander jerked the gun back for the twelfth time, he ripped the weapon out of my grasp. My fingers clenched the empty air. No, it couldn't be over.

"Ha!" Leander crowed, aiming it at me. Sweat glistened off his forehead and dampened strands of his cropped black hair. The sheen of the metallic gun cast fragments of light on the wall. "Thanks for making up my mind, Nessie. You'll be the first to die." Eric froze in horror, his mouth open. "Don't worry, you won't be alone for long."

That was it. My dream was becoming reality.

He flipped off the safety and pulled the trigger. There it was—that flash of red. I was sure it was my own blood spurting graphically everywhere. All those late nights watching crime shows, I'd become an expert—isn't that what usually happened? It was all wrong, so wrong. I should have died from appendicitis like Theodore Strider said. Everything happened so quickly, the scene playing out like snippets of a movie pasted together.

Leander screamed something unintelligible, tears streaming down his horrified face. He brought his hands up to his mouth, dropping the weapon at his feet. Odd. Eric was at my side, stroking my hair and telling me everything was going to be fine. Well, I was dying, so not entirely accurate, but thanks for trying, Eric. But the most out-of-place scene was my pink-haired roommate, my trusty Mystical Unicorn, lying dead beside me.

That's when the realization dawned on me; there was no flash of red, no graphic blood spray. It was hot pink hair attached to Unicorn's body as she dove in front to take the bullet meant for me.

Leander was hunched over Unicorn's still body, sobbing. "I loved her! I loved her so much!"

But I didn't have time to mourn or figure out Leander's cryptic words. I was too busy watching it all go down like a bad Shakespearean tragedy. Eric stopped petting my hair and focused on Mystical Unicorn's fallen figure. He stood to his feet, raising the gun level with Leander's chest.

"No, Eri—" My words were muffled by the blast of his gun. The ammo slammed into Leander, dropping his body like a cow in Idaho. Clanking and shouting echoed from the open door, preceding the fleet of specially-trained Spoon soldiers that flooded the room. I gasped, crying out when they raised their weapons and shot Eric. He fell to the ground with a thud beside me, but my time for grief was limited. A guard decked in a purple and lime military uniform with a fork emblazoned on his chest aimed at me and fired.

When the bullet hit, it was a relief. I was so tired of all the fighting and the sorrow, so very tired. I calmly counted my breaths until the once-warm glow from the fire had turned into obsidian nothingness. *Well, this was lame.* And with that, I died.

Chapter 29

Now, I know what you're thinking: *Dead people can't write.* Well, guess what? You're correct. I, for one, have never read a story written by a dead person—at least a tale written by someone who died *before* they wrote it—and I hope I'm never faced with that experience, since it would be a little creepy.

I don't know what Nessie might have told you about me; I'm sure they were bad things. A lot of people get me wrong, judging me as a thug. They think, *Veli? Sounds like a jerk.*

Well, just because I'm snarky doesn't mean I'm a bad guy. Even though I wasn't there to protect my brother or the girl he fell in love with. Oh, and that hippie lady, too.

From the get-go, our plan was going to crumble into pieces. I was heading for Leander to distract him when that thieving ruffian, Robert Hood, tried to steal my watch and earned a black eye from yours truly. The guards came to arrest him and that's when I saw Miss Sea-Green Nessie and my older brother running away with the king.

Chaos erupted. It was impossible to follow Leander or Nessie in that crowd. Mystical Unicorn disappeared in some secret passageway hidden by the bathroom, Felicia was trying to get out of the way of the panicked soldiers, and I was left completely lost.

So I wasn't there when Nessie had her big tell-all or when Leander came in all smirky with his gun, which was not as big as Nessie made it out to be— she was always a bit dramatic. I didn't get to see the fight over the weapons or when everyone ended up getting shot. But when all the smoke cleared, and I found the still-very-alive king in the armory, this is what I saw: a bunch of people on the floor, slumped over.

Don't tell anyone tears welled in my eyes when I knelt by my fallen brother, touching his warm forehead and fluffy hair. His death rattle shook his frame, and he—I did a double-take. *Death rattle? Sounded more like a snore.* Jumping up to avoid looking like a chump, I took note of the four bodies, their chests rising up and down in slow rhythm. Once I thought about it, there wasn't any blood in a place where four people had been shot...

King Kermit was giving orders to a group of soldiers when I interrupted him with my confusion. "They're not—"

"Dead?" He howled with laughter, his wrinkly jowls shaking. "Land's sakes! No, my boy! You think we carry around bullets like they're candy? This isn't the Mafia, for crying out loud." The king leaned over slowly, bending to the floor. He picked up Eric's hand and let it flop lifelessly, triggering another chuckle. "Tranquilizer darts are just as useful for bringing down criminals. No one has to go sleeping with the fishes quite yet."

A frown crossed my lips. "But, what about my brother and—"

"Yes, the good guys. I know." His bones creaked when he put his hands on his knees and pushed himself up. "Except I don't know yet who the real good guys are, which is why everyone was put out for a nap, at least until we can straighten this all out."

It still didn't make any sense. "What about the gun Eric got from the armory wall or the one Leander brought in? How did those have tranquilizers, too?"

"Haven't you seen those public service announcements about leaving guns near children? You know how many kids come to the armory on field trips? We make sure all of these guns," he plodded over to the wall and pulled a rifle off the wall, "are loaded with tranquilizers instead of ammo in case a kiddie decides to play 'war hero' with his friend. Yes, we thought about leaving them completely empty, but if weapons were needed, like now, a dart could at least hold the enemy off for a little bit. As for Leander's gun," he rubbed his white beard thoughtfully, "that must have been a miracle. I'm not exactly sure how that happened."

So, you see, the moral of this story is that you should never put the cart before the horse. Or maybe it's something about burning chickens before they hatch. At any rate, you should learn that Nessie exaggerates a lot. I guess now that she's finally awake, she can tell you the rest.

Chapter 30

Okay, don't be mad. I mean, if you saw a giant bazooka aimed at you and your world started going black, you'd think you died, too.

The fluffy, white blankets on the bed in the guest chambers scared me at first. It was like being in a cloud—not a great feeling for someone who thought they kicked the bucket. However, my view of the blue, morning sky through the clear ceiling told me I was very much alive.

Happy day! I could run and jump and sing and kiss Eric—Eric…My fingers balled the sheets between them. Was he alive or did my memory of him taking a bullet and falling to the ground prove true? There was only one way to find out. I pulled down the soft covers, taking notice of the long silk nightgown I wore. Nope, wasn't going to think about how I got in it. Moving on from that embarrassing thought. My bare foot peeked out of the sheets and tested out the plush red carpet. Wow, what was that made out of? Baby angels? I could—

"Hello there!" King Kermit's wrinkly face popped out from behind the dresser, and my scream filled the small room. Good grief! How long had he been hiding there?

He held up his gnarled hands defensively. "Relax, dear. Everything's okay."

I leapt to my feet. "Eric? Is he…alive?"

The king's words came out slowly. "There was nothing more we could do for him."

No…I fell to my knees. After everything, how could he just be gone? How would I ever forg—

"Because he was completely fine! Perfect bill of health," Kermit grinned.

What a sneaky butt the king was turning out to be. He clapped his hand roughly on my shoulder. "Now you're awake, let's start untangling this mess."

Easier said than done. Our investigation proved to be difficult. At first, Leander's motto was, 'Deny everything' and he was quite a convincing liar. However, too many soldiers knew his plans; too much evidence existed, and too many victims were more than happy to point the finger.

The turning point came when King Kermit reminded him he shot Mystical Unicorn. There in a dirty prison cell, the prideful Leander—now complete with haggard stubble—burst into uncontrollable sobs. He morphed from an arrogant, stubborn commander to a remorseful, broken soul in a matter of seconds.

"If I had known, I never would have…" Leander trailed off in his blubbering. He wiped his face on the purple and lime military uniform, soiled with dungeon grime. "I hadn't even known that she was still alive after all these years." After that statement, he completely broke down and no one could make out any further intelligible words.

Not a pretty sight.

So, I paid my roomie a visit down the hall. It was comforting to see her sitting cross-legged on her bed, her long pink hair cascading down her back and pooling onto the white comforter. She had found her cheetah print clothes and, even though the pattern clashed with the blue flower wallpaper, she was rocking them out. That had to be a good sign of things returning to normal.

"Nessie!" She leapt off the bed, somehow missing the corner of the vanity next to her, and squeezed me in a boa constrictor embrace. "It's so good to see you're alive!"

And it was good to be alive, dressed in my tunic and reacquainted with the comfort of my sword in its sheath. My lungs struggled for air in her crushing grip. "The feeling is mutual," I rasped, "especially after I saw you take that bullet for me."

"Oh, sorry," she apologized, releasing me at last. "But does it still count as heroic if it just turns out to be a tranquilizer dart instead of a bullet?"

Shrugging, I sat on the edge of her bed. "I'll let you have it this time."

"Even if I replaced his bullets with the tranquilizer darts in the first place?" she smirked and recounted how she'd made the switch when she had busted me out of Leander's study. "I figured it wouldn't hurt to be safe. Luckily, he didn't check his weapons before using them." She sat down at the vanity, lifting a silver brush on the table to her pink tresses.

"Yeah, thank God for that." Now for the hard conversation. "But I have another question for you."

"Okay, answers are five dollars. Correct answers are ten," she teased, winking in the mirror at me.

What a dork. My hand stretched to deal a noogie, but she leaned out of reach. "And how much for an explanation of what's going on with Leander and you?"

She lowered the hairbrush into her lap, staring at her hands. "Well, that is quite an expensive one."

"You can just put it on my tab."

We don't have time to transcribe the three-hour long conversation that commenced after this, complete with laughter, sobbing, and two pints of ice cream, but I'll sum it up for you. Mystical Unicorn discussed growing up in the kingdom of Forks—where apparently everyone has vibrantly colored hair—until she was old enough to train as one of King Alfonso's personal bodyguards. Excuse my laugh, but the image of my hippy, nature-communing roomie as a thug was humorous. She went on to recount the story of meeting Leander while she was spying on the Spoon Armed Forces and how they had started courting. Dating Leander—the thought made me cringe, despite her assurances he'd been quite the gentleman at first.

"I was…I was starting to love him," Unicorn confided with a bittersweet smile. "But when he asked me to marry him, I knew it would never work out. For one, our kingdoms feuded which would be uncomfortable for our families. But, there were other, bigger issues. He didn't know who I really was.

"Leander doesn't know I was a spy. I'm not anymore, in case you're wondering. When I fell in love with Leander, I realized the people of Spoons were just like us, and my conscience didn't sit well with sneaking around their villages. I even started helping out openly in the palace, catching criminals and such which the guards were grateful for, but Leander's growing pride pushed me away from him…from this place." She stood from the vanity and plopped down beside me on the bed.

"On one of my previous spying sessions, I'd overheard King Kermit talking to the Duke of Burntbread about this new portal to some parallel universe. It sounded better than anything else, so I vowed to find a way to follow Eric and start a new life. Through my extensive research, I learned the Blades of Remiel weren't the only way to get to other universes; you could create portals out of low-energy kitchen appliances, which is how I ended up in your world." Low-energy kitchen appliances? This parallel universe thing was too complicated.

"When I first got there, I lived with a bunch of earth people in some commune until they ran out of money and went their separate ways. Without money, I had to get a job at a bookstore and look for a place of my own, which is how I met you." She patted my hand. "When you talked about parallel universes, I started getting antsy for home. And then you left and my homesickness was utterly unbearable."

A sighed escaped her lips, her voice cracking. "But I witnessed what had become of Leander and all the monstrosities he had created. It was obvious I was to blame. Any awful thing that happened to the half-breeds only happened because of me." She wrung the sheets between her fingers. "Maybe I should have just married Leander, but I knew his pride became too large for his own good.

In the early days, he was considerate and generous, even humble, but as he got stronger and more confident, he often told me that he could get by on his own. He was headed for a collision, and I didn't want to be in the passenger seat when it happened."

Poor Unicorn. "You can't beat yourself up for Leander's choices. If it hadn't happened because of you, it would have been something else. Maybe…" I fidgeted with the hilt of my sword, "maybe you should talk to him. You know, he thinks he killed you. He's going crazy with grief, so maybe he's starting to understand the weight of all of the harm he's caused."

"I don't know. Maybe it's better for him to think I'm dead, and we can all just move on with our lives," Mystical Unicorn said.

"It's your call." I stood from the bed and left it at that.

§ § §

A quail-shaped bush loomed over me. The castle courtyard was much less intimidating—but definitely still random—now that I wasn't trying to escape from Leander through it. A gray sky stretched out overhead, puffy clouds swollen with moisture. Veli combed a hand through his blond hair, shifting back and forth on his feet. You'd think the muscular lug was nervous, if that was even possible for him.

"This is it," he said, the words husky with emotion. Veli leaned forward and wrapped his thick arms around me. I thought I was dreaming again, but he was more than happy to pinch my arm to convince me of reality. He looked at his feet, fiddling with the dagger at his side. "Well, Felicia needs to get back before her kids start to worry too much, and I'm going to make sure she gets there okay."

I craned my neck around the quail bush to see the ponytailed blonde chatting animatedly with Eric and Unicorn. She sat on the edge of the dolphin fountain, swinging her feet and laughing whenever the porpoise statue squirted her with water. Looked like someone had finally loosened up about the whole parallel universe thing. "Sure you are. And if you just happen to find a place there, get to know her and her kids more, and eventually settle down, then that's just a perk?"

He put his hands in his pockets and headed towards the fountain. "I guess you could say I'm going to take an extended vacation and see what happens."

My eyes teared, but happiness overwhelmed me at the sight of the mature, snarky, smiling Veli in front of me. He'd finally made peace with his brother. There he was, growing up and starting to love. It was too much.

"Unicorn rigged up a portal out of a sertav-maker for us."

"That sounds…dangerous," I frowned, hurrying to catch up with his long legs. "Do me a favor and take care of yourself. And don't forget to lighten up and live a little. After all, when you visit Felicia, you're going to have four little kids running around, talking and crying and snotting and whining and loving you."

He punched me playfully on the shoulder. "Don't worry. I had plenty of practice taking care of you. Besides, I kind of like kids."

Never would have seen that coming.

"There you are!" Felicia caught sight of us. She pushed herself off the fountain's edge and linked arms with Veli. "We're going to be late for the…" Her nose scrunched. "What was it called again?"

"The solar flare influx!" Mystical Unicorn chimed in. "That's the prime time to travel by sertav-portals."

Of course it was. With hugs and well wishes, I bade them goodbye. Well, not quite goodbye. Felicia was my next door neighbor after all.

"Oh, this is utterly divine, darling," a voice crooned from the thick hedge behind me. No, it couldn't be. I crouched down and rustled a few branches in the hedge to get a better view. Sure enough, Betty was in a pink-sun dress, sitting on a picnic cloth and offering a piece of a bundt cake to Elbert, sans Ferny. Betty's unique laughter filled the courtyard. "Oh, Bertie! You're such a card."

With that glow on her face, Betty wouldn't be returning home any time soon. Perhaps Spoons could be saved from her craziness as long as a whisk was in her hand and the gentle Elbert was at her side.

On a positive note, I'd seen Leander and Unicorn strolling the gardens. According to my roomie's reports, he was a completely different person, apologizing for his mistakes, giving back to the people that he had taken so much from, even using his own personal money to revamp the entire Spork society. Good for him, though I wouldn't be going to any tea parties with him any time soon. It would take some time before his face stopped haunting my nightmares.

Still, King Kermit was so impressed by his turnaround he considered keeping him around as Commander, but, of course, after King Kermit was ready to retire. His recent adventures ignited a spark inside the wise monarch. I saw him roaming the castle grounds speaking with soldiers and villagers, that serious, firm look on his face and new zeal in his eyes.

As for Mystical Unicorn, every time I ran into her she was grinning like a possum. A super happy possum that just won the lottery. If possums had pants, she would be a possum that peed her pants because she was so happy.

"So, tell me," a deep voice broke my possum thoughts. "Did the Nessie Monster live happily ever after now that she saved the day?" Eric appeared at my side, sliding his arm around my back.

"Only time will tell, Bran Muffin." I basked in the warmth of his embrace, inhaling his clean, cinnamon scent, something I hadn't appreciated on our adventures. In fact, now we weren't running for our lives, I noticed some more awesome things about him, like how his chin was so stately and elbows was so perfectly elbow-y.

His lips gently kissed the top of my head. "Only time, huh?"

My hands tenderly reached for his face. "Well, I'll let you in on a little secret." He drew nearer until the space between us evaporated. His face leaned in close, lips parting for a warm, sweet kiss. "My sources tell me that the ending is looking very favorable indeed."

Epilogue

The blistering, hot air of the summer day invaded my car, and I pressed the gas pedal harder in hopes of stirring a breeze. Why was I too cheap to run the air conditioning? My speed-produced fan worked pretty well until a cop pulled up behind me with flashing lights.

Rats. My already-nauseated stomach didn't need a speeding ticket to raise the stress of this miserable day. The good thing about Spoons was no speed limits—a rule I wished worked across universes when the officer got out of his car, notepad in hand. Could I help that it was hard to remember what rules applied when Eric and I were always traveling back and forth between the universes? The frowning police officer didn't seem sympathetic to my confusion.

"Hello, officer," I smiled innocently at the mustachioed law-enforcer, hoping my sweetness masked the desire to vomit.

He pushed down his reflective sunglasses. "Ma'am, are you aware that you were going 53 in a 45?" He hastily scrawled on the notepad. "Need I remind you how dangerous speeding is? Do you know that there are little creatures in these woods, waiting to cross the road?" His eyes widened, crossing when he pointed to the side of the street. "Look now, there comes Peter Rabbit on his way to his grandmother's house! All he has to do is get across this road and he'll be sitting at granny's table eating carrots and milk. But, no. Here you come going 53 miles per hour and then—bam!" He smacked his hands together. "You knock poor Peter's head off. His grandmother just finds the headless body twitching in the road. Is that what you want?!"

Someone was a bit touchy. I looked down at my lap. "Why didn't Peter Rabbit look both ways before crossing the street?"

"You sicken me," he spat out and slammed the ticket in my hand before retreating to his squad car.

Ugh. Not what I needed, especially when I was already ten minutes late for my date with Eric. Our date night of dinner—made by yours truly—and renting a movie sounded a lot better before I'd started feeling so crappy.

Wanting to look especially nice since it was my first time cooking for Eric—okay, actually, first time cooking ever—I had stopped by Salon D'Veli for some sprucing up. Yes, Veli finally listened to his true calling to open up a

197

beauty parlor. He was doing a fantastic job, especially with his betrothed, Felicia, working as the receptionist, and her four little kids running around doing errands.

But now I was late. As soon as the cop turned the other direction, I pushed the gas a little harder—I mean, you can't get two speeding tickets in one day, right? My car leaned into the curve and a pair of cute, beady eyes peered up at me from the middle of the road. "Peter Rabbit!" I screamed. "Run! Run!"

But he didn't run. In fact, I was the one that ran…right over top of him. Oh, the tears squeezed from my tender soul, but there was nothing more that could be done. Really, wasn't the person to blame stupid Peter Rabbit's mother? Didn't she ever tell him not to play in the street? And what about that grandmother? What granny makes her grandchild cross a death trap just for some carrots? The thought made me want to lose my lunch again.

It was okay. Soon, I'd be curled up with Eric on our couch watching a pointless comedy—a fact that would have been true if my tire hadn't decided to go flat. Of all the horrible luck. No, I had not hit Peter Rabbit; Peter Rabbit was for normal people to run over with their minivans and SUVs. My car hit weird animals I didn't know were native to the city until a few minutes ago when the quills of poor Peter Porcupine slashed my tire. Sure enough, I looked back in the road and there was a dead porcupine with his tongue sticking out.

Slowly and nauseatingly, the tire was changed and I returned to the safety of my apartment where Eric was waiting outside. It was time to let go of all the stress and crappiness. My one mission: spaghetti. The directions on the box were pretty straightforward—this cooking thing was a cinch—and the pasta turned out perfect. I was born to boil water, and you don't even know the skills I have when it comes to pouring the noodles in a pot and stirring.

This was so easy; why had I never cooked before?

I winced, clutching my stomach. There was that pain again, shooting across my abdomen. Surely my lunch at the taco truck was to blame.

"Are you okay?" Eric asked.

"Never better." *Just don't barf on his shoes and everything will be okay.* The pasta stirred round and round, fueling the dizziness that kicked up in my brain—not a big help for the nausea.

"You look warm," Eric reached out and touched my forehead. "Do you have a fever? Maybe you should lie down for a while."

"No!" I protested, stamping my foot. "This is my first dinner I've ever made you and I want it to go right. It's just those tacos from lunch coming back to haunt me. Now tell me if this noodle is done."

His thumbs up was enough for me to transfer the spaghetti into my prettiest serving dish and open the jar of sauce. Hey, I cooked the spaghetti already—no one said I had to make the sauce, too. The pungent tomato smell filled the room, wafting up to my nose, increasing the pain in my stomach.

Do. Not. Vomit. You can do this. But why was the kitchen so hot? Sweat dotted my brow. After mixing the concoction, I proudly thrust the bowl out to Eric. "Doesn't it look great?"

He beamed, putting a hand on my shoulder. "Can't wait to eat it, Ness."

But it was too late. "I'm gonna throw up," I blurted and grabbed the closest bowl, which just happened to be the one I was holding. Leave it to me to puke all over my perfect spaghetti. There it was—that sharp pain in my right abdomen. "Oh my goodness, Eric!" I screamed when realization sunk in. Theodore Strider had called it in the third grade. "We need to go to the hospital now!"

"What?!" Eric went into panic mode, a flurry of motion as he rushed to the couch, filling his arms with my purse, our jackets, and a few throw pillows. "Why? What's wrong?"

"Ahh! We don't have a lot of time. Just do it!" I yelled, throwing my car keys at him.

However, my fears intensified when we arrived in the bland waiting area of the emergency room. It was a frightening sight to have a nurse with gold hoop earrings, diamond studded press-on nails, who was blowing bubbles with her gum.

"What kind of a hospital is this?" I scolded Eric, plopping into a tattered chair. The nurse looked up from her copy of *People* and handed him a clipboard.

"What's your problem?" she snapped. I'm not sure what else I expected from a hospital that looked like its furniture was salvaged from a dumpster. Which bodily fluids were those on the couch next to me? And was it wrong to ask for artwork that didn't look like cover art for Metallica albums? Not exactly my idea of comforting.

"Excuse me?" Eric asked the nurse in disbelief.

"I asked the lady what was the matter with her," the sassy lady pushed herself onto the edge of the desk so she could sit and examine her fingernails.

"Can't you see that I'm dying?" I shouted grabbing my side with another coursing pain.

"In that case, can you do it a little more quietly?" she muttered, pointing to the television behind the desk. "I was watching Oprah before you got here."

My lack of faith in the medical system was increasing exponentially, though my doctor, a man who looked like George Clooney if he let himself go, seemed more stable when he met me in the exam room. He calmly explained we would be going back to surgery soon because of my—wait for it—appendicitis! I could only pray the surgeons were of a different breed than my nurse when they wheeled me away.

Eric gave me a kiss before I left and whispered he loved me. Oh, the warmth and calm generated by that statement. His smile was tender. He leaned in close, his lips brushing against my forehead one more time. "I was hoping this night would go a little differently."

Yeah, me, too, but nearly-exploding organs were a little needy. Thank you, Theodore Strider. Thank you for your graphic slideshow of appendicitis operations in the third grade. You might have just saved my life.

§ § §

"Is it lunchtime yet?" I grumped, trying to push myself up on the lumpy hospital bed. The machines hooked up to me beeped annoyingly to let me know I was still alive. Sunlight streamed through the gray curtains, brightening the dismal room.

"Thank goodness you're going home soon," the nurse mumbled after scanning my sutures.

If I wasn't hooked up to machines… "Give me a break, lady! I've been through an ordeal and deserve some food."

"You can eat when you go home," she snipped and marched out of the door.

"Can you believe that?" I gasped, turning to Eric who was perched on the arm of a beaten up armchair and clutching his jacket against the chilly draft. "She should have worked at the IRS or somewhere you're expected to be mean."

"Don't let it get you down," Eric grinned, which only made me grumpier. Didn't he know he was talking to a ravenous woman? "I have a surprise for you."

Well…surprises were good. Maybe it was a cookie…or a pony.

He lifted his jacket to reveal a covered tray. "I got it from the cafeteria when she wasn't looking," he whispered with a wink.

"You're so sweet," I beamed with the love that can only come from a hungry woman who's been offered food. But when he removed the cover, I started laughing. "Is this what they're really serving in the cafeteria?"

A piece of toast rested on the white plate with a diamond ring perched on top. On closer inspection, the bread had been strategically burned to read, "Will you marry me?"

Would I marry him? The laughter stopped and a firm frown pulled my lips tight. "I'm sorry, Eric, I can't marry you."

His face froze. I could have sworn he stopped breathing beside me. The only sound in the hospital room was him exhaling, long and heavy. "Oh."

"C'mon, Eric. Everyone knows I can't cook. How will I ever get married if I can't cook?"

A smile relit his face, and Eric energetically ruffled my pixie cut. "We'll just order out."

"In that case," I extended my hand, "Yes."

Eric leaned down for a sweet, slow kiss, and I giggled when he ended up entrapped in the embrace of hospital cords. Oh, well. Just a way to make sure he stayed close.

"For the record," he murmured, his warm breath tickling my ear, "your spaghetti looked pretty good before you threw up all over it."

And I don't think Betty Crocker herself could have gotten a better compliment.